Advance Praise for *The Cheesemaker's Daughter*

"*The Cheesemaker's Daughter* takes us to Pag, an island where sheep's milk becomes curds, partners become rivals, exes become new possibilities, and one woman finally becomes who she was meant to be. Deeply researched and fully inhabited, this novel is a thrilling, transformative read."

—Julia Phillips, bestselling author of *Disappearing Earth*, finalist for the National Book Award

"Kristin Vuković's captivating debut novel delves into the intricate tapestry of familial bonds, self-discovery, and web of obligations that entangle so many immigrants. Vuković skillfully crafts a sophisticated and graceful narrative, weaving a tale of a woman's transformative journey. I loved this novel!"

—Jean Kwok, *New York Times* bestselling author of *Girl in Translation* and *The Leftover Woman*

"*The Cheesemaker's Daughter* is a beautiful exploration of family, identity, and the connections and responsibilities we have to those who came before us. Kristin Vuković writes an elegant novel about a woman who blossoms into the person she was always meant to be."

—Jill Santopolo, *New York Times* bestselling author of *Stars in an Italian Sky* and *The Light We Lost*

"Where do we really belong and why? While still reeling from a devastating miscarriage and a fracturing marriage, New Yorker Marina is also forced to reckon with her roots and her culture, reluctantly returning to her native Croatia to help save her family's cheese business. Set against the backdrop of Croatia's dark history and the rich, fascinating world of cheesemaking, this is a literary page-turner with unforgettable heart."

—Caroline Leavitt, *New York Times* bestselling author of *Pictures of You* and *With or Without You*

"A magical debut, *The Cheesemaker's Daughter* is a sensual exploration of cultural identity, loss, and love. Shattered by her broken marriage, thirty-four-year-old Marina, a Yugoslav refugee, leaves her life in New York City and returns to her island home in Croatia, where she becomes entangled in saving her family's failing cheese factory and legacy. Amid the backdrop of Croatia's war-torn history, Kristin Vuković conjures up the island's wild landscape—its glittering sea, sheep-dotted hills, extreme weather, and complex scents of antiquity—with spellbinding beauty."

—Jessica Brilliant Keener, author of *Strangers in Budapest*, an Indie Next pick

"Kristin Vuković's tender and elegant novel is a tale of coming home and of coming to terms, of filial affection and heartbreak, and of wanting, waiting, and fierce island winds. It's a story about Croatia, but it's meant for all of us, wherever we are, because the story at its heart is one about the struggle to belong and to heal."

—James Sturz, author of *Underjungle*

"Kristin Vuković knows that cheese contains multitudes: history, identity, loss, and love. In *The Cheesemaker's Daughter*, she weaves a richly delicious story about one woman's return to her family's cheesemaking factory on Pag, a Croatian island, to save her family's cheese—and then, herself. I couldn't put it down."

—Hannah Howard, Amazon bestselling author of *Plenty: A Memoir of Food and Family*

The Cheesemaker's Daughter

KRISTIN VUKOVIĆ

A REGALO PRESS BOOK
ISBN: 979-8-88845-682-8
ISBN (eBook): 979-8-88845-401-5

The Cheesemaker's Daughter
© 2024 by Kristin Vuković
All Rights Reserved

Cover Design by Jim Villaflores
Interior design and composition by Alana Mills

Publishing Team:
Founder and Publisher – Gretchen Young
Editorial Assistant – Caitlyn Limbaugh
Managing Editor – Aleigha Koss
Production Manager – Alana Mills
Production Editor – Rachel Hoge
Associate Production Manager – Kate Harris

As part of the mission of Regalo Press, a donation is being made to the Croatian
Scholarship Fund, as chosen by the author. Find out more about this organization
at: http://www.croatianscholarship.org

Regalo Press
New York • Nashville
regalopress.com

Published in the United States of America
1 2 3 4 5 6 7 8 9 10

For my Croatian grandparents, Ivan and Ana Vuković,
who made America home

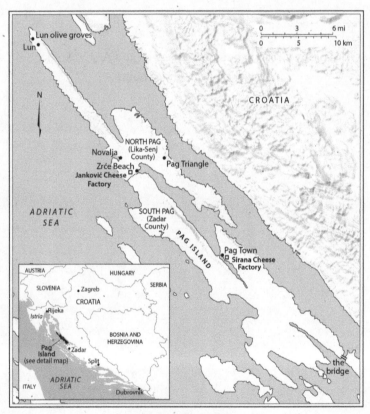

Map by Bill L. Nelson

He only says, "Good fences make good neighbors."
—Robert Frost, "Mending Wall"
(*North of Boston*, 1914)

"A cheese may disappoint. It may be dull, it may be naive, it may be oversophisticated. Yet it remains cheese, milk's leap toward immortality."
—Clifton Fadiman, *Any Number Can Play*
(Cleveland/New York: The World Publishing Company, 1957)

Chapter One

Marina gripped the rental car's wheel just as the heavens opened. Rain shivered across the windows like tadpoles swimming upstream. The windshield wipers were useless. They didn't really wipe anything away, they only moved it somewhere else, leaving dirty half-moon streaks. Croatian *klapa* music blasted on the radio. The haunting, deep, a cappella singing moistened her eyes. Homesickness for the country she'd left washed over her. But this time, she wasn't looking forward to returning.

Through the blurry window, she watched village after village pass by. Like her own family's house in Pag Town, every house had a vegetable garden. Vines grew wild and unrestrained, bearing crooked zucchini and dimpled tomatoes that would never be acceptable in American supermarkets. In America, produce was perfect and tasteless. She liked irregular, misshapen things. Maybe it was the pressure she'd always felt to be perfect, to live up to her family's reputation as a pillar of the community. Maybe it was the weight of her father's expectations. When she came back home to visit, things always seemed simpler here, but she knew they were just as complicated, in different ways.

Her father's words echoed in her head: *Sirana is in crisis*. Sirana was her family's cheese factory, their livelihood. It was the way they'd made it through Yugoslavia's civil war, the way they'd always made it through tough times. Inside those walls, she felt safe, like nothing could hurt her. It was the one thing she had counted on to remain constant, since everything else had changed. She craved a cigarette, but she didn't want to come home smelling like an ashtray. Despite it being her father's bad habit, he didn't like it when she smoked.

Nikola was not the type of man to ask for help, not even from his daughter. On the phone, his voice had frightened her; he was always steady, even during the war. She'd felt so helpless. She'd booked the next flight out. She dreaded having to explain Marko's absence. They usually arrived to Croatia together, just before the fourth of July, to take advantage of the long, American holiday weekend. She knew she was running from one disaster to another, but she hoped this one could be fixed.

Pag Bridge emerged, a narrow concrete arch suspended above the sea. The pelting water on the rental car's roof sounded like tiny explosions, raising hairs on her neck. Every time she crossed from the mainland to her island, she thought about the bombing of their bridge by the Yugoslav army, after the Serbs had seized control of it. Her family had taken shelter in Sirana, protected by thick concrete walls, the pungent smell of sheep's milk cheese filling their noses as they prayed. Miraculously, the bridge had held, and Pag Island was not bombed. Would she hold? She felt shaky as she passed over the bridge and onto Pag.

Near the bridge, the Fortica ruins continued crumbling, edging towards decay. When she was a girl, her father told her that the limestone fortress had been protecting their island since the

Middle Ages. But now, looking down at the walls, they appeared as only ruined piles of rubble, stones that had lost their places, slowly returning themselves to Pag's barren, rocky landscape, giving way to the harsh *bura* wind. "Only the stubborn and strong survive here," the elders had told her. "You'll grow up to be a strong girl."

She had to be strong, for her father. Sirana had to survive.

Sirana came into view, the weight of her country's history seeping through its concrete façade. A hulking Yugoslav relic, the post-WWII cheese factory looked like another failed communist promise. The sign was cracked now, its pale-blue lettering fading into the dull, gray background, a kind of shrug against the moody sky.

Her father had spent years inside these walls. Sirana was his second home, his employees a second family. Her second family, too. She parked and rushed to escape the rain. She heaved open the metal door and entered the hallway leading to the production room. White lab coats—the required uniform for the production room—looked ghostly lined up on hooks, as if the humans they belonged to would appear at any moment and occupy the clothes.

The rusty door creaked open. Moist, warm air greeted her; she inhaled the gamey, primal scent of fresh sheep's milk cheese, the aroma of her childhood. The whir of machinery groaned. Everything was white, from the tile floors to the shower caps to the rubber gloves and rain boots. Men stuffed blocks of white curds, fresh off the line, into white plastic molds. Marina stared at the puddled, curd-littered floor, strewn with cast-off cheese that didn't fit the molds, curled like fallen crescent moons. She closed her eyes. Cocooned by thick factory walls, she was filled with the certainty that season after season there would be cheese—even during war. In the familiar environment, her breathing slowed.

From her father's upstairs office she could watch milk transform into cheese like magic. Marina had had a fantasy as a child of jumping into the vat, floating on her back in litres of sheep's milk. Sometimes Nikola had taken her downstairs to visit the production room. He would give her a shower cap and an adult-sized lab coat that skimmed her ankles. She would watch men stir milk with aluminum poles and stuff curds into molds with their fists. In the aging room, towering planks with wheels of cheese were stacked one on top of the other to the ceiling. Marina called it her cheese castle. She grew up with the cheese, aged batches marking birthdays, special wheels imprinted with her initials, M.M.

She trudged up the stairs, which her young legs had sprinted up and down countless times.

"*Tata*?" Marina said, knocking on her father's door.

Nikola was deep in thought, leaning back in his chair and puffing out his belly, a cigarette with long ash dangling from his fingers. His thinning gray hair was slicked against his scalp, his shirt sweat-stained. Marina didn't know if he kept the air conditioning off because of money or *propuh*, the draft that Croatians believed brought on all kinds of maladies from muscle aches to headaches to colds. Seeing her father, she fought back tears.

"*Mala*," Nikola said, rising from his chair, embracing her and kissing her on both cheeks.

"You can't call me that anymore, *Tata*, I'm thirty-four," Marina said, wrapping her arms around her father's thick girth. She wanted to hold onto him forever.

"You'll always be my little one," Nikola said. "How was your flight?"

"Tiring." She had a feeling of whiplash, a departure from one life and entry to another, a return to the past. The jet lag and lack of sleep made her disoriented and unsteady. She wanted her father to tell her everything was going to be fine like he did when she was little, even if she no longer believed him.

"You're home now, you can rest," Nikola said, shuffling to the coffee machine. He pressed a button.

"This rain," Marina said, dabbing her face with a tissue and wiping the black mascara from underneath her eyes.

"When it rains, it pours," Nikola said with an ironic smile. "Anyway, we needed it to cool down. It's been a hot June so far."

"How are the sheep faring?" Marina said.

"Milk production is down a little. We're nearing the end of the season, though, so it's to be expected. Where's Marko? Did he go to his family's house already?"

"No," she said carefully. She knew her father could read her face. She wanted to avoid talking about Marko for as long as possible. Her father had never liked him.

Nikola frowned, handing her a cup of black coffee with sugar, just how she liked it. "Oh?"

Marina took a deep breath. "He couldn't get time off."

"*Ej*, The American is always working."

Behind his back, Nikola referred to Marko as "The American." According to her father, Marko wasn't Croatian because he was born in America, to parents who had left.

"Speaking about work. Tell me how I can help, *Tata*." She welcomed any distraction. She wanted to distance herself from the life she'd left behind in New York. If she kept moving, kept doing, maybe she could push through.

"Why so eager? Sit down, have your coffee," Nikola said. "And have a taste first," he added, cutting her a slice of Pag cheese from a wedge on his desk with a pocketknife. "Just out of the aging room. It's our best batch this year."

Marina sat across from her father's desk. She bit into the familiar cheese, its nutty flavor awakening her taste buds, savoring the essence of wild herbs dusted with sea salt that blanketed their island's rocky pastures in spring like an afghan. She closed her eyes. For a moment, the cheese made her forget about her problems. But, like a hazy memory, it was lacking something she couldn't quite discern, something ineffable that could have made it extraordinary. Was it the method? Was it the milk?

"So?" Nikola said.

"It brings me back to simpler times," she said, swallowing.

Cheese was her comfort food. And right now, she could eat an entire wheel.

Their sheep, like their people, were tough. Pag's flocks faced extremes, their milk made potent by scarcity, a triumph of survival each season. She had to remember that. She had to remember where she'd come from. But she was no longer a child playing in her father's cheese factory. She wanted to tell him everything, but he was burdened with enough problems of his own.

"You didn't say much over the phone. What's going on?" Marina said.

Her father preferred to have important conversations in person. He was still paranoid from Yugoslav times, when telephone tapping was a widespread method of mass surveillance. He was always worried someone was listening in.

Nikola sighed, pointing to a mountain of paperwork labeled *SAPARD 2013: The Special Accession Programme for Agricultural and Rural Development.* "It's all in English. You'll need to translate. These European Union funds can help us save Sirana, if we can get them before next summer when Croatia joins the EU. Things will change after that."

"And if we don't get them?"

Nikola stubbed out the butt in an overflowing ashtray. "It would be a problem."

"Why?" Marina pressed.

"We'll talk about it tomorrow."

Sutra, sutra, sutra. In Croatia, everything was always tomorrow. What would tomorrow bring for Sirana?

"How bad is it, *Tata*?" she said.

Nikola lowered his eyes. "It's possible we could…" His mustache twitched. "We could lose the factory."

Her stomach dropped. She felt the ground beneath her feet move, her heart swirling in uncertainty. It was the same rush of feelings she'd had when her father told her he was sending her to America; unsure about the war's end and their country's future, he'd wanted his only daughter to leave while it was still possible.

In New York, she'd lost count of how many times she had changed apartments, shifting from one rental to another after staying with cousins in Queens during college. No matter how much change she experienced in America, no matter how much her country had changed, she took comfort in the idea that she could come back to Sirana, that somewhere things were always the same.

Her father appeared frailer than she remembered. His strong shoulders had rounded, his knuckles were bony. Since she was a girl, in her eyes, he was invincible. He could lift stacked wheels of cheese with ease, sling bags of feed for the sheep on his back like they were filled with feathers. She couldn't imagine losing Sirana, the spine of Pag Town, which sustained their family and neighbors by providing jobs and supporting the community. Her hands turned clammy.

"*Mala*?" Nikola said, putting his hand gently on her shoulder.

"How much time do we have?" Marina said finally.

"A year," Nikola said.

Marina shuddered. She knew how long it took to get things done in Croatia. It wasn't like America. Croatian bureaucracy would make anyone throw up their hands. And she sensed Sirana was in even more trouble than her father let on.

Nikola paced behind his desk, running his palm over his balding head. She had never seen her father this distressed. He lit another cigarette, inhaling deeply, his forehead creasing. Her chest tightened.

"Does Mama know?" Marina said.

"You know how she worries."

"And Franko?"

"Your brother can't keep anything quiet."

She knew Sirana had been struggling, but she didn't know how bad things had become. Her father, proud and set in his old ways, still did things the same as in Yugoslav times, while everyone else was moving on. She'd heard the rumors. Josip Janković, her father's former friend and previous chief dairy technologist, was making better cheese in the northern part of the island—all the islanders knew it, and even those southerners who had allegiance to Sirana had to admit that Janković's cheese was superior. Marina loved her father, and she didn't want to hurt him by pointing out his mistakes. But someone had to step in.

Marina had studied marketing and management in college on a scholarship, and Marko was a management consultant who turned around businesses for a living. She'd thought they would become a New York power couple, but that hadn't happened. Still, from her American education and her husband, she'd learned the necessary skills to help her father, who didn't speak English and couldn't write convincingly about why Sirana needed EU assistance. If she couldn't save her marriage, at least she could help save Sirana. At least her life in America wouldn't have been a complete failure.

"Go see your mother now, she's waiting," Nikola said. "And on your way, pick up some milk from Konzum, will you? I'll just finish up here."

"See you at dinner," she said, kissing her father and taking the opportunity to exit. She didn't look forward to facing her mother's interrogation, but she couldn't stay at Sirana any longer. All she wanted to do was go home.

The rental car was sweltering. Marina rolled down the windows and turned onto the road, gazing at the hill in the distance. Pag Town residents had the reputation of being closed-minded because they lived sandwiched between two hills on the southern part of the island. When Marina was little, Nikola told her, "Those are northern rumors, it's only jealousy," waving his hand in the air as if to brush away any limited vision.

Her father had told her that wealthy merchants and nobility had settled in Pag Town when it was the center of the island's lucrative salt trade in the fifteenth century, causing jealousy in the poor northern fishing villages—and that envy had persisted for centuries. And now, islanders on both sides of Pag were jealous of the cheesemaker's daughter, who had left for America during the war and had the opportunity to start over. As their country was crumbling, Marina had carried that guilt all the way to America like her ancestors had carried precious bags of salt on their bent backs.

When she was a teenager, even before the war, everyone thought she would escape to New York, maybe become a famous model and marry some millionaire. Nobody told them being a bit pretty wasn't nearly enough. Nobody told them half those "models" worked as cocktail waitresses in nightclubs or seedy places just to get by. She certainly hadn't married a millionaire, and she hadn't found her way in the big, cold city that never forgave her accent.

Nikola had had different dreams for his daughter: an education, success in a serious profession. She had high marks, always placing at the top of her class, striving to meet her father's expectations. He did not consider marketing to be serious enough, and she felt like a disappointment. Now, he needed her help. And she needed her family. Without Marko, they were all she had left.

After stopping for milk at Konzum, Marina left the rental car in the supermarket parking lot and walked the short distance home through the town center, marked by the steeple of the Church of St. Mary's Assumption, where her family attended Mass and where she'd married Marko. How happy she'd been that day, filled with grand expectations for their life together. Against her father's wishes she'd decided to marry him, under the eyes of God. She didn't believe God was on her side now.

In Marko and Marina's living room in Astoria hung a framed piece of *Paška čipka* attached to a piece of creased cerulean paper, a gift from his grandmother. At the end of their annual summer visit last year, when they were packing their bags to leave Croatia, Marko told Marina not to put it in her suitcase, but she was hurried and stuffed everything in. Her makeup bag had crushed it on the trip back to New York. "You've ruined it," he'd said, stomping out of the bedroom.

The intricate doily-like lace was attached to the paper like an artery; it was impossible to remove without damaging the design. If the threads were accidentally cut, the lace would begin to unravel. Months of his grandmother's labor would be transformed into crumpled thread.

Their life had unraveled; she was left holding strings.

She grasped the doorknob of the house where she'd spent the first seventeen years of her life. Each summer, she felt more like a visitor. This year, she realized, she had lived as many years in America as she had in Croatia, her identity split neatly in half.

"Mama?" Marina said, pushing the door open.

Dragica emerged from the kitchen wearing a flowered pink apron. The strings did not wrap around her waist twice, as they once did. Her flaxen hair was swept into a bun on the top of her head. She kissed her daughter briskly on both cheeks. "Your flight landed earlier. You didn't call."

Always the accusations. At least her mother could have offered a welcome home first, since they hadn't seen each other in a year.

"I stopped for milk," Marina said, handing it to her mother. "*Tata* said you were out."

"*Hvala*," Dragica said. She stuck her head outside. "Where's Marko?"

"Working." She smiled and tried not to feel like her face was cracking. The veneer came back easily, the false front she had practiced her entire life in America that concealed her sadness, her loneliness. Acting had allowed her to survive.

"That boy is always too busy," Dragica said, clucking her tongue.

"So busy," Marina said. She'd perfected this smile, acting like everything was fine, at times almost fooling herself. It was her way of coping when things were falling apart, a weapon against feelings that could drown her.

She tried not to think of the woman Marko had been with or how many times. She tried not to think of how he'd made love to that woman.

"Come in, come in," Dragica said, ushering her inside.

From year to year, nothing changed. Even the crocheted tablecloth was the same, painstakingly crafted by her father's mother, the late *Nana* Maržić. Possibly the only thing that had been altered since she'd moved to America was the photo of Nikola and his former best friend, Josip, that used to hang in the living room.

Her father had removed it after Josip left Sirana. Around the space where the frame hung, the cream paint was faded, a ghostly absence punctuated by a hole where a nail once resided.

Grandma Badurina sat at the table, her olive-wood cane propped against a chair. The stately old woman frowned as she sipped her glass of *rakija*. "Marina, you look too thin."

"All that stress in America," Dragica said. "Not good for making babies."

Her mother always had something critical to say, some way to make her feel like a failure. Marina was too tired to fight. "Where's Franko?" she said instead.

She was surprised her father had beat her home. Nikola glanced at his watch. "He should be back from Zagreb by now," he said, hobbling to his chair. His limp seemed worse this year, and she wondered if his old war injury was bothering him.

"I thought he'd be on the field," Marina said, a hint of disgust seeping through her tone. Her brother, still harboring dreams of becoming professional, was always playing soccer. The field was a place to release pent-up aggression—from the war, from being left behind. Croatians were fierce about soccer, and games often turned violent. In Croatia, God and soccer ruled.

"I sent Franko to show his face. We need to get payments from our distributors," Nikola said, sighing out a stream of smoke.

"This isn't Yugoslavia," Grandma Badurina said. "They shouldn't pay late."

"It's still Croatia, what do you expect?" Nikola grunted.

"I heard you're doing payments in cheese again," Grandma Badurina said.

Marina glanced at her father. Nikola's eyebrows furrowed.

"I've been pressing our distributors," he said.

"Press them harder," Grandma Badurina said.

"Mama, let him be," Dragica said.

"It won't matter," Nikola said.

"Why not?" Grandma Badurina said.

Nikola sighed. "Let's not talk about this now. Marina is home, so let's have a nice dinner."

Marina couldn't have a nice dinner even if she tried. She stared at her empty plate.

"What is it, Nikola? I've been hearing rumors," Dragica said.

Nikola threw up his hands and ground the butt into the ashtray. "I'm not going to be able to make payroll again. I'll have to lay off some of our workers."

"There must be another way," Dragica said.

"Draga, I've run the numbers. I've tried everything. I know how much Sirana means to our family, to this town."

"Sirana is part of this family," Dragica said. "We have to do whatever it takes."

Nikola lowered his eyes and cleared his throat. "I know," he said, his face contorting into a painful grimace. "I might as well tell you now. I had to put the house up as collateral."

Dragica gasped. Grandma Badurina's jaw dropped. Under the table, Marina pressed her nails into her palms. She couldn't believe things could possibly get worse.

"We could lose our home?" Marina almost whispered. She felt herself shutting down, the walls inside her rising, barricading her.

Franko burst in the door. "Welcome home, *sestro!*" He surveyed the grim room. "Who died?"

"Sirana is in trouble," Grandma Badurina said.

"I got some money from Zagreb," Franko said. "That should help."

"It won't be enough," Nikola sighed.

"How much do we need?" Franko said.

Dragica poured shots of *rakija*. Nikola retrieved a dented tin box from his pocket and rolled a cigarette. The grandfather clock struck eight.

"Well?" Franko said.

"Oh, for heaven's sake. Your father took a bank loan with this house to try to save the factory," Grandma Badurina said.

"Are you crazy?" Franko said, turning to his father, wide-eyed. His face fell. Marina could tell he wanted to swallow back the words. She wished that this was all a bad dream.

"Franko, don't speak to your father that way," Dragica said. She still treated him like he was a teenager, coddling him and doing his laundry. He could do no wrong. He was the son who had stayed.

Nikola's eyebrows curled into angry caterpillars. He glared at Franko, slamming his fist on the table, causing the glasses to shake. "How dare you speak to me like that! You haven't even taken an interest in the business. This conversation is over."

Marina didn't think anything was over, certainly not the conversation about Sirana, but that would have to wait until tomorrow. Her father had let problems pile up, had tried, in his desperation, to fix one thing with another: a house for a factory. Marina understood that kind of desperation, wanting to save something at any cost.

"Dinner should be ready soon. Marina, come help," Dragica said anxiously, then hurried into the kitchen.

Marina trailed behind, eager to leave. She hated the way her mother was constantly slaving over the stove. Marina had promised herself never to be like her, on a constant rotation of cooking and cleaning. It had been difficult at first to adjust to life in America, with take-out food and coffee to go, but Marina appreciated the freedom from domestic expectations. After writing pitch decks for clients all day, she was too exhausted to cut vegetables or fuss with a marinade. But parts of cooking were satisfying after hard days or fights with Marko. She enjoyed tenderizing meat, pounding a mallet on raw flesh.

"Mama, did you know it was this dire?" Marina whispered.

"Your father will handle it," Dragica said, peering through the oven window.

"It's our house, Mama," Marina said.

"I said he'll handle it," Dragica said firmly. "Any news?" She glanced at Marina and raised her eyebrow, pulling the roast out of the oven.

Marina felt her anger flare. She knew exactly what Dragica meant. Leave it to her mother to shift the conversation from one difficult subject to another. She knew this interrogation was coming, but she thought her mother would at least wait until tomorrow.

"No news," Marina said, crossing her arms.

"Are you trying?" Dragica said.

"I don't want to talk about it."

"You're older now, you should—"

"I told you, I don't want to talk about it," Marina snapped.

"It's about time," her mother said, handing Marina a jug of homemade wine.

At thirty-four, Marina was on the older side already, a year from a "geriatric" pregnancy. Dragica always found something to blame: Marina was working too hard, she was too stressed, food in America wasn't healthy or pure, not good for growing a baby.

Dragica set the platter of meat on Grandma Maržić's crocheted tablecloth, the years of wear evident from stains that never fully disappeared with bleach. The aroma reminded Marina of happier years before the war, when her mother made special dinners more often. *Dalmatinska pašticada* took hours to prepare; Dragica had roasted garlic, cloves, carrots, and bacon, then salted and marinated the beef in vinegar overnight. Then she had cooked it with onions, parsley root, nutmeg, prunes, tomato paste, water, and sweet *Prošek* wine. During the war, they never ate beef. There were no cows on the island, and any good meat from their region went to the troops. On holidays they had eaten lamb, but Marina could hardly bear to have one of her beloved pets for dinner, especially the lambs she'd named.

Since she'd turned thirty, Croatia had called Marina back like a siren, her strong roots stretching across an ocean and a sea. The novelty of Starbucks had worn off, and she missed sitting at Café Zec for long coffees with friends, before her father sent her to New York, before she was a refugee, before she was lost. But she'd never expected to return for more than a summer visit, and certainly not like this.

"Well, now that you're home, you can help your father," Dragica said, turning to Marina. "He's been working too hard lately, coming home late."

Nikola glanced at Marina. "You can translate some documents for me, help me prepare for the SAPARD interviews. Come tomorrow morning, I'll show you."

Marina chewed and nodded, grateful she wouldn't need to make up an excuse and explain to her mother why she was spending so much time at Sirana. Maybe helping her father with the funding paperwork would provide just the distraction she needed. Maybe it would help her find her way.

Chapter Two

Marina awoke to church bells. She'd only been home a week, but it already felt like an eternity. The faded, flowered sheets enveloped her body like a cocoon. She slept on these same sheets when she was a girl. It felt like she'd woken up in the past, as if her life in America was a dream. She almost expected to turn on the radio and hear news about the war. But she wasn't a teenager anymore, and it wasn't wartime.

She pulled the sheet over her face. Light streamed through cracks on the sides of the blinds, illuminating a strip of flowers. How many times had her mother washed these old pieces of cloth, which absorbed her sweat and tears, the blood from her first period. She had been so frightened to awake to that thick, sticky sensation. Her mother had swiftly and wordlessly changed the sheets, rubbing them raw over a ribbed washing board. The fabric became thin but never tore, even after all those years. One day she woke up and noticed that the sheets were threadbare, the flowers no longer bright.

The window let in fresh air and the shade rapped against the peeling wood. Nikola had had air conditioners installed because everyone on Pag was getting them; this was the modern way of living, and he didn't want to be left behind. But they almost never used them. Her mother didn't like running the air-conditioning for fear everyone would catch a cold. She was afraid of *propuh* that blew through cracks.

"Marina?" Her mother knocked, then opened the door without waiting for an answer.

Through the translucent sheet, Marina saw Dragica's shadowy outline sit on the tiny stool where Marina used to put her shoes on before school. Marina pulled the sheet down to her chest, determined to face the day, starting with her mother.

"I thought you would never wake up," Dragica said.

"Where's *Tata*?" Marina said.

"Sirana."

"He's at work on a Sunday? I should go help him," Marina said, swinging her legs over the side of the bed.

"Don't disturb him. He's going over Sirana's numbers today, and he won't need your help with that."

Marina tried to hide her disappointment. Ever since Josip's wife Sanja had left Sirana, Nikola hadn't let a woman touch their books.

"And Franko?" Marina asked.

"Where else?" Dragica said. Of course: Her younger brother would be on the soccer field. Thirty-two and still playing with a ball, not facing any kind of responsibility.

"Have you spoken with Marko? When is he coming?" her mother demanded.

"He's not coming," Marina said, sitting up in bed.

"Why?"

Marina stiffened. "We've been having issues."

"What do you mean?" Her mother wiped her hands on the apron.

Better to say it now. She'd staved off her mother for days, making excuses about Marko's work, how he was busy with clients. He hadn't called, and she hadn't either. She was sick of the veneer.

"I left him, Mama. He's having an affair." It was the first time she'd said it aloud. *Affair*. Her husband was having an affair. Her stomach twisted.

"*Ajme*." Dragica put her hand to her heart.

Marina didn't understand how the years had passed and somehow she'd woken up right where she began, to find all that she thought she had built destroyed, the future uncertain—as uncertain as she'd felt when she started a new life in America as a teenager, far away from her homeland and family. She wanted to hide under the sheets and not come out like she used to do after school when she'd had a bad day.

"It will all work out," Dragica said after a minute.

"You always say that," Marina said. She knew her mother was trying to help in her own way, but Dragica could never give her the support she needed. Marina didn't know what she needed. Maybe just a hug. She crossed her arms over her chest. Her mother wasn't the hugging type.

"I'm always right. Now get up, no use moping in bed," Dragica said brusquely. "Come, have some coffee."

Her mother rose from the chair. Marina trailed behind, feeling like a scolded child. Like most Croatians, her family didn't like talking about their emotions.

Grandma Badurina was in her usual seat at the dining table, sipping Turkish coffee and reading *Free Dalmatia*. Her silver hair was swept up in a bun like Dragica's, and her wire-frame reading glasses sat low on her nose.

"Mama, Marina left her husband," Dragica said. Her face was ashen.

"What now?" Grandma Badurina said, looking up from the newspaper.

"She left Marko," Dragica said, louder.

Grandma Badurina sighed. "I told you she shouldn't have married an American."

"*Nana*, his parents are from Pag," Marina said, and immediately regretted it. She was done defending Marko to her family.

"Northerners have always caused trouble for this family," Grandma Badurina said, waving her hand as if to shoo a fly. "What happened?"

"He had an affair," Marina said.

"If he were southern, I'd say live and let live."

"Mama!" Dragica exclaimed.

Grandma Badurina shrugged. "She's not a girl anymore, Draga."

"You won't try to repair it?" Dragica said, sipping her coffee.

Her mother seemed to think their marriage could be fixed, like Sirana's machines. She didn't know if she loved Marko anymore, or if she could love him ever again. It wasn't just the affair. They weren't the same people anymore.

"Why should I, Mama?" Marina said, blood rising to her cheeks. Why was it hers to fix? Her mother blamed her for everything.

"He's your husband," Dragica said.

"He's not acting like one." How had her life turned out like this? How could he have done this, after what they'd been through? If her mother only knew.

"What will people say?" Dragica exclaimed.

"I don't care what people will say."

"You should."

"What's that supposed to mean?" Marina fumed.

"You're not a young lamb any longer," her mother snapped.

Dragica knew how to hurt her—bringing up her age, and babies. Ever since she'd left for America all those years ago, Dragica's carping had intensified. Although Dragica had never been to New York, she'd heard enough stories. Her mother thought New York was extravagant; designer shoes in stores on Madison Avenue cost a month of a line worker's salary, and she complained that people frittered away money on overpriced drinks and fancy restaurant food. She'd refused to visit Marina, preferring to stay at home on Pag, where she wouldn't have to venture outside her comfort zone or see how anyone else lived. Besides, Astoria, Queens, was hardly the New York of Dragica's dreams.

Marina had the sense that her mother hadn't actually wanted a better life for her. Dragica had wanted her to stay on Pag, to carry on tradition. She'd wanted Marina to suffer, as Dragica had. She'd wanted Marina to be under her husband's thumb, as she had been under Nikola's, having to ask for money like a child asks for allowance because she made no money of her own. Marina had a marketing job, but it was still hard to support herself in an expensive city. Before she married Marko, she'd had roommates in Astoria, barely making rent each month. They'd eaten a lot of instant ramen. Marina remembered those times fondly, even as she tired of the noodles; warm conversation and the support of her friends was the best nutrition. But those friends had faded into the background when she'd met Marko. He became her center.

When she'd married Marko, Dragica was pleased, as if marrying was the highest achievement Marina could have accomplished in America. Having her daughter settled was important for Dragica, even if she'd married a Croatian-American man with parents who had northern roots. Even if Marko sprawled out on the couch after work, watching television, ignoring her and eating potato chips, leaving crumbs for Marina to vacuum. Even if he said he didn't expect Marina to do all the cooking and cleaning, and then changed his mind once they were married. Even if he said he loved her, and then found someone else.

Dragica removed the Turkish coffee from the burner and poured a small cup from the beaker, handing it to her.

"At least have some breakfast," Dragica said.

"Fine," Marina sighed. "I'll have some toast."

"You should try to make up with your husband," Dragica said.

Marina felt her cheeks flush. "Forget the toast, Mama," she said, taking her coffee and slamming her bedroom door. She sat on her bed and gulped down the coffee, trying to calm herself. She wanted to talk to someone, but she didn't know who to call. Who would understand? She stared into the thick coffee grounds. Her father always said *a man could get lost in those grounds*, fearful of what fortunes the patterns could reveal. All she saw was blackness.

In the late morning light, Marina walked along the edge of the sea, passing rusty, mushroom-shaped posts with coiled ropes knotted tightly to keep boats tethered. Sheep dotted chalky hills. In the distance, the slate-gray Velebit mountain range loomed. The scent of herbs—sage, rosemary, and basil—peppered the salty Mediterranean air. A network of drystone walls divided the terrain into uneven segments, the jagged outline of their stones like teeth against the pale morning sky. Pag's dramatic, craggy hills seemed to undulate forever, revealing winks of shimmering sea. Alone in the rugged beauty, she realized she was adrift in her midthirties with no plan. She felt trapped, suddenly aware that she was surrounded by water. The thick coffee jostled in her empty stomach.

The seaweed was jet black, a slash across the shore's cheek. Two old men in a noisy motorboat passed under the small bridge connecting one side of the town to the other, blushes of terracotta roofs flanking both sides. The breeze carried a faint smell of decaying fish. Seagulls barked.

She sat on a slatted wooden bench by the water. Old tires stacked beneath planks of wood created makeshift piers that extended into the bay, and colorful buoys were randomly scattered across its calm, glass-like surface. There was so much life happening beneath, another world she couldn't see. What she couldn't see made her uneasy.

She swiped her phone alive and scanned her list of favorites, pressing Marko's name and sliding her finger left until the red "delete" button appeared. She wanted to delete him from her life, but she knew it was impossible to erase those years, to wipe away their memories.

Somehow life had become a series of logistics, arranged in neat columns like the numbers in Marko's spreadsheets. Each cell led to the next, which led to the next, in an efficient, joyless order. When was the last time they laughed together? She had to think. It must have been two years ago, when he came home with surprise tickets to a comedy show in the city. Usually, Marina didn't enjoy comedy shows, but Marko insisted she'd like it. The comedian riffed on immigrant stereotypes; at first, Marina was shocked, even offended. As he exaggerated cultural norms, she found herself chuckling, then crying because she was laughing so hard. Afterwards, they'd stopped at a bar in the city, drinking to the point where they were both tipsy. They returned home and made love like they had in the early days, all heat and passion.

Her finger hovered over the "delete" button. She paused, lifted her finger, and tapped the screen instead.

"Marina?"

Marko's voice sounded far away. She considered hanging up.

"How long has it been going on?" Marina demanded.

She hadn't suspected the affair—she'd taken him at his word that he was hanging out late with the boys at the bar, avoiding having to face her and their shared grief. They were both running from it in their own ways. She'd started drinking a bottle of red wine almost every night. It didn't really dull the pain, but it helped lull her into a restless sleep. Sometimes she stirred when he entered their bedroom, but other nights she didn't hear him come home. She felt stupid now, not suspecting. She thought the crumpled Victoria's Secret receipt she'd found in the trash was a surprise gift for their summer trip to Croatia. But Marko hadn't bought the lingerie for Marina.

"Well?" she said more loudly than she'd meant to, startling a seagull.

She was irritated she couldn't see his face. His silence enraged her.

"After...you know."

Marina felt chilled. The affair had started after they'd lost their baby. Of course it had. They hadn't had sex for weeks after it happened. Only the doctor had spoken the word aloud: *miscarriage*. They had talked around it. They had talked about letting their baby go. "The healing process takes time," the doctor had said.

"How could you?" Marina said, her voice wavering. She wanted to sob and scream.

"Mina, it just happened," Marko said.

Mina, his nickname for her, because Americans loved nicknames. It made her feel diminutive.

"Don't call me that. And things like that don't just happen."

"We talked a lot, she listened—I'm not saying it's an excuse, but you just shut me out," he said.

"You shut *me* out," Marina said, clenching her fingers around the phone. "You could barely even look at me."

"You wouldn't let me touch you."

"I can't believe you! You make everything about you," Marina sputtered.

He was so selfish. He'd left her alone in her grief, and couldn't face his own.

"Who is she?" Marina said.

"No one you know," Marko said.

Marina wondered if he thought it would make her feel better that the woman was a stranger. It didn't. That nameless, faceless woman. Had he met her at the bar, or at work? Or online? A stranger had been sleeping with her husband, and he had come home to their bed every night without showering. She felt like vomiting.

Marina sucked in her breath. "I'm not coming back," she said hoarsely.

"You were gone anyway, even when you were here," he said.

"How can you blame me for that, when you constantly tune me out?" she shouted.

"Stay, then," he said flatly.

She inhaled sharply and hung up, throwing the phone on the pebbles. A rock punctured the screen like shrapnel. Tears welled in her eyes, a soft wail escaping her lips. She lightly ran her fingers over her abdomen, the soft ripple of stretched skin. Early black-and-white scans flashed through her memory, the barely human figure the size of an olive curled inside her womb, and later, defined images that revealed tiny, perfect hands and feet. Her daughter had been the size of a pomegranate; the fruit of the dead.

Nearly halfway through her second trimester, at a routine prenatal visit, the baby's heartbeat had disappeared. Surrounded by the screams of live babies on the labor and delivery floor, Marina gave birth to a girl who would never take a breath.

She leaned over and hugged the wings of her narrow hip bones, too narrow for children, according to her mother. She remembered how Marko used to praise her body, cataloging its curves with his pointer finger. But after the miscarriage, on the rare occasions they had sex, he turned off the light, as if darkness would make their loss disappear.

In a daze, Marina drove north. She glanced in the rearview mirror at Pag Town growing smaller, her angular face and brown eyes dramatic in the soft light.

It was an hour's drive from Pag Town to the northern olive groves. *Suhozidi*—drystone walls built from pieces of limestone that fit together like puzzles—snaked across the land. One of the drystone walls marked the division between north and south, but Marina could never remember which one. They all looked the same. Her father always found a way to bring up their island's great divide. More and more, he told her, residents from Pag Town were leaving to work in the north for better pay and opportunities. Old island divisions were being resurrected with the new wealth in the north. Money had a way of creating sides. "Yugoslavia was better, with socialism," Nikola often lamented. Marina also fought against nostalgia, that phantom life where people were happier and better, where countries and promises and marriages remained unbroken.

The northern beach bordered the centuries-old olive grove, filled with gnarled trees whose ages surpassed even the oldest island elders. This grove had always been her sanctuary. Before the war, her father had taken her there to pick olives for their homemade oil. Those afternoons felt like yesterday, but twenty-one years had passed. The war began that summer in 1991, on a sticky June day. Picking olives with her father that fall was the last time she remembered feeling unburdened.

Back then, she'd swum with her friends, flaunting their bronzed bodies and flirting with forbidden northern boys. Luka had kissed her for the first time under the shade of the oldest tree, pressing her back against the bark. She shivered, recalling his hands on her body, tracing the edges of her bikini, finding the curves of her breasts. In the light of the setting sun, his blue eyes had pierced through her, as if he wanted to consume her completely. He was her first love. Luka and Marina had dated for a year before she was sent away, with too many words left unsaid.

She didn't think she'd ever fall in love again, but then, she'd met Marko. What had happened to that charming man who came up behind her at a Croatian bar in New York and lightly touched his warm fingers on the nape of her neck, who said, without introducing himself, "I want you to be my wife"? She'd spun around on the stool and laughed. What a line! This was Astoria, not Pag. But she'd agreed to see him the next day. And the next.

What if she hadn't agreed to see him again? What if she had chosen to marry someone else? Her heart fluttered with nostalgia. *Luka.* She undressed behind a tree, letting her sundress crumple in a pile on the stones. As she changed into her bikini, her hand grazed her abdomen and she winced. She leaned against the tree for a moment, unsure her own legs could support her.

Their trees in the northern olive grove were marked with "M" for Maržić, deep peaks like the two hills that hugged Pag Town, painted in white and enclosed in a circle, as if to protect the letter or punctuate ownership—northern land owned by southerners. The oldest olive tree had stood witness to generations fighting over land. Rooted in God's ground, the tree had no argument with men. It was impartial to the changing of borders and empires. The grove had survived the Venetians, who cut down all the other trees to build their floating city but had let the stubborn olive trees live. Survival came from deep beneath the poor soil and limestone rock, between crevices. During wartime, Nikola said the 400-year-old tree was a reminder of their people's fortitude. She tried to remember her own.

The azure Adriatic sparkled in the distance, beckoning her. She needed a baptism in its waters, to feel saltwater on her skin. She wanted everything to wash away.

Swimming made her feel free. Easing into the buoyant water, the sea enveloped her as it had almost every summer for her entire life. She floated on her back until her fingers pruned, letting her body drop into the water, just low enough so her nostrils could still suck in air. Occasionally, a small wave pushed seawater into her nose and she sputtered and coughed. She gasped and held her breath and dove.

When had she become so lost? Returning to Pag this year had made her question her decisions, her life suddenly in microscopic focus. Maybe she hadn't fully acknowledged her rebellion against her family—dating Luka, and then marrying Marko, with their northern blood. Why did she choose partners her parents didn't approve of?

Marina wrapped herself in a towel, licking salt-coated lips. She returned to the grove to escape the Mediterranean sun, taking care to avoid the thistles, their spiny violet flowers a wild, dangerous beauty. Maybe she'd become like thistle: prickly and full of spikes, so no one could get close. Silvery-green leaves winked in the breeze. Other than the chirping cicadas, the landscape was silent, until she heard footsteps on gravel.

A girl, maybe seven or eight years old, peeked out from behind a thick olive tree, her bright-blue dress exposing scraped knees.

"Hello. What's your name?" Marina asked.

"Kata," the girl said, dancing around the tree. "What's yours?"

"Marina."

"Do you live here?" Kata said.

Marina wondered if the girl was trying to determine whether Marina was from the north or south, if Kata was already aware of their island's divide. But the question was not easy to answer. Did Marina live here?

"I'm from Pag Town, but I lived in America," Marina said. She realized her use of the past tense. *Lived.*

"Where do you live now?"

Marina paused. "I don't know. Here, for now." She didn't like uncertainty, the feeling of being a nomad, wandering without a home. She didn't know where she belonged.

"Why?" Kata said.

"This is still my home," Marina said. *And I have nowhere else to go.*

"I'm friends with the trees," Kata said suddenly. "This is Ivo. Do you want to meet him?"

"Sure," Marina said. At least she wouldn't have to explain herself to a tree.

Kata ran over and reached for Marina's hand. The girl led her to the wide trunk and pressed Marina's palm on a knot in the bark.

"Ivo, this is Marina," Kata said. "She lived in America. That's very far away. But now she lives here."

Marina stared at Kata. Her pale skin was sunburned, her blue eyes wild. For a moment, Marina allowed herself to wonder what her daughter would have looked like at that age.

They sat down at the base of the tree, avoiding sharp stones jutting out of the parched terrain. The tree's roots bore into the ground like determined veins. Kata picked at a scab on her knee.

"Ivo is sad," Kata said.

"Why?" Marina said.

"Because you're sad," she said.

"Ivo is right. I am sad," Marina finally said. She had been sad for a long time. "I've lost something." She couldn't believe she was saying this to a child.

"Can Ivo help you find it?" Kata said.

Her inquisitive eyes were so clear that Marina feared she might fall into them.

"No." Marina felt a tear slide down her face behind her sunglasses.

"Someday Ivo will help you find what you're looking for," Kata said.

The girl reached over and hugged Marina around the waist. She didn't let go.

Marina wrapped her arms around Kata and wept. It was as if someone had pressed a release valve. The girl didn't know what Marina had lost, and she could never understand. But right then, Kata's embrace was everything she needed. They sat under Ivo's shade on the barren land where only olive trees grew. Marina's eyelids were impossibly heavy, her face wet. She leaned against Ivo and fell asleep.

When she awoke, Kata was gone. Marina wondered if she had been dreaming. She stood up and studied the way Ivo's body twisted, growing in every direction but straight upward. She marveled at his ancient bark, smooth and rough in places. He was split and scarred by bitter cold, dry and hollowed by the unforgiving sun. Ivo, a thing of beauty, had survived all these years. His leaves fluttered in the salty wind. Late afternoon rays illuminated the jagged landscape, turning it golden. In that moment everything was so touched with fire that she barely recognized the shadows.

Chapter Three

The July sun bore down on Pag's white stone, intensifying the already unbearable heat. Marina sat at a table with a ballet slipper-shaped cake in Pag Town's main square, across from the Church of St. Mary's Assumption. Clusters of bright-pink balloons, stretched taut like her best friend Ivana's stomach, swayed from ribbons held down by stones. Ivana's five-year-old daughter pranced around the square like a ballerina, though awkward in her movements. Marina smiled with appreciation at how she was wholly ungraceful and yet full of joy.

"*Teta* Marina, come dance with me!" Mia said, grabbing Marina's hand and pulling her from her chair. *Teta* Marina, the childless aunt. Marina smiled at Mia, forcing herself to her feet.

One of the mothers played a recording of Croatian folk music. Women and girls joined hands in a circle dance, their shoes brushing and stomping on blocks of chalky limestone. Ivana beamed at Mia, her belly bouncing in time to the beats. When the song came to an end, the chain of hands broke. Girls screamed for cake.

Ivana lit candles sunk deep into the slipper's toe. Mia took a deep breath and blew out the flames.

"Here, my birthday girl," Ivana said, kissing Mia on the forehead and handing her a slice of cake. She cut pieces for the rest of the girls. "Marina, let's have some, too."

Mothers were busy tending to their children, wiping pink frosting from fingers and noses. Marina caught herself staring.

"Sure, thank you," Marina said, accepting a plate of cake and glancing away. She took a sip of coffee. "I still can't believe Café Zec is gone. We basically grew up there."

"Everything changes," Ivana said, rubbing her pregnant belly.

Marina thought about how many things had changed since she'd left. She'd been dreaming about the war years, waking up in a sweat, wondering what would have happened if her father hadn't sent her away near the end of that awful conflict.

Mia tugged on Ivana's dress. "Can we color?"

"Of course," Ivana said. She handed her daughter coloring books and Caran d'Ache colored pencils, but first removed one and wagged it at Marina. "You know, you were my first friend. You always stood up for me, even when I didn't belong here."

Marina could trace twenty years of friendship to a single pencil. A year into the civil war in Yugoslavia, they were on the verge of turning fourteen, that tender age where the wrong glance from a popular girl could mean alienation. In their small class of twenty, Marina was friends with the popular girls, although she didn't think of herself as popular. When the refugees came from the mainland, their class swelled to thirty. There were not enough desks, so some of them sat on folding chairs and took notes on borrowed books stacked on their laps. Ivana, a slight girl with thin raven hair, struggled to write with a pencil stub.

"We're collecting pencils and notebooks for the refugees," the teacher had said. "Everyone be nice to them, and please give something."

Marina's treasured set of Swiss Caran d'Ache graphite pencils was a gift from one of her father's Serbian business contacts before the war. She loved those pencils; imported items like that were rare in Yugoslavia. She took two from the tin and brought the rest to the front of the classroom. Others followed.

After class, Marina gave one of her two remaining pencils to Ivana. "I wanted to make sure you got one," Marina said.

Ivana clutched the pencil like a life raft. Marina would never forget Ivana's wistful eyes, how lost she looked. Marina remembered looking away, feeling guilty for her own settled circumstances, the protected island life she had inherited but not earned. She could have been Ivana; Ivana could have been her. Chance circumstances defined their lives, and Marina was lucky. She had always been lucky, until now.

The mothers stole furtive glances in her direction. Word of her separation with Marko had spread. Rumors on Pag swirled like the *bura* wind, building strength from the mighty Velebit, tumbling down its steep slopes and exploding on Pag Town. Local gossip, often fueled by jealousy, caught on like frenzied bleats in a herd of sheep. Ivana had told her on one summer visit, "You left, like the rest of us wanted to."

Her father had turned her sails in that western direction, months before the fighting ended in Croatia in 1995. Everyone knew Nikola had used his brother's political connections to help secure a refugee scholarship for Marina at City College in New York. None of them knew what lay ahead, across the sea and ocean, but her father believed it must be better than what she was leaving behind. Everyone did.

"Tell me about that night, when you came here," Marina said.

Ivana raised her eyebrows. She tucked a strand of raven hair behind her ear, something she did when she was nervous. No one liked talking about the war. "What made you think about that?"

"I've been thinking about that time a lot lately. Before I left," Marina said, "I was afraid to ask you about it back then. It was so fresh."

Ivana sighed and rubbed her belly. "It feels like long ago, and also yesterday. I remember my sister lost her sandal running over the hill from our village. We got separated. I ran faster than I ever had in my life, away from the Serbs and the shelling and snipers. It was like the *bura* was behind my back, pushing me across the bridge towards Pag. My sister cried over her sandal. She didn't understand there were much bigger things we could have lost."

It seemed like another lifetime ago. Refugees from villages on the mainland flooded the square, congregating in front of the Church of St. Mary's Assumption. Pag was her island; she hadn't needed to run. She'd felt sheltered on Pag, even during the early months of the conflict, even when the Serbian-led Yugoslavian army lashed out after Slovenia and Croatia declared independence from Yugoslavia in 1991. As a teenager it was difficult for her to grasp, their country turning on itself, neighbors becoming enemies seemingly overnight.

Marina had been spared the shellings and snipers, the displacement and losses others suffered. Even she felt it wasn't fair that she had obtained refugee status. She was never in any real danger. Lucky ones like her had escaped to Canada or America, or somewhere else where they had a chance to start anew, even if they didn't know the cost of that yet, even if they didn't realize what they'd left behind.

Americans called Marina a refugee. They sometimes called her Russian because of her accent, and she didn't correct them.

Explaining where she was from was difficult. Americans didn't understand what had happened in Yugoslavia, and sometimes neither did she. Sometimes, she wanted to say, "I'm from no-man's-land." A land in between.

"I was jealous of you," Ivana said. "Your house with heating instead of a wood stove, your Caran d'Ache pencils. You had things. We had what we had from Caritas, but nothing ever really felt like ours. It all felt borrowed. A borrowed life."

Marina donated her old clothing to Caritas. She never experienced what it was like to dig through other people's clothes to find something that fit. Sometimes, she would see a mainland refugee in class with her sweater, or skirt, or pair of socks. On a different body, the clothes took on a new form.

"I found one of your sweaters, once," Ivana said. "I knew it was yours because I saw you wear it. It was light blue with silver flecks, like the sky on a clear day. I never wore it to school. I didn't want people to recognize me in your old clothes. But I wanted to see what it felt like to be you, to wear something beautiful that you once had."

"You never told me that," Marina said, blushing. She remembered that sweater; one of Sirana's distributors had bought it for her in Italy, before the war broke out. It was made of Italian wool, and the silver flecks felt itchy against her skin. Her father complained she was too sensitive.

"We all have secrets," Ivana said. "You and Marko still aren't speaking?" She started clearing the table of plates smeared with chunks of frosting and half-eaten cake.

"I think it's really over," Marina said, picking up plates and throwing them in the trash. She thought about how everything was disposable now: plates and people.

"Give it time," Ivana said.

"You know about the problems we've had over the years. But this is different. I don't think I'll be able to forgive his affair, and—"

Marina held her breath. *And... Our daughter died. The baby I wanted so badly died and left a hole so gigantic we don't know how to fill it.*

"We're just broken," Marina said instead.

"Every relationship has problems," Ivana said. "Marriage is something you have to work on every day."

"You're sounding like a sermon," Marina said, trying to lighten the mood.

Marina tossed the last of the plates into the trash bag. Tears streamed down her face. Ivana dropped the bag and hugged her. Marina felt the baby pressed against her, which made the tears come harder.

"I always thought you'd end up with Luka," Ivana said. "But the war made other plans for you."

"I thought America was finally home. I thought Marko was home."

When Marina had first arrived in Astoria as a teenager learning American customs, English felt like a mouth of sawdust. Articles in front of words felt alien. People laughed when she made mistakes, jesting in their American way: *Want to go to cinema?* So she'd tempered her accent, learned how to blend in—mostly.

America left its mark and she was split, halved like a summer fig. She no longer knew which parts of her belonged. Marko never understood her other half. Maybe she'd known, deep down, that they weren't quite right for each other, that he'd never really understand who she'd been. Or who she might grow to become.

Now Marina was back here, where her life began, on the island that so many still wished to leave. She wanted to tell them that if they went, they would never come back the same. *Don't leave*, she wanted to tell them. *Don't leave.*

"Are you going to church today?" Ivana said. "Seriously, maybe it would help to pray for guidance."

Ivana was a good Croatian Catholic, but Marina didn't think prayers could help her.

"I'm not sure," Marina said. She wasn't sure she could face herself, let alone God. She should pray for Sirana, since she didn't know if her marriage could be saved, or if she even wanted to try to save it. But she definitely didn't want to face the town gossipers at church.

"Are you avoiding church because of the rumors about Sirana's bankruptcy?" Ivana said.

Ivana could always read her mind, the way her husband never could.

"Probably," Marina said. "But I can't really talk about Sirana."

"You know I won't say anything," Ivana said.

"I know. We're going through a difficult time, and you know how *Tata* is."

"Is it true he's paying people in cheese?"

Marina hesitated. She wanted to confide in her friend, to tell Ivana how overwhelmed she'd been with the endless SAPARD paperwork and the disarray she'd discovered at Sirana, but they were within earshot of others. And Marina knew how fast more rumors would spread.

"Just for now." Marina hoped the cheese payment was temporary.

"I'm here for you if you need me," Ivana said, squeezing Marina's hand.

Marina felt eyes boring into her back and had the sudden urge to leave. "Thanks, love. I should go, I'm late to help *Tata* with some things at Sirana," she blurted, immediately regretting the lie. On Pag, it was important to keep up appearances. She smiled, kissing her friend on both cheeks.

On her way home, Marina stopped for an espresso. The old Café Zec was now run by Albanians who didn't serve any liquor, much to the dismay of the locals, who were used to having a shot of *rakija* before their morning coffee. Hearing the American tinge in her accent, they charged her the tourist price for coffee. She paused before paying, then set down the *kunas* on the counter.

"*Ej*, Marina Maržić, bless your dad and Sirana to give us work in these changing times," a line worker from the factory said, raising his cup of coffee at a table behind her. She turned and smiled, but couldn't help herself from worrying. Would they be able to keep employing their workers?

The Albanians, recognizing her surname and realizing her father was Nikola, apologized and tried to give her a complimentary coffee. "It's fine," Marina said, and paid the local price. Still, it stung to be considered a foreigner—even by foreigners. She'd heard rumors from Ivana that people were calling her "The American." She'd been gone for half her life; maybe she was more American than Croatian now.

Who was she? She didn't know anymore. A woman divided, from a divided country. When she was in Croatia, she missed life in New York. When she was in New York, she missed life in Croatia. She felt suspended somewhere over the Atlantic, drowning under waves of the war's making. Yugoslavia no longer existed; after she'd left for America half a lifetime ago, it was erased from maps but not her memories. Almost every summer since then, she'd returned to a country of a different name, a splinter of fragmented homeland surrounded by sea. Could she re-form herself like Croatia had, or would she remain fractured inside forever?

In the following weeks, Marina spent long days in the factory with her father, poring over paperwork and prepping him for interviews with the SAPARD committee. They'd submitted the EU funding paperwork just before the deadline. It reminded Marina of "cramming" before exams in college, a term she'd learned in America. When she tried to describe it to her father, he raised an eyebrow. There was a saying in Croatian about being last-minute—*uhvatiti zadnji vlak*, to take the last train. But her father, despite all his concerns about being on time, had kept Sirana's troubles to himself until it was almost too late, letting pride get in the way of progress.

Marina took comfort in watching the cheesemaking process from the window of her father's upstairs office, the hum of machinery a salve for her frayed nerves. Since she was a girl, Sirana's methods hadn't changed. Twice a day, the sheep's milk was funneled into the factory from the refrigerated tank outside, where shepherds deposited their milk. Then, the milk was pasteurized, and salt and rennet were added.

Rennet was the springboard of cheesemaking: In a slow process, rennet coagulated the milk, producing kernel-sized curds that were then formed into slabs and cut into white blocks, which were then hand-packed into cylindrical molds, drained, and submerged in the *salamura* for a salty bath to help develop the rind. Finally, the wheels were shipped off to the aging room—Marina's cheese castle—where they slumbered on planks for months, each patiently waiting their turn to be rotated and rubbed with oil.

In their applications, Marina had made a plea to the EU agricultural assistance program for new machines, citing unreliable Soviet equipment that desperately needed to be replaced. A few days before the applications were due, the cutter broke. The line workers were forced to hand-cut blocks of curd with bread knives, which considerably slowed down production and led to overtime hours Sirana couldn't afford. For the factory to survive, they needed to streamline production. They could all feel Janković's breath on their necks. Josip's competing cheese factory in the north had already received EU funds, and they were steps ahead of Sirana.

It took weeks to schedule a repairman from the mainland to fix the cutter. Marina had forgotten how people got caught in *fjaka's* hot jaws—a Dalmatian state of mind that rendered a person incapable of doing anything. Her previous visits with Marko only allowed for two weeks' vacation, enough time to relax but not sufficient to succumb to Pag's summer torpor, induced by the Mediterranean sun's intense gaze bearing down on their island. The southern part of the island, including Pag Town, belonged to Dalmatia, a region which had the lion's share of the Croatian coastline. Dalmatians were a particular sort. Some called them lazy, but she felt that was unfair. People on Pag worked in cycles, which were driven by the seasons: There was a time for milking and making cheese, and there was a time for *fjaka*.

The milking season started in January and lasted through the beginning of July, and during that time, shepherds milked the sheep twice a day—once in the morning and once in the afternoon. It was only during these months that Sirana produced cheese, and after that, Nikola liked to joke that the sheep went on vacation. But it was not a vacation for Sirana's cheese family; in the off-season, workers diligently tended to the cheese, rubbing it with oil and turning it as it aged on planks. In the packing room, they cut wheels of cheese into wedges and vacuum-packed them for shipping. Machines were cleaned and repaired. They prepared for upcoming cheese festivals and fairs. And the shepherds didn't get a break, either: They awoke every morning at dawn to make sure the sheep had enough to eat and drink. November brought new lambs, completing the circle of life, which meant the milking season would begin again in January.

One sweltering August day, Marina meandered along Tale Bay on her way to the factory, wiping sweat from her brow. Her phone buzzed—she recognized the 212 area code. She had ignored calls from her office in New York. They knew she'd be away for the summer on extended leave due to a family emergency, but she had written an email to her boss asking to extend her time in Croatia even further and work remotely for the fall. She wasn't sure how she would handle two jobs, especially since the work at Sirana had been so consuming, but she felt compelled to try to keep her position in New York. She couldn't bring herself to quit and wanted to keep her options open.

Marina's boss, like Marina, didn't have children. She was at least a decade older than Marina, probably in her late forties. Her boss didn't believe in regular business hours. She expected her employees to jump when she called, even on weekends. She often took credit for Marina's ideas, presenting them as her own. It seemed no matter what Marina did, she couldn't progress. Marko said Marina's boss felt threatened, but he was a hindrance to Marina's career as well, expecting Marina to come straight home to cook dinner while her boss and other members of the team bonded and brainstormed over after-work drinks. Marina also wondered if her boss disliked that she was an immigrant. Marina's previous boss had been interested in her Croatian background, but this new boss only hired Americans that shared the same cultural references and frowned when Marina spoke Croatian on the phone while eating lunch alone at her desk.

Her boss left a voicemail in a clipped tone informing her they would have to let her go if she didn't return to the office right after Labor Day. Marina didn't blame them; it had been nearly two months since she'd left. Still, she felt disposable, like everything in America. Replaceable.

But returning to New York by Labor Day was impossible. There was still so much to do at Sirana, and she couldn't let her father down. Besides, where would she live if she went back to New York? Certainly not with Marko. Her friends had all married and moved on, and many of them had children. At least on Pag, she had her family. And a routine at Sirana that helped keep her sane.

Feeling heavy, Marina started typing a draft email. *I regret to inform you my family needs me to stay longer.* Her phone buzzed again, her father's number this time.

"He's finally here," Nikola said. "Hurry."

She opened the production room door and held her hand under her nose. Even in the off-season, Marina's acute olfactory sense was overwhelmed. She had become aware of her fine nose in New York, when friends praised her ability to discern obscure notes at wine tastings.

"Third repair this year, *ej?*" the young repairman said, squinting at his clipboard.

"Maybe third time is the charm," Nikola said, forcing a smile.

"I don't even know if I can get this part anymore," he said.

Nikola frowned. "Davor always managed."

"Davor retired. I don't know where he sourced these old things."

"What are our options?" Marina said.

"If I can't find it, I can make the part custom," the repairman said. "But it won't come cheap."

Nikola sighed. "How much will it be?"

"I'll have to talk to my boss. But why don't you think about investing in new machines? I installed some over at Janković's last year. You'd need even fewer workers, so much is automated nowadays."

"We'll always need our people," Nikola said solemnly, handing the man a stack of *kunas*.

Marina knew her father couldn't bear to lay off more workers. The day he was forced to let seven workers go, he'd come home and poured seven shots of *rakija* in succession, a silent tribute to those men and women who made Sirana's cheese.

It was fall before anyone realized summer had slipped away, the last tendrils of unseasonably warm weather reaching into October. Straggling tourists undeterred by the quiet that had settled over the island lounged on a patch of sand near Tale Bay, roasting their pink bodies under the weakening Mediterranean sun. Except for a few local businesses that stayed open year-round, on the first of October, the entire island closed their hunter green shutters and prepared for the long winter ahead.

Marina wasn't sure how long she would stay on Pag, but the longer she stayed, the more convinced she was that she couldn't go back to her New York life. No job, no apartment, no husband. She wondered if Marko was still with the other woman. If her body kept him warm at night in their Astoria apartment. If he loved her.

On her short daily walk to Sirana she passed fishing boats lined up like soldiers along Tale Bay and breathed in deeply the fresh, salty air. She felt imbued with Pag cheese, from the time she woke up to the time she went to bed. Even though she worked from an office above the cheese factory, as much as she washed her hair, she couldn't rid herself of that earthy smell, which emanated from the aging room.

Her name meant "of the sea." Since she was small, she watched the winds mold the Adriatic into lashing tongues that beat upon the land. Waves of melancholy seized her like violent storms. Maybe her destiny was to live adrift, obedient to the sea's ebbs and flows. Still, she questioned what her life would have been like if she had never been sent away. Would the cheese factory have been her life had she stayed? Did all roads lead to the same place? What if Nikola hadn't sent her to America, what if she'd married Luka instead of Marko? What if she had her daughter?

"You're late," Nikola said.

Marina looked at her watch: quarter past seven. Unlike most Croatians, her father was obsessed with punctuality, owing to his years as a line worker at Sirana. She hung her purse on the back of the office door.

"I'm sorry, I thought I had more time," she said.

Nikola clucked his tongue, stubbing out his cigarette. He retrieved a dented tin box from his pocket and rolled a new cigarette, licking the paper to seal in the loose tobacco.

"*Tata*, this smoking—"

"*Bože moj*, I get enough from your mother." Nikola lit the cigarette and exhaled smoke through his nostrils, dragon-like. He took a sip of macchiato, which left a trace of white on his mustache like sea foam.

Dr. Miletić had warned Nikola to quit or at least reduce his pack-a-day habit, but Nikola was a lifelong smoker. "We aren't Croatian without our cigarettes, Comrade," he said. Smoking was how most people got through the war—and through life.

Marina sighed. "So, where are we today?"

"All these European Union regulations," Nikola said, taking a drag. "They're making us change the way we make cheese, and we haven't even joined yet. They don't want us to age on wooden planks anymore because of bacteria. Don't they know cheese is bacteria?" He laughed, and then coughed.

"I think we have a good chance of getting the funds for next year," Marina said.

She wanted to reassure herself and her father that everything would be fine. She didn't want to think about the alternative. Losing Sirana and their house couldn't be an option. But it was.

"I hope so. We need to upgrade Sirana's equipment to compete with Janković." Nikola's expression darkened. He took a long drag.

Marina took a deep breath. "I have an idea, and I want you to hear me out, okay?"

Nikola stared at her, blowing out a stream of smoke. Her father looked skeptical.

"I want to focus on our marketing," she continued. "I want Sirana's cheese to become known outside of Croatia. Our future is with Western Europe and America."

After months of translating documents and filing paperwork, Marina had come to understand that when Croatia became a part of the European Union, with fluid borders, they could bypass Croatian bureaucracy and easily export their goods. How would Sirana's *Paški sir* compete in an international market, up against famous French, Italian, and Spanish cheeses? Pag cheese was famous within Croatia, but Sirana was a small producer compared to Europe or the rest of the world. She worried about competing against Manchego in particular, as their cheese was often compared to it. "Croatian Manchego" some tourists would remark, and she would cringe.

She'd already made plans for them to attend several of the upcoming cheese fairs, most importantly the World Cheese Awards.

"The World Cheese Awards are being held in London," Marina said. "It's important for us to attend, for Sirana to get exposure. I heard Janković is going."

Nikola grimaced at the mention of his former friend's factory. "How much will it cost?"

"Don't worry. I'll figure out how to do it cheaply."

"We need to save our money for the workers and repairs," he said.

"But if we don't go, Janković will steal the spotlight. He'll expand his brand and sell more cheese than us. Global distributors will be there, too."

Nikola nodded. "If Janković will be there, we have to go."

Marina went to her desk and pulled out a pamphlet with a new logo and slogan she'd been working on for weeks. Nikola studied the paper, fingering his mustache. He ran his hand over the brochure's glossy surface, pausing over gold lettering, "SIRANA: Adriatic Gold," embossed on a white doily-like pattern meant to represent Pag lace, which was set on an ice blue background.

Nikola didn't speak or read English but he recognized the gold logo on their island's famous lace; the juxtaposition was perfect. Marina had designed a new beginning for Sirana with an old island symbol, a tribute to its maker's patient, self-sacrificing nature, the skill of a pair of hands. She also hoped it would be a new beginning for herself.

"Well?" Marina said, eagerness edging its way into her voice.

"I think it might be better than Josip's," he said, a smile slowly spreading across his face.

Marina knew her father wouldn't be outdone by his rival. The Janković factory was doing well, and Nikola finally admitted it might have something to do with their clever marketing and tagline, "*Samo Srce*"—Only Heart. The famous Croatian symbol, a heart-shaped gingerbread biscuit glazed red with white accents, made for a clever, eye-catching label.

Writing the marketing material for Sirana, she thought about how, just a few months before, she used to write copy for large technology companies and car manufacturers, talking with executives to try to get their messages across. She sculpted pitches to convey their ideas, to influence buyers and investors. At the end of the day, she felt drained, her ideas eventually chipped away by her boss and the clients into something unrecognizable. This was different; she knew Pag's cheese story in her bones. She could do it her way.

Nikola pointed to the copy on the brochure, which was written in English. "Read it to me."

"Sirana is a taste of history," Marina read. "Some say cheesemaking on Pag dates back to the first century BC, when the Illyrians first settled the island. Making *Paški* cheese is still one of the most important occupations on Pag, and Sirana is the oldest producer."

"The oldest, and the *best*," Nikola said, looking at her with approval. "Add that."

Chapter Four

London's skies were filled with clouds that hung over the city like wet wool. Marina had never seen so much rain. This city, steeped in grays and browns like the teas she consumed for warmth, possessed another kind of chill. Black umbrellas bobbed in sharp waves as people brushed by in a hurry. They walked like people in New York, briskly and with purpose. On Pag, people stopped to greet each other or at least exchange a quick "*Bok.*" Marina clutched her umbrella tighter. The November cold penetrated deep into her bones, settling in the marrow and turning her body icy.

Her father had refused to come. "I can't be in the same room with that man," he said, knowing his rival Josip Janković would be there representing his cheese, boasting about how his was the best. "You should go alone. I'm an old man and you have a young, bright face." Marina begged him to reconsider, but her father's decision was final.

She took the Tube to the behemoth conference center in the Docklands, an endless series of buildings that was a city unto itself. People poured out of the station and moved in an ant-like procession onto the escalators and ramps. She looked at her watch—late as usual, the Croatian part of her that never changed. Picking up her pace, she followed signs with the World Cheese Awards logo, a globe punctured by a gavel, and entered a great hall with ceilings twice as high as Sirana's production room and fluorescent lighting that hurt her eyes.

"Which country?" a man asked. His badge read: Harry, Cheesemonger Herder.

"Croatia," Marina said.

"Happy to help," Harry said. His accent sounded funny to her half-American ears.

He led her through the maze of tables with white tablecloths, each covered with wedges and wheels of different colors and sizes, thick rinds of burnt orange, canary yellow, and deep burgundy, pieces of a dairy sunset. They passed Spain and France, countries that occupied dozens of tables with different cheeses displayed neatly on each.

"Here we are," Harry said.

Croatia shared a single table with two of its former Yugoslav neighbors, Bosnia and Herzegovina, and Serbia. Marina thought how they could never escape their geography, South Slavs forever grouped together. When Marina was growing up, Nikola had tried to explain their country's history to her but she had trouble following it.

The fall Marina turned twelve, after that year's olive harvest, war was all people could talk about. News stations reported that President Tuđman was planning Croatia's secession from Yugoslavia. She didn't understand why Serbian friends were suddenly no longer invited for dinner.

Nikola wanted Marina to understand her place in the world. "Yugoslavia is surrounded with BRIGAMA," Nikola said, explaining how their neighbors—Bulgaria, Romania, Italy, Greece, Austria, Mađarska (how Croatians called Hungary), and Albania—brought about worries and concerns. Given their history, there was always reason for suspicion.

Every few months he made her draw a map of Yugoslavia and its republics from memory. In pencil, so that she could erase if she made a mistake, she sketched borders between the republics: Slovenia, Croatia, Bosnia and Herzegovina, Serbia, Montenegro, and Macedonia. Then, with a thick marker, she retraced the irregular lines that delineated each area of land. Croatia, crowned by Slovenia, hugged Bosnia and Herzegovina like a boomerang; Croatia's right shoulder nudged Serbia, its left reclining in the Adriatic Sea. She colored the whole of Yugoslavia with blue crayon.

Marina's map was often revised over the years. The summer before she turned fourteen, Slovenia and Croatia declared their independence from Yugoslavia. At the time, she didn't know what that meant, but it made her father and all the other adults nervous.

Slovenia and Croatia were shaded in purple crayon to indicate their independence. Macedonia followed. Then Bosnia and Herzegovina declared independence. Marina decided that Serbia and Montenegro, the federation that controlled Yugoslavia after its breakup, should be colored crimson, isolated in angry red to indicate the turbulence and violence of war. And Serbia and Montenegro eventually split as well.

At the cheese competition, the Serbian representative was explaining to a judge how Kashkaval was traditionally dried by attaching two gourd-shaped balls of the cheese with a single rope hung from a wooden pole. "As if placed on a horse's back," the Serb said, "Because 'Kashkaval' comes from the Latin *caseus*, cheese, and *caballus*, horse." Each cheese contained a story.

When Marina glanced away, she saw him. There was Luka, carefully arranging Janković Pag cheese with its red heart logo. He glanced up, his intense blue eyes catching hers. He smiled and the past rushed in: playing together as children in Sirana, when they were innocent and their country was whole. She felt something inside her stir, but quickly tamped it down.

"Welcome to our little corner of Croatia," Luka said, grandly gesturing to their sliver of table.

"Hello to you, too," said Marina, eyeing the table, noticing that he had taken up more than his fair share of space. *Typical Janković.* Marina busied herself with arranging her pamphlets on the table. Sirana's airy blue-and-white brochures contrasted with Janković's red heart, set against a black background. Both had gold lettering, and she was relieved her father had sprung for the metallic gold ink.

"Is your father coming?" Luka said.

"No. Yours?"

"No. And my daughter had a fever so Zara stayed home with her."

"Sorry to hear," Marina said.

The judge finished writing his notes on the Serbian Kashkaval and moved to Slovenia.

"Do you want gum? It helps with nerves," Luka said.

"Thanks," Marina said, shaking her head.

No gum could help her forget what she felt when she looked at him.

"How about some cheese, then?" he said, spearing a piece for her to try.

Marina met his eyes, narrowing hers as she accepted the toothpick and bit off the slice of cheese. It was the kind of cheese she'd grown up with, the kind Sirana used to produce. It emanated their land. She inhaled their island's aromatic herbs and savored the salt melting on her tongue, releasing the complex flavors of history.

"With sage this strong, this cheese was made in spring," Marina said, closing her eyes.

"You've always had an exceptional palate," Luka said, smiling.

"Immortelle didn't have a good season up north, though."

"I can't believe you can taste that in the cheese," he said, shaking his head.

"Croatia?" The judge's tag read, Martin: Chief Cheesemonger, British Cheese Society.

"Yes," Marina and Luka said simultaneously.

She watched the judge's eyes scan their materials and spear a slice of Sirana's cheese with a toothpick. He chewed and scribbled some notes. Marina studied his face, watching for any change in expression. He speared a slice of Janković cheese.

"The same sheep's cheese?" the judge said.

"It's from the same island," Marina said quickly.

"Hmmm," the judge murmured.

Marina watched his pen move across the page. She couldn't make out his chicken scratches, but noted an exclamation point. In an effort to cut costs, her father had instructed the workers to rub Sirana's wheels with sunflower oil instead of olive oil as the cheese aged. She knew Janković still used olive oil. What else made their cheese different? Why was the judge so impressed?

"Do you have any questions for us?" Luka asked.

Us. There is no us. Not anymore.

"Just one," Martin said. "Do you both use the same milk?"

"The secret is in the milk, which contains the essence of our island," Luka said. "Our milk is from the northern part, so our sheep might graze on some different herbs. The southern part is barren in places because of the *bura*."

The man looked confused. "The *bura*?"

"Our strong northern wind that can reach hurricane speeds," Luka said.

Marina cut in, "We also have potent herbs in the south, where Sirana's cheese is made."

"There are probably more herbs in the north, though," Luka said.

"The entire island has patches of salt-coated herbs that contribute to making the flavor so unique," Marina said, forcing a smile. "And Sirana has been making cheese on Pag since the end of WWII." She sounded exactly like their marketing materials. But she wanted the judge to know that their history mattered.

"Interesting," Martin said, scribbling. "Thank you."

Luka and Marina watched as he moved on to the cheeses of France.

"How could you say there are more herbs in the north?" Marina said, turning to face Luka.

"It's true," Luka said.

"You make it sound like we don't have anything in the south!" Marina fumed. She felt her cheeks warming.

"I didn't mean it that way," he said.

"Of course you did," she snapped.

"I don't want to fight like our fathers. Let's start over," he said, extending his hand.

"Is that possible?" Marina wondered aloud. She had been wondering if it was possible to start over ever since she'd moved back to Pag. How do you begin again when the past threatens to drown you; how do you resist the pull to the soft floor of the sea?

As their palms met, she felt a strong current overtake her, an undeniable rush, the same sensation she'd felt when they kissed and groped as teenagers in the olive grove. They held each other's hands for longer than necessary until Marina was forced to look away.

Marina spent the rest of the day answering questions about Pag cheese and Sirana's philosophy and cheesemaking techniques. Luka's voice was confident and smooth, just like his father's, which she remembered so well, hearing it for years in Sirana's production room when Josip and her father had worked together—when they were friends, not rivals.

She tried to focus, reciting phrases and information she had prepared, digging into her brain for more information. With the overbearing lights and stream of people asking questions, she began to feel overwhelmed, her head heavy with memories.

"Our family has made cheese for generations," Luka told a London purveyor. "My father started making cheese out of his garage in 1997, and we opened a brand new state-of-the-art factory just a year ago, with European Union funds."

Marina bristled. That was only half the truth: Luka's family had made cheese for generations, but not alone.

"Right. And you're the only producer of this particular cheese?" the man asked.

"Sirana is the oldest producer of Pag cheese on the island," Marina said before Luka could respond, handing the man a brochure.

Marina read the man's name tag: John: Dissa, Borough Market, London.

"Where is Dissa?" she said.

"We're opening next year near London Bridge," John said. "I'm looking to import some cheeses from your region so I'll keep you both in mind. I should say, one of you in mind. Since it's the same type of cheese, we can only have one."

Luka glanced at Marina.

"We'll look forward to hearing from you," Luka said, shaking John's hand like they were old friends.

"Yes, looking forward," Marina said, shaking John's hand. She wouldn't let a Janković get the last word.

The last of the judges and buyers trickled out. As Marina packed up, she noticed Luka didn't have many leftover pamphlets and wondered if he'd brought less or if people had taken more. Either way it made her stomach turn. Had people preferred Janković's cheese? She couldn't stand the thought.

For years, her father had insisted that Sirana's cheese was better than Josip's. "Janković is just a showman with no substance," Nikola said. Even before she'd moved back to Pag, Marina had pressed her father about spending more money on marketing. He'd just said with a deep belly guffaw, "You want us to be stupid like Josip, spending all his money on ads and fancy new labels that eat up profits?"

But Nikola couldn't deny it: Josip's cheese was selling. Only when he heard that Josip was entering his cheese in the World Cheese Awards did he approve new ads and packaging. Her father told her Sirana's success was already in its flavor, in their decades of experience, but if they needed new labels and brochures to catch the flighty eyes of judges and buyers, "So be it," Nikola had said, slamming his fist on his desk.

"Want to grab a drink?" Luka said, packing up the last of his materials.

"Actually, I'm meeting a friend for dinner, but thanks," Marina lied.

"Come on, just a quick one."

Looking up at him, she felt exposed under the fluorescent lighting, as if he could sense her lie. "I need to get these back to the hotel," she said, awkwardly scooping the rest of her pamphlets into a box.

"That's a lot to carry," Luka said. "I'll help you. Where are you staying?"

"Chelsea."

"I'm in Kensington. It's not far from there. Come on." Luka picked up the heavy box with ease. She couldn't help but notice his fine build, how his biceps flexed under his black T-shirt.

Marina walked alongside him, trying not to stare at his profile. He was always tall, now a full head taller than her, a giant like his father. In his presence she felt diminished. She was so preoccupied she barely noticed they'd missed the Tube station.

"*Ej*, where are we going?" Marina said.

"It's easier if we grab a taxi," Luka said. "Too many transfers on the Tube, and it's going to rain."

"That will cost a fortune!"

"*Nema problema*, it's on Janković."

Marina stopped walking. "I can't," she said. She felt guilty even being near him.

"What?"

"I can't accept favors from you or your family."

"Don't be crazy."

"If my father found out he'd never forgive me. I shouldn't even be talking to you."

"I won't tell if you won't." Luka brought his index finger to his lips, smiling.

Marina hesitated, then nodded. She felt like a rebellious teenager again.

Luka hailed a taxi. A fine mist enveloped them, dusting tiny droplets on their faces and coats.

"Where to?" the driver said through the intercom.

"Builders Arms in Chelsea," Luka said, with the authority of someone who'd been there.

"So we *are* getting that drink," she said, flashing him a smile. She'd forgotten what it felt like to flirt.

Marina watched as the droplets gathered on the windows, magnifying a darkening sky. She felt a heady mix of excitement and adrenaline. In this foreign city she felt like a different version of herself, more powerful, bold. No one knew her here; she was anonymous. She could be anyone.

They passed a park where children were playing hide-and-seek, shrieking in the rain.

"Do you remember playing hide-and-seek in Sirana's cheese castle?" Luka said.

"Of course," she said, her cheeks flushing. She did remember: running through the cheese castle's dairy lanes filled with rows of stacked wheels, sitting together in the worker's lunchroom eating slices of Sirana's cheese with crusty white bread. Their furtive teenage meetups during the war, Luka in the northern olive groves, pressing her against gnarled trunks, his soft lips on her skin, his hands memorizing her body.

"I remember those days, before everything happened," Luka said.

"Everything worked out for you," she said.

Luka looked down. "Most things."

For a moment, Marina thought about getting out of the taxi, standing with her box of pamphlets in the drizzle without an umbrella. *We can't go back.* After Luka's father had betrayed them and left Sirana to start Janković, her father had said, *The past is the past. Let's leave it there.* When Marina looked at Luka, the past didn't feel so far away.

Inside the Builders Arms pub, crystal chandeliers hung over mismatched couches and chairs. The worn hardwood floors looked at least a century old. It was cozy and familiar, the kind of place you couldn't help but feel welcome. An illuminated sign above a wine barrel table read, "Beer today gone tomorrow."

Luka ordered for both of them. "Two pints of Guinness," he said.

The bartender poured velvety beer with thick white foam into two pint glasses. Luka reached for his wallet.

"It's on me," Marina said.

"No chance," he said.

Luka paid before she could protest any further and handed her a glass, grinning. Her father wasn't far from her thoughts; he would be furious. So would Marko. He was always the jealous type. Did she care what Marko thought or did anymore? They were separated now. The terms of their separation were murky, but to appease their parents, they had agreed to give it until next summer before filing for divorce.

"Remember how you used to think my father was Klek the Giant?" Luka said, interrupting her thoughts.

"I can't believe I ever told you that!"

"You told me a lot of things," Luka said.

"I remember the day you snuck a fistful of curds from the vat," Marina said.

"My father gave me a slap across the face."

"Curds went flying across the floor!"

They laughed. The heady mix of beer and memories made Marina feel lightheaded, or maybe just lighter. They drained pint after pint, so many she lost count. Loud laughter echoed in her ears. She never drank this much. Talking with Luka was so easy. Marina recognized his boyhood mischievousness in the way he looked at her, playfulness gleaming in his eyes.

"So, your husband is in America?" Luka said.

"You must have heard the rumors. I left him." The words felt bitter in her mouth. She took a large sip from her glass.

"I'm sorry," Luka said, putting his hand on hers.

"Don't be." His warm palm felt safe.

They nursed their beers in silence.

"Any children?" Luka said.

Marina felt her body tense. Luka didn't know, how could he? How could anyone.

"No," she said. "And I heard you have a daughter?"

"She makes everything worth it," Luka said, taking out his phone and showing her his screensaver.

Marina stared at the screen. She shivered. The girl from the olive groves. Marina remembered her wild, bright eyes.

"She has a strong spirit," Marina said, struggling to keep her voice even.

"Not unlike someone I used to know, before she left our little island for America," Luka said, winking.

"She got her mother's good looks," Marina jested, studying Kata's features. "And your eyes."

Luka rotated the pint glass on the bar and took a sip.

"Yes," he said quietly. He paused and studied the glass. "You know we are good friends with Zara's family. My father arranged the marriage. After Branko died, I would have done anything for my father."

Marina took a sip of beer. Her mother had called her in New York—a rare thing with the cost of long-distance calls—weeping, after Nikola and Franko had left to fight in Operation Storm. Josip, Luka, and Branko had joined the fight for Croatia, too. Men and boys became soldiers, something to which most were ill-suited.

"I'm sorry about Branko," Marina said in a low voice.

"That bullet was meant for me."

"Don't say that."

"Branko jumped in front of me, knocked me to the ground. He protected me, made sure his little brother didn't get shot."

Marina didn't know what to say. "I'm so sorry," she said.

"My father shot that Serb dead, so he couldn't kill anyone else," Luka said. "You don't understand until someone close to you dies."

Marina took a breath. "I had a miscarriage. Second trimester. I know."

"I'm sorry. That's terrible," Luka said.

"It was. It is. Of course, it's not the same as losing a brother."

"You lost a life," Luka said.

They drank in silence. Marina felt like collapsing on Luka's shoulder. The beer made her feel heavy and slow. Being with him felt like old times. But they were both in different places in their lives now.

"I should go," she said, rising from the stool. "Big day tomorrow, and we should get some rest."

"I'll help you," Luka said, picking up the box.

"I'm fine, really. A taxi shouldn't be too expensive from here."

"Do you think I'm going to let you go alone in the rain at this hour?"

Marina looked at her watch. How was it nearly midnight already?

The drizzle had turned heavier. Luka opened his large umbrella and they huddled under it. Marina was too exhausted to argue. He hailed a taxi.

"Chelsea House Hotel, please," she said.

Marina couldn't wait to get back to her room. The alcohol made her feel disoriented. So did Luka.

He held the door for her. They entered the lobby and stood under a bright brass chandelier. He tapped the umbrella and set it in the stand.

"I can get that," she said, opening her arms to receive the box.

Luka smiled and shook his head, ascending the carpeted stairwell.

Marina followed. She wanted to tell him not to come up, that she could carry the box herself, but the words stuck in her throat. The stairs creaked under their weight. The Victorian house had been opulent once, but it had fallen from grace. Now a budget hotel, it was a skeleton of its former self. Would this be Sirana's fate? She could not let their beloved cheese factory become a relic. She wouldn't let a Janković into their lives again. She chided herself for being so open with Luka.

"Which floor?" Luka said.

"The top," Marina said. Her mouth felt dry from the alcohol.

When she turned around Luka was staring at her. She felt blood rush to her cheeks. He took a step toward her, reached down, and cupped her face in his large hands. Before she knew what was happening, he leaned down to kiss her. Swept up by the past, she turned her face and let his lips brush the edge of her mouth.

Marina felt her whole body tremble. He had been her first lover. His hands knew the curve of her clavicle, the shape of her breasts. She had buried the memories under shame and guilt. *I'm a good Catholic girl, I'm a good Catholic girl*, Marina remembered repeating to herself when they were younger. She felt transported back to that moment on the beach when they were teenagers, cloaked by a hot summer night, only their breath and bodies guiding them.

"We can't," Marina said, pulling away.

"Seeing you," Luka said, his voice hushed. "Seeing you again…I didn't know I still felt this way. That I could still feel this way."

He ran his hand through his hair, a gesture he did when he was nervous. He looked distressed.

She was distressed, too. Something inside her, long dormant, had awakened. Trancelike, she couldn't take her eyes off him, couldn't break his gaze.

"I didn't either," Marina said finally. She heard herself saying the words, but couldn't believe she was saying them, the truth of what she felt. She'd thought of him many times over the years. Those sleepless nights in Astoria, she'd wondered what her life would have been like if she'd stayed.

She wanted to let herself go, but she knew what would happen if she did. It was a line she couldn't cross again.

"It's been a long night," Marina said. "Let's both get some sleep."

She tried to tamp down the beast that had unleashed itself inside her. It took every imaginable restraint not to fall into him.

"Don't you ever wonder?" The way he looked at her made her feel as if he could see through her.

"What?" she said. But she knew.

"If you hadn't left—"

"But I did."

"I never connected with anyone like I did with you," he said. "I miss our conversations. I miss—"

"Luka, don't."

She closed her eyes. The anguish returned, as fresh as when she'd left, knowing she would have a different life than the one they'd imagined together—a life in America. A life without him, far away from the war and the rivalry between their families. Far away from the raw intimacy they'd shared. Leaving him had almost broken her.

"You should go," Marina said, pushing the door open.

"I want to stay right here," he said.

His eyes. Those bright, beautiful eyes. She couldn't bear to look at him any longer.

"Go," she whispered, shutting the door softly behind her.

Later, alone in her room, when Marina crawled into bed and turned off the light, all she could see was Luka's gaze, his warm hands cupping her face. She thought of all the secrets contained inside her body, how they moved like hungry shadows, quickening the beating of her heart.

That night, she dreamed she was on a plane back to America. In her mind's eye she saw herself opening the red emergency exit, watched as her body was sucked through the door, disappearing into a thick pillow of clouds. She fell through the fog, engulfed in white mist. Luka's hands were on her skin, moving her hips in a gentle rhythm, her legs splayed wide. Every muscle alert with vibration, followed by an ache that simultaneously ripped her apart and filled her up inside.

The next day, the enormous room of the convention center was filled with palpable tension, nervous cheesemakers who had slaved over their wheels, tenderly rubbing them with oil as though they were caring for babies. Now their children would be judged.

Marina was late, as usual. She hadn't slept well, waking up from the dream in a sweat. It had felt so real.

Luka was already talking to a judge, his charisma perceptible even from a distance. She held her breath and took her place at their table.

"*Jutro,*" Luka said, turning his gaze towards her for a moment before returning to his conversation with the judge.

"Morning," she said, averting her eyes.

She tried to concentrate, but she couldn't stop the old memories from replaying in her head. Luka's hands on her body. Limbs intertwined. Sand. Sweat. Luka represented everything she left behind when life felt boundless. For a moment last night, she was that more hopeful, unbroken version of herself. The past came, quick and urgent, like seawater rushing through cracks. She swallowed mouthfuls, unaware that, like saltwater, it would just make her thirstier.

Judges and purveyors made their second rounds. "Cheese has personality," Marina overheard one of the judges say. "Sometimes when you first encounter a cheese you can find it offensive. It's important to give it another try, on a different day, in case either of you were in a mood." She studied the judges' faces, trying to discern which cheeses excited their palate on a second go-round. Most had perfected a poker face. The judge left and Luka turned to her. "Listen, about last night—"

"Let's just forget it," Marina said, knowing it was impossible even before she spoke the words.

"I can't."

"*Bonjour*," a woman said, approaching their table. She had a smart brown bob and intelligent, curious eyes. Marina could look into eyes and see stories; she always recognized the particular strained hue of trauma reflected in her own.

The woman looked at them curiously, studying their faces. "Sorry, I'm interrupting?"

"Not at all. How can I help you?" Marina said.

"Tell me about Croatia," she said, her eyes wide with youth. "I'm Céline, from Basque—French Basque Country."

"I'm Marina, and this is Luka, from the island of Pag in Croatia."

"You work together?"

"No," Marina and Luka said simultaneously.

"But you are making the same cheese, this *Paz̆ki seer*?"

"We both make it," Luka said. "Different factories."

"We make sheep's milk cheese in the Pyrenees Mountains, near the French and Spanish border," Céline said. "My father is the cheesemaker of Petit Agour. You must know it?"

"No," Marina said.

"Have you been to France?" Céline said.

"No," Marina said. "But I will be going in April with my father, to SIAL in Paris."

"Oh, you must come, and not just to Paris for *Salon International de l'Agroalimentaire*," Céline said. "Our mountains are beautiful. They have snow hats—how do you say in English?"

"Snow caps?" Marina offered.

"*Oui*. I must come to your island. I have never been to Croatia. Maybe we could exchange, you know, you come to our factory and I come to yours."

Marina was taken aback by the young woman's presumption. Marina remembered herself at that age in New York, when she hadn't yet suffered crushing disappointments and rejections. She had been bold and tenacious once, too. And she felt her boldness coming back.

"We don't work with other producers," Luka said flatly.

Céline raised her eyebrows.

"He's afraid that someone might steal their secret cheesemaking techniques," Marina said, realizing her tone was slightly acerbic. "Our dairy technologist is Tomislav. I'm not a cheesemaker—I help with marketing at Sirana. We are Pag's oldest cheese factory."

"Well, then your Tomislav must come to learn about our French cheese," Céline said.

"I would need to check with my father," Marina said. "He's the boss."

"I give you my card. Please call or email. *Bonne chance!*" her new friend said.

An announcement boomed over the loudspeakers: "Best Central and Eastern European Sheep's Milk Cheese, please proceed to South Gallery Meeting Room twenty-nine."

"That's us," Marina whispered, realizing too late the unintended choice of "us." She blushed.

Luka didn't seem to notice. "Let's go."

They walked through long hallways and filed into the meeting room. A panel of five judges sat on the stage behind a table.

"Welcome," the man holding the microphone said. "And thank you to our panel of distinguished judges. It gives me great pleasure to announce the winners of the 2012 World Cheese Awards in the Best Central and Eastern European Sheep's Milk Cheese category."

She didn't want to sit next to him, but their chairs were already assigned. Being close to him felt kinetic. Marina clutched the armrest. Luka rubbed his hands on his thighs.

"For third place, Jovanović Kashkaval cheese from Pirot, Serbia. Congratulations on a total score of forty-one."

The lanky Serb bounded up the stairs to accept the award, a wide smile exposing his poor teeth. Marina could hardly concentrate. Sirana had so much riding on this competition. She hoped it would be their time to shine.

"For second place, Kovač Bovec cheese from Bovec, Slovenia. Congratulations on a total score of forty-six."

A woman with cherub cheeks and a wide girth took her place on the stage. Marina's stomach sank. She'd sampled Slovenia's masterful cheese, with a distinctive aroma and piquant flavor, and thought it might win. If that impressive cheese placed second, did Sirana stand a chance?

"And the winner of the 2012 World Cheese Awards in the Best Central and Eastern European Sheep's Milk Cheese category is..."

Marina sucked in her breath.

"…Janković Pag cheese from Pag Island, Croatia."

The room erupted in applause. Luka rose from his chair, glancing back at Marina. She couldn't read his expression, a mixture of elation and apprehension. He ascended the stage and shook the announcer's hand, accepting the golden globe-shaped award.

"Congratulations on your gold award, with a nearly perfect score of forty-eight," the announcer said, shaking Luka's hand and handing him the microphone.

Luka looked out into the crowd, hand over his eyes like a visor, searching. Marina gripped the chair's arms harder. She stared blankly at the stage. Her heart pounded in her ears with rage at Luka's father's betrayal. Luka wouldn't be standing there accepting an award if it wasn't for Sirana, and for her father. She couldn't believe she allowed herself to get swept up in the memory of their torrid teenage romance.

"This award means so much to me and my family," Luka said. "My father started making cheese in his garage fifteen years ago, and I am honored that our cheese made it this far. We are in good company with these exceptional cheeses from our region. Thank you to the judges, and congratulations to everyone."

Under the bright lights, Luka shook hands with the Serb and Slovene. Marina stood up and made her way to the door before Luka could follow her. At the Tube station, Marina watched people get off the train. *What if they didn't receive EU funding? What if Sirana declared bankruptcy, what if it didn't survive? What if they lost their home?* She closed her eyes to shut out the world. *My father. This would kill him.*

"I wanted to catch you before you left." The female voice was high-pitched, breathless.

Marina's eyes snapped open. Céline was standing in front of her.

"Quickly, hop on," Céline said, grabbing Marina by the arm as the doors closed behind them.

"Where are you headed?" Marina said.

"I thought we could have a drink," Céline said. "I saw you leave. I was there, in the back of the room. You left so suddenly, you must need some cheering up."

Marina's cheeks flushed. "It's a disappointment, obviously. We are planning to make some changes at Sirana, but—" She stopped herself. She didn't want to reveal Sirana's financial troubles to a stranger.

"But I just started helping my father with the business a few months ago," Marina said instead.

"It's your first time here?" Céline said.

"It's that obvious?" Marina said, fidgeting with the button on her jacket.

"I hadn't seen you at the World Cheese Awards before is all. My father has been interested in Eastern European cheeses for some time now, particularly Croatian."

"Why Croatia?" Marina said.

"Well, for one thing, you'll be part of the European Union soon," Céline said. "He is thinking about investments."

"What kind?" Marina said.

"Real estate, maybe other things," Céline said. "Shall we get off here and find a pub? I'm not sure where you're headed."

"Chelsea. But this is my transfer."

They exited at Tower Hill station. Céline walked with purpose. She looked up at a sign: The Liberty Bounds. "How about this?" she said.

"Why not?" Marina pulled her coat tighter around her.

The pub hummed. Crimson carpeting was patterned with golden anchors and nautical knots. Rich oak paneling and a floor-to-ceiling wall of books flanked a grand staircase.

Céline walked directly to the bar and held up a hand to signal the bartender.

"I'll have a Pinot Noir," Céline said.

"Same," Marina said.

"It's on me. You had a difficult day," Céline said. They clinked glasses. "At least their win will bring attention to your island and your cheese also?"

"Maybe," Marina said, taking a long sip of wine. She realized, out of nervousness, she hadn't eaten. The wine went straight to her head.

"You and Luka, you're friends?"

Marina blushed. "Not exactly. Our families have history."

"Oh, I thought—you seemed friendly," Céline said.

"We used to be friends," Marina said, taking another sip.

"I used to have someone like that. My father didn't approve," Céline said.

Marina swallowed the wine, leaving her throat dry. "What happened?"

"He didn't think the guy was good enough for me. My father said if I married him, I wouldn't inherit our family's cheese business. I had to choose."

"That must have been difficult," Marina said quietly, fingering the stem of her wine glass.

"He's with someone else now. Life moves on."

"Does it?" Marina wondered aloud.

"My father taught me you have to keep moving forward," Céline said. "Don't look back. These awards are over. You have next year, and the next, to become better."

Marina liked this girl. Céline knew what she wanted. Marina admired her decisiveness, her ability to focus on the path ahead.

"Thanks for the wine—and advice," Marina said, kissing Céline on both cheeks before they left.

Céline rushed to the curb and hailed a taxi. "Tell me what your father says about the exchange!" she said over her shoulder.

What would her father say, Marina wondered. And what about the competition, Sirana's loss and Janković's win? Marina closed her eyes at the thought of telling him, but Céline's words echoed in her ears: *Life moves on.* There would be more competitions, more cheese. Maybe their cheese could be improved. And maybe Céline could help them. Marina was more determined than ever to make Sirana succeed.

Chapter Five

Marina gazed out the kitchen window at the stark December landscape. Stripped of its sparse foliage by the *bura*, the Velebit mountain range was a naked giant lying in wait for spring. She felt a chill and pulled her sweater tighter around herself, nursing her cup of tea.

Gossip had spread quickly. Pag Town was already abuzz with the news of Sirana's loss at the World Cheese Awards last month. The numbers were not good. Vendors in Zagreb, Split, Dubrovnik, and Rijeka owed them money, and they needed to collect. Sales were lower than expected. Now, with Janković winning the award, the demand for Josip's cheese would be even higher. Sirana needed to find an edge.

To nurse her family's disappointment after the defeat, Dragica had prepared *pašticada*. She rolled gnocchi from an island of potatoes, folding in snowfalls of flour until the dough became light.

"Can you pass me more flour?" Dragica said, startling Marina.

Marina handed her the bag. Here she was, cooking in the kitchen with her mother—a place she'd vowed she'd never be.

"Your father hasn't been sleeping well," Dragica said.

"Poor *Tata*," Marina said.

Marina didn't add that she hadn't been sleeping well either. She hoped her late-night calls with Marko hadn't kept Nikola up. She didn't know why she answered his calls; they were both hanging onto something, their familiarity a salve. Marko sometimes called after work, when it was after midnight on Pag; the six-hour time difference made phone calls inconvenient. When they texted, there were often misunderstandings, leading Marko to erupt in bright bursts of anger. They'd agreed to keep texting to a minimum. Often when they spoke, the lonely line hummed in waves of silence.

Marina studied her mother: Dragica's arms were strong from rolling countless mounds of dough, lifting pans of *pašticada* with her stubby fingers that Marina thankfully had not inherited. She didn't look like her mother, except for her eyes, in shape and color. Maybe in a couple decades she would begin to look like Dragica, take on her hunched posture.

"I heard you on the phone late. You've been talking with Marko?" Dragica said, dusting the countertop with flour.

"I wouldn't call it talking."

"How long is this going to go on?"

"I already told you. We said we'd wait until summer."

Dragica sighed and leaned her weight into the rolling pin.

"Do you think I wanted this, Mama?" Marina said, feeling her chest tense. "Do you think I wanted—"

Marina didn't finish the sentence. She had not wanted to lose her baby. She had not wanted to lose her husband. She had not wanted to lose herself. Her time in America seemed to bring her further from the person she was, the person she wanted to be. For a brief moment, she considered telling her mother about her miscarriage, the piece of herself that was missing and the hole it had created in her relationship with Marko. She was realizing, slowly, that the absence could never really be filled.

"I didn't want to lose everything," Marina said, washing her hands.

"You haven't," Dragica said. "You have us. But what are your plans, Marina?"

Marina rolled a gnocchi with a fork. "I don't know."

"I can't imagine you'll stay here forever. Why can't you two sort this out?"

"He wants me to be someone I'm not!" Marina exploded, surprising herself and her mother. For seven years, Marina had been trapped in a role that didn't fit. She was so used to pleasing everyone around her that she no longer knew what she wanted.

Franko entered with a rush of cold air, his cheeks flushed. He'd inherited Nikola's solid build, but soccer kept him in shape.

"Shoes off," Dragica said, not turning around from the stove.

"Yes, Mama," Franko said, unlacing his muddy cleats.

"Nice of you to show up. Care to help?" Marina said, glaring at her brother and shoving him a stack of plates to set the table.

"I always help," he grinned, taking the plates from her and sticking out his tongue.

"Of course you do," Marina said, rolling her eyes. Her brother still acted like a teenager. He rubbed off on Marina, who sometimes regressed into juvenile behavior herself.

"*Pašticada?*" he said, leaning over Dragica's shoulder.

"Shoo," she said, hitting him with a dish towel.

Franko retrieved two bottles of Karlovačko from the fridge and handed one to Nikola, who was sitting at the dining table, immersed in the paper.

"How was practice?" Dragica said, emerging from the kitchen. Marina followed her with a jug of water.

"Good. I scored a goal," Franko said.

"I need to go over Sirana's numbers with you tomorrow, since we're nearing the end of the year," Nikola said, popping open the beer.

Marina fumed. Even though she'd helped her father with the funding applications, Nikola wanted to share Sirana's finances with Franko. Their island was patriarchal, and this deep-seated chauvinism made her boil. Marina had accepted it growing up, but after spending time in America, she could no longer turn a blind eye to some of the dated beliefs entrenched in Pag. She cared about Sirana's survival, and wanted to be involved in all aspects of the business. She was all in.

"*Nema problema,*" Franko said breezily. He ran his fingers through his hair and leaned back in the chair so it balanced on two legs, taking a long sip of beer.

"This year has been a catastrophe, with repairs and late payments," Nikola said.

"They pay eventually," Franko said, filling up a glass of water from the jug.

"Franko, you need to take this seriously."

"I know, we'll figure it out, *Tata,*" Franko said. "Tomorrow."

"*Sutra, sutra, sutra,*" Nikola said, sighing. "Everything is always tomorrow."

Marina slid into her favorite black pumps. Nearly half a year had passed, and soon it would be Christmas, and then a new year; she hoped 2013 would not be unlucky. Then her thirty-fifth birthday in February. The thought filled her with dread. She would be officially geriatric, by pregnancy standards. As a college graduate with a new American life, she had imagined she'd be settled by this age, married with a family. Back then, so many choices were ahead of her. And now, waking up every day alone in her childhood bedroom, she wondered how many moves she had left.

Marina turned the knob to the office.

"*Jutro*," Nikola said, lighting the tip of a freshly rolled cigarette.

Marina spun around. "Good morning! I didn't expect to see you here so early. I thought you were still asleep."

She kissed her father's head and sat in the chair across from his desk.

"You couldn't sleep either?" he said, exhaling a cloud of smoke.

"Not a wink."

"I've been thinking about what to say to the workers. You're good with words, *Mala*. I'll need some good words. I'm going to have to fire Tomislav."

"But who will make our cheese?" Marina said. She knew money was tight, but her father didn't remember enough about cheesemaking to run the production room. It had been almost two decades since he'd made cheese with Josip.

"I should be able to secure a temporary dairy technologist for cheap, maybe a student in training. We have a month before the milking season begins." Nikola fingered his mustache and frowned. "But I'm worried about you, *Mala*."

"I'm fine, *Tata*. Don't worry."

Marina couldn't meet his eyes, turning instead to look at the production room below. She wasn't fine, and her father knew it. He'd probably overheard through the thin walls her late-night, long-distance fights with Marko.

Every morning, she woke up feeling like her head was just above water. The day was spent treading, and by bedtime, she felt as if she was being pulled under, exhausted from fighting the tide.

Marina looked at the clock. The workers would arrive in less than an hour.

"I want to show you something," she said.

Marina pulled Céline's business card out of her purse and handed it to her father.

"I met the daughter of a French cheesemaker who makes Petit Agour. She's young, but her father is an expert, and she learned from him. She's ambitious. Maybe she could help us temporarily for the season."

Nikola turned over the card, squinting.

"I really liked her," Marina added.

"The French do make very good cheese," Nikola said.

"The best."

"She would expect a high pay? In euros?"

"I think she would do it for room and board, maybe a small stipend. She wants to learn about Croatia and our cheese. But I would need to ask."

Nikola exhaled a stream of smoke. "Do it," he said, stubbing out the cigarette. "If she's no good, we can always send her back."

In the production room, thirty workers formed a semicircle around Nikola, who was like a commander rallying his troops. Marina watched from the door, and she wondered if her father had looked like this when he went off to fight in Operation Storm: chest puffed, chin raised, bold and inspiring. The necessary confidence of a man facing death.

In a normal year, Nikola called a meeting like this only once, at the end of the milking season. But given Sirana's performance at the World Cheese Awards, he asked everyone to gather. There was work to be done in preparation for the beginning of the milking season in January.

"I'm sure you're all disappointed, but we will come back stronger," Nikola began, his voice steady. Marina pictured her handwritten scribbles, the speech she'd written for him that morning. "Our cheese has a long history on this island, and many of our fathers and grandfathers worked in this factory. Sirana made the best cheese in Yugoslavia, and the name *Paški sir* was known. It is still famous, and it will become more famous—in Europe and even around the world. We are going to get help and advice from the best French cheesemakers, who make sheep's milk cheese in the mountains."

The workers whispered among themselves. Marina had spoken with Céline, who was delighted at the prospect of coming to Pag, and agreed to work for room and board and a modest monthly salary. She would stay through the milking and production season, from January through early July. Croatia was slated to become a member of the European Union on the first of July, and on that day, Nikola planned that Sirana would unveil its improved cheese.

"This season will require hard work from all of you, but together, we can do it," Nikola continued. "We are like family— some of us are actually family. Igor, Stjepan, you are my cousins by blood and my brothers in war."

Igor and Stjepan nodded solemnly.

"We want to be proud of our cheese, made from the fruits of our land. It represents our country, all the richness and complexity we have to offer. Let's show them what Croatia can be, and what it has always been."

The workers applauded. Marina smiled. Their cheese family, however imperfect, was loyal.

"Alright, back to work," Nikola boomed.

The whir of machinery filled the room.

"Tomislav, please come to my office," Nikola said in a low voice. "Marina, you too."

Tomislav followed him through the maze of concrete hallways and up the stairs. Nikola sat down at his desk, and Tomislav sat across from him. The poor man looked like a pale, trapped animal. His wispy white hair blended into the wall. Tomislav tapped his boot on the floor, his knee bobbing up and down. Nikola rolled a cigarette.

"I'm sorry, Tomislav," Nikola said, striking a match. "We talked about this before, and it's time."

"Can't you keep me on for a little longer?" Tomislav said.

"You've put in a good many years here," Nikola said. "And we, all of us at Sirana, thank you. It's time for you to retire."

"*Ej*, Nikola, but you know the pensions aren't the same as they were in Yugoslavia. It's already lean living. What am I going to do?"

"I can give you three extra months, but that's all I can do, I'm sorry. Marina will give you the severance paperwork."

Tomislav's boot tapping sped up. Marina's heart broke. Tomislav and Nikola went so far back. Tomislav had become Nikola's friend when Josip had betrayed him, and he stood by her father all these years, making Sirana's cheese in the same way, albeit with no improvements. But even without seeing the numbers, she knew they couldn't afford to keep him on. It wasn't just the money. They needed someone with fresh, new ideas for the business to survive.

"Maybe we can send Tomislav to France," Marina said, thinking out loud. "It would at least get him through this season."

Nikola smoothed his mustache. "I suppose that could work," he said slowly. "Maybe they would feel like they got a fair exchange then, too. Tomislav, would you like to go to France for a few months to work and show them some of our methods?"

"I believe they would pay you a healthy stipend in euros," Marina interjected.

For a moment, Tomislav's creased face looked hopeful, but then it fell. "But what happens after? What do I tell Gabrijela?"

"Tell her I told you to enjoy retired life. You could go back to Slavonia. Get a place by a lake, in the woods. Relax." Nikola set his cigarette on the ashtray, stood up, and shook Tomislav's hand. "Thank you for all the good years you gave us."

Tomislav looked grateful. Marina was sad to see him go, but she knew change was necessary—for Sirana and herself.

Chapter Six

Nikola wanted Marina to go to Istria while he took care of some business in Split. When Marina slipped and called the Croatian peninsula Istra by its English name, Istria, Nikola's caterpillar eyebrows had jolted up in surprise. *Half here, half there,* Marina thought. She didn't know where that left her.

Istria's heart-shaped peninsula jutted into the Adriatic, a dangling mass of land that had left itself vulnerable to shifting empires throughout the centuries. Sandwiched between two gulfs—Kvarner to the east and Venice to the west—Istria, at one point ruled by Mussolini, was home to Italian minorities, and the local dialect was peppered with Italian words.

Marina often thought about how their small country had been fought over, again and again. So many divisions, so many names for their homeland. Her great-grandfather on her mother's side, who had lived on the Dalmatian Coast, had resided in six different countries in his lifetime: the Austro-Hungarian Empire; the Kingdom of Serbs, Croats, and Slovenes; the Kingdom of Yugoslavia; the Independent State of Croatia, a German puppet state; the Federation of Yugoslavia; and, finally, Croatia, where he died.

She hadn't been back to Istria since she was a teenager. Her father had driven her through what was then Yugoslavia to Italy, and she'd flown alone from Trieste to Rome to New York. It was near the end of the war—though they didn't know it then—and she thought she'd been blessed with this new beginning in America. If only she'd known what leaving would mean. She didn't realize then she would never be fully Croatian ever again, that even her own family would consider her foreign. When she came back, people said she walked differently, talked differently. Many things had stayed the same, but she felt out of step with her own culture, a stranger at home.

Marina remembered they hadn't spoken much during those long hours winding through the Istrian peninsula on the way to her American dream. She could tell her father had been nervous by the number of cigarettes he smoked; the ashtray of what was then his new car, a shiny red Yugo, was overflowing with butts by the time they had arrived at the Italian checkpoint. She had cried as they crossed that boundary, a line that seemed to separate her past from her future. She had realized there was no turning back, and that in that moment, she was leaving everything she'd ever known. Her father had told her she was a lucky girl, and she should always remember that: She would have the opportunity to study in a great city where there would be other foreigners and immigrants like her, where every morning the entire world would spill onto the streets in anticipation of a better life.

The war would end sooner than everyone expected. She was swept up in the pulse of New York, and then somehow ten years passed and she'd met Marko, which changed everything. Maybe if she had moved back home, she would have had a child by now. Maybe Luka would be her husband. Maybe she would have a different life, away from those relentless, churning streets of possibility, their false promises filled with potholes.

But a life with Luka wouldn't have been possible for so many reasons, even before Josip left Sirana and betrayed Nikola. Her father had loved Luka's mother. Nikola never spoke of it, but one night during the war, between trips to the mainland to fight, he woke up everyone in the house by screaming her name. *Sanja!* When Marina asked her mother about it the next morning, Dragica's drained face told her not to ask questions.

Nikola had heard a rumor that Josip was trying to dominate the market in Istria, the gateway to Italy. And Nikola was sure it was true; he knew his former best friend well enough to understand his strategy. On the same side, they would have been such a team.

It wouldn't be long before they would all be part of the European Union, competing against other countries, and Nikola wanted to be prepared. He knew that if Josip could make Pag cheese famous in the north of Croatia, he could reach Trieste, and from there, start to compete among Italian hard cheeses like Pecorino Romano, the legendary cheese created centuries ago in the Roman countryside and known worldwide.

So Nikola wanted Marina to travel around Istria and convince vendors to sell Sirana's cheese instead of Janković's. He told her he didn't want only the Pag cheese name to be known outside their country; he wanted Sirana's name to be famous.

Josip would send Luka to the Motovun Truffle Festival, just as he did for the World Cheese Awards. Marina dreaded running into Luka again. After London, they had both gone back to their respective sides of the island, which might just as well have been their own islands. All the same, Marina missed him. She missed their candid conversations, the way he understood her like no one else did. But she couldn't allow herself to think of him in that way, romanticizing the past. He was married now, and worse, the son of her father's enemy.

Packing her suitcase, the same blue hard-shell in which she had packed her few precious belongings when she traveled to America all those years ago, she felt weighted by her decisions, and those decisions that had been made for her. Earlier in their relationship she would have talked to Marko. He held her when she cried, when she told him she felt like a fraud, not a real refugee, because she hadn't truly experienced the conflict. No snipers had shot at her; she had not been displaced from her house due to Serbian occupation of her hometown. She had not lost family. But Marko was born in America, not sent there; he could never understand leaving your country, especially one at war.

Marina put moisturizer on her face, feeling the fine bones underneath her skin, delicate like a bird's. She put on foundation, smoothing out the unevenness of her complexion, under-eye concealer to make her look less tired, and blush to make her look more alive. Mascara to make her eyes appear alert to the world. She slid off her underwear and noticed a streak of blood. That time of the month again. A period reminding her that her unused womb was shedding again.

Nikola sat at the table smoking a cigarette and reading *Free Dalmatia*. The headlines were still celebrating Gotovina's overturned war crimes convictions, which were reversed by a United Nations appeals court in the Hague in November, just a couple weeks before. Many Croatians celebrated his release, and welcomed him home as a hero.

After his release, Marina had read the story online in the *New York Times*:

> A United Nations appeals court in The Hague on Friday unexpectedly overturned the war crimes convictions of two Croatian generals who led a 1995 campaign that helped end the wars involving Serbia, Bosnia and Croatia but also left several hundred Serbian civilians dead and drove more than 150,000 from their homes.

She was baffled at how differently the information was relayed in Croatia. General Gotovina was a homeland hero, while Americans seemed to believe he had contributed to a campaign that left hundreds of Serbian civilians dead and drove thousands from their homes. She didn't know what to think, but now that she was home, she felt compelled to celebrate his release along with everyone else.

Nikola tilted his head down when Marina entered, looking over the edge of his reading glasses.

"Ready?" he said.

She nodded, pointing to the newspaper. "They're still celebrating his release?"

"He is a great man," Nikola said. "He led us to victory in Operation Storm. He took back our land from the Serbs."

Her father had a biased view of the conflict, having fought for Croatia during the war. But Marina knew things in their region were hardly black and white.

"Did you ever meet him?"

"He and Josip...I met him, after he congratulated Josip." His brow furrowed.

Dragica poked her head out of the kitchen. "Do you want some breakfast before you leave?"

"I'm not hungry, Mama," Marina said.

"Have some coffee, at least," Dragica said, handing her a cup of thick Turkish brew.

Marina stirred in sugar. She pressed her fingers to her temples. A headache was coming on, or maybe a cold.

Dragica wiped her hands on her apron. "I told him he should go with you to the truffle festival. Especially after the World Cheese Awards," she said, nodding at Nikola.

Marina clenched her hands under the table. "It wouldn't have mattered, Mama," she said.

"*Ej*, maybe if the boss was there, who knows about those judges," she said, shrugging.

"Why do you always have to blame me?" Marina exploded.

Dragica took a towel out of her apron pocket, turned, and started drying dishes from the rack. "It might have made a difference," she said.

Marina felt like a little girl again. How could her mother make her feel so small and insignificant, even now?

She hadn't been looking forward to traveling by herself. She didn't want to have all that time to think. Alone with her thoughts, she was afraid of where they would take her. Maybe it would be better if her father came along. Plus, he connected with the buyers, who were all men. And men made the decisions.

Nikola took another drag of his cigarette, then stubbed the butt in the ashtray. "Of course you'd be fine on your own, but let's go to Motovun together. It's only for the weekend, and I can catch up with our contacts in Split next week. Besides, I love truffles, and Istra has the best," he said.

"I was planning to leave this morning," Marina said.

"I just need a few minutes," Nikola said, rising from the table and coughing as he headed for his bedroom.

Marina sat down with a thud on the hard, wooden chair. She picked up the copy of *Free Dalmatia* her father had been reading, and turned to a page about corruption and Croatia's imminent accession into the European Union. Many Croatians felt that joining the EU would lend a kind of legitimacy to their small country.

"It's better he's going with you," Dragica said.

"You think everything is better when *Tata* does it," Marina said.

"Marina, you know how things are done in America, but here—you were young when you left," Dragica said.

"This is still my home," Marina said, clenching her jaw.

Nikola emerged from the bedroom carrying a small suitcase. Dragica kissed him, in the casual way two people who have been married for too long say goodbye.

Marina didn't kiss her mother, but retrieved her own suitcase from the entryway and followed her father out the door. She was determined to prove her mother—and everyone else who doubted her—wrong.

Nikola's faded bumper sticker read: "Kiss me hard before Yugo." Her father always idealized Yugoslavia; no matter how many times the car was washed, her father refused to remove the peeling sticker. "Those were better times, where everyone had jobs and enough money to live," he would often say. "We produced things. Now we just import things. Even our food, we don't grow most of it here ourselves, despite our fertile eastern farmland in Slavonia."

The sky was slate gray over a dead landscape. The *bura* whipped down the Velebit slopes, nearly knocking Marina off her feet as she tossed her suitcase into the back seat. Cold air filled her lungs. What a terrible time to visit Istria. It would have been so much nicer to go in spring, when young asparagus budded and warm Adriatic breezes swept over the seaside towns. At least they would be away from the icy Adriatic winds in Istria's green interior, which wouldn't be green this time of year.

It was early and the road was empty. A few sheep grazed on the hills near Dinjiška, where, when she was a child, they would stop for lamb freshly roasted on a roadside spit. Driving over Pag Bridge, she felt it shake a little. The *bura* wind wasn't yet strong enough to close the bridge, which happened a few times every winter, preventing anyone from leaving the island.

Every summer when she visited Pag with Marko, they pretended the bridge didn't exist, and that they were on an island far out in the sea, rather than on a long strip of land a stone's throw from the mainland. They would visit friends in Zadar, and sometimes drove further south to Split, but they never went to Istria. "Istrians are a different breed," Marko used to say. Marina thought but never said: *You are, too.*

There were so many things she never said, or if they had been drinking, she would say terrible things, sharp words that hung in the air like splinters. The next day would find them both riddled with invisible scars.

"We'll stop for a few hours in Rijeka, have a chat with our friends at the Dairy Pavilion," Nikola said. "We'll make it to Motovun by dark."

"Did you tell them we're coming?" Marina asked.

"It's nothing formal, they know we're stopping by. Our trucks just dropped off a shipment and I want to make sure everything is fine. You know how business is done here. Everything is solved over coffee or alcohol."

"And smoking. The fuel of our nation," Marina joked. For a moment, she actually felt like laughing.

Her father took a drag on his cigarette. Marina inhaled, transported back to the smoke-filled rooms of her childhood. Marko never smoked. She used to smoke occasionally, but stopped when she moved to New York. It seemed like nearly everyone in Croatia smoked, and in America, she was surprised most people didn't.

"Your brother should be coming to these things. Eventually he'll inherit the business, and he doesn't have any idea how to run it," Nikola said, exhaling a stream of smoke.

Marina bristled. "I guess he'll have to learn." *But why him? Why not me?*

She had grown up in this patriarchal culture and knew the rules. When she had returned, her father uttered, for the first time in her memory, that she was a feminist when she'd wondered aloud why a woman couldn't lead their country. He had said it like it was a bad word. He couldn't have imagined that in just a few years Croatia would elect its first female president.

The ancient red Yugo lurched ahead. They sat in silence. Nikola turned on the radio. A pop song from the throaty singer Severina vibrated through the fuzzy speakers.

"I haven't asked you how you're doing lately," Nikola said. "We've been so busy with Sirana."

"I'm fine," Marina said, almost automatically.

"Are you?"

She took a breath. "Sure."

"A lot has happened since you've been back home," Nikola said.

Every morning she woke up with a pounding, racing heart. A cup of strong Turkish coffee first thing in the morning didn't help quell her anxiety. Before the onslaught of her cheese-filled days, away from the hum of the office and the chatter of colleagues, her life felt painfully empty. She had never felt so alone.

"It's been an adjustment, being back," Marina said.

"When you described your life in New York, I always thought, I wouldn't want to live that way. So much rushing around, for what?"

"It's different. There are things that I miss. And people."

"Do you think you will go back to him?" Nikola said, flicking his cigarette out the window. Cold air rushed into the car.

"You never even liked him."

"But you did. And I want what's best for you. That's all I've ever wanted."

"We're not going to make it," she said quietly.

"Marriage is hard. It's work," Nikola said, smoothing his mustache. He lit another cigarette.

"I know. But it's not working."

Nikola cracked the window and exhaled a stream of smoke. Marina felt the chill on her cheek.

"Sometimes you have to find a way to make it work," Nikola said.

"We're not like you and Mama," Marina said.

Her parents, who went about their days with the same old script. Her father, who could have had a chance at real love with Sanja but let old island divisions get in the way. And here she was, thinking she had created a new life in America, only to discover that she had married a man who couldn't ever really love her because he couldn't ever really understand her.

It started to rain. First softly, then steady streams of heavy drops that pummeled the old metal. Marina felt her eyes flood and the road became blurry. She thought of her lost baby, how the baby might have changed her life, her marriage. She might have had a daughter. But she didn't have a daughter.

Her father took a drag. He sighed out a long exhale. "*Mala*, you never know what a marriage is like unless you're inside it. You have to do what you have to do to make it survive."

"It's dead," Marina said. The words thudded in her chest. Tears overflowed, creating dark rivers on her cheeks. "I had a miscarriage in my second trimester, *Tata*. I lost the baby in the worst way. Marko will never forgive me for it. And we were—we were over even before that. Now, we can't talk. We are just too broken."

Saying the words out loud made something thud in her stomach. But then, a wave of relief washed over her.

"I'm sorry, *Mala*," Nikola said quietly.

"We can't go on, how we've been going," Marina said.

Nikola sighed. "I hear what you're saying. But think first what you're doing, Marina. Think."

"Please don't tell Mama," she said.

Nikola nodded and exhaled a mouthful of smoke, slow and deliberate. "Take your time," he said. "Everything becomes clearer with time."

The planned stop in the seaport city of Rijeka was longer than expected. By the time Nikola and Marina left, the ashtray was overflowing and *rakija* glasses had been refilled more times than she could count. Marina watched her father's face get red and his voice boom deeper with each shot. The fiery homemade spirit warmed her throat and her bones. She had stopped on her second glass, begging out of future pours with the excuse of driving, since her father clearly wasn't fit to take the wheel. They still had one hour left, and the local roads were winding and dangerous in the dark.

Marina slid into the driver's seat and started the engine. It had been a while since she'd driven her father's stick shift. Nikola limped to the car and lowered himself into the passenger seat; his weight tilted the small vehicle.

"That seems to have gone well," Marina said.

Nikola lit a cigarette. The tip glowed.

"I got some of the payment, at least," Nikola said, reaching in his pocket to pull out a wad of folded *kunas*. He counted them slowly, his movements slowed from drink. "They still owe us."

Marina shook her head, turning on the Yugo's headlights and following a road leading away from the sea. "It's crazy. I never fully understood how business was done here. It's so different in America—they would just start a lawsuit for nonpayment."

"If they started lawsuits for nonpayment here, the courts would be tied up for centuries," Nikola coughed, his lips curling into a smile.

"Speaking of courts," Marina said slowly. "Gotovina's release, it's still all over the news. It's even been written up in the *New York Times*."

"They shouldn't have charged Gotovina in the first place," Nikola said.

"*Tata*, what about the Serbian civilians?" Marina asked tentatively.

"Lies," Nikola said, puffing out smoke.

"Civilians weren't killed?"

"We were at war, and Serbs were on our land."

"But some said there were acts of vengeance, and civilians weren't fighting," Marina said carefully. She wanted to understand what had happened after she'd left.

"They reversed the convictions, *didn't they*?" Nikola said, his words slurring.

"They did." Marina turned on *klapa* music on low volume, the men's deep, resonant voices blending together in spiraling harmony, the same haunting tones emanating from many throats.

"Gotovina did what needed to be done. Nobody was doing anything, we didn't get any help for so long, and finally in the end the Americans helped us with Storm. It was a success, and then they have the nerve to call Gotovina a war criminal. No one knows the truth of what happened. I know, I was there. I was fighting for Croatia."

"I know, *Tata*," Marina said, using the mollifying voice she often used with Marko during their fights.

"You don't know. You don't know what happened," he said, fuming.

Marina didn't have to look at her father's face to know it was starting to turn red.

"You think the Serbs played fair? Let me tell you how fair. A damned Serb shot Branko, and he almost shot me, too."

Marina flashed back to the London pub, to Luka telling her about Branko taking a bullet for him. She imagined Branko jumping in front of Luka to shield him, his arms spread wide like Jesus's.

"A Serb shot Branko, and I shot that Serb," Nikola said, his voice rising. "If we didn't stop them, they would have shot us all. They would have kept pushing into our land."

"You shot him?" Marina said slowly.

"I was close and I had a clear shot. Josip's hands were shaking. What a coward, he didn't even raise his rifle. I shot that Serb, but of course I let Josip get the credit. It was his own son who died. Josip got to look like the hero. And the Serb gave me this souvenir," Nikola said, pointing to his leg.

"You shot him," Marina repeated.

"Of course, Josip was the one who shook Gotovina's hand at the end of Operation Storm. Josip always takes what isn't his."

Marina wondered if her father was referring to Josip stealing Sirana's milk or to Sanja, but she didn't dare ask.

"And Luka? What happened to Luka?" Marina asked instead.

"Branko knocked Luka to the ground, and that saved his life. He didn't see anything. Kid still thinks his father saved him."

"But *you* did," Marina said softly, sucking in her breath. Nikola had protected Luka.

Nikola exhaled a stream of smoke. "I was in the right place. I had the shot. In war, sometimes you don't have time to think too much about it. You never know which day is going to be your last. You do what you need to do to survive. That's what Gotovina did. He saved us. And he saved our country."

Marina swallowed the revelation that her father had killed the Serb who had killed Branko. Nikola had saved Josip and Luka by killing him, too. One of them would have certainly been next. In the driver's seat of her father's old Yugo, the beam of headlights guided her, catapulting into some unknown future. The Maržić and Janković fates were bound together like the intricate stitches in Pag lace; some patterns were visible and some threads were hidden behind the backdrop in a divine design yet to be determined.

They reached Motovun by dusk. Marina navigated the Yugo up the twisting road that led to the medieval town. Perched at the top of the hill, Motovun sprawled out like a giant serpent, its red-tile rooftops lightly dusted with snow and glittering in the fading light like frosted scales. She parked in front of an old winery converted into a bed and breakfast, and they entered through the arched stone doorway. Checking into a lonely hotel in the dead of winter seemed like a certain kind of punishment.

"Maržić," Marina said, trying to hold herself back from sighing. She was suddenly so tired she felt like falling asleep right there on the floor.

"Just one room?" the receptionist asked, glancing at her and her father.

"There is only one reservation, but my father has also come, so he needs a room too. We assumed you'd have space at this time of year," Marina said.

The receptionist scanned the ledger, as if a delegation was scheduled to arrive.

"Is it a problem?" Nikola said, with a shade of annoyance.

"We have room," the receptionist said, handing him a key. "Second floor."

"Third floor, for you," the woman said, handing her another heavy key that looked like it could open a lock the size of a grown sheep's head.

Marina regarded the steep stone steps. At least her room was on the top floor, and she wouldn't have anyone walking over her head. "Good night, *Tata*," Marina said, picking up her suitcase.

"See you tomorrow morning, early," her father said. "Sleep well."

Marina ascended the stairs, grasping the olive-wood handrail for balance. Her eyes adjusted to the dim hallway light.

"Marina?" Luka stood in front of a door marked thirty-four, ready to turn the key.

She looked at her key: thirty-three. Her stomach dropped.

A familiar sensation washed over her body, hairs standing on end. Her fingers loosened on the key, almost slipping from her grasp.

"Luka," she whispered, with as steady a voice as she could muster. She wanted to run to him, and away from him.

"I thought you might be staying here," he said, taking a step towards her. "There aren't many places in town open this time of year."

"I thought I'd maybe see you tomorrow, at the festival," Marina said. How was it possible that she had simultaneously dreaded and looked forward to seeing him?

He shifted his weight. "I thought about calling. I can't stop thinking about you," he said, his voice hushed.

"You're married, Luka," Marina said. "You have a daughter. And our families..." Her breath caught short. "Where is your father?" Marina hoped Nikola wouldn't hear their voices carry down the stairwell.

"The Cheese Pavilion. He probably decided to stay the night in Rijeka, sleep it off."

"We were there, too, earlier. We must have just missed you," Marina said. They were always just missing each other. She crossed her arms. She wanted to protect her heart.

"Look, I didn't expect you to turn up in my life again," Luka said.

"It was a long time ago. Let's just move on," Marina said. She surprised herself by the bitterness in her voice.

"We could talk about what happened, or what didn't happen—what *could* have happened," he said.

Marina stared at him. "'What could have happened,' Luka? What's the point of talking about that?"

She felt the blood rise up in her. He had a way of getting underneath her skin. But when she looked at him, anger transformed to lust in a flurry of emotion. Her father's words echoed in her ears: *We never know which day will be our last.* What if this were her last day? What would she regret? A flicker of desire crossed Luka's eyes like a passing cloud. She wanted to disappear into him.

His lips were sweet and tasted of *rakija*. He smelled of smoke from the Dairy Pavilion, and she breathed him in, pressed herself against him. She felt his body respond and the key dropped on the hard stone. The rattle startled both of them, but she didn't open her eyes, didn't want to see, only to feel, to drink in his skin and smoke and *rakija* like a beast.

He pulled away, bewildered. She brought her hand to her lips.

"Not here," he said.

"I can't believe I did that," she said incredulously.

"I want to, but—we know too many people. It's a small town," he said.

"We can't," Marina said, stepping further away as her Catholic guilt washed over her. "I'm sure I'll regret this in the morning."

"I won't," Luka said.

They stood in the hallway, staring at each other for what seemed like eternity. Her legs wouldn't move. A cleaning lady rounded the corner and Marina quickly retreated into her room, shutting the door and standing with her back pressed against it. Her heartbeats wouldn't slow. She was so beautifully, brilliantly alive.

Chapter Seven

arina parted the curtain; a view of the valley was emerging into focus in the soft dawn. A thin blanket of snow covered the landscape, barren trees and shrubs poking up from the ground. Overcome by fatigue, she crawled back into bed and let the stiff sheets envelop her body.

She'd been up most of the night thinking about Luka. She mulled over his words: *What could have happened, a long time ago.* When her father had sent her West, their paths diverged, and they'd created new lives. They had both changed. But she loved him; she always would. She wanted to exist in this bubble a little longer, feeling so completely understood, but she knew it couldn't last.

The bedside alarm startled her. She looked at the red digital numbers: 6:30 a.m. She had never been a morning person. Life molds us into a shape we no longer recognize, and we forget what we were, the original blueprint buried deep within us under layers and layers of other people's expectations.

In the mirror, under bright and unforgiving fluorescent lighting, she noticed wrinkles she hadn't mapped before. Her skin appeared sallow; she'd lost some weight in recent months, and her face was thinner. She wondered if people noticed. Not much escaped local gossip: who was pregnant, who had gained weight, who was having money trouble. She splashed some cold water on her skin and turned on the shower.

Getting ready took longer these days: applying eyeliner to make herself look more awake; under-eye concealer to hide the dark circles that never seemed to fade, even with a good night's sleep; blush to her cheeks to enliven pale winter skin. She remembered walking into a Rite Aid in Astoria soon after she had arrived in the US, overwhelmed by aisles upon aisles of cosmetics. She had been struck by the number of choices she could make, and spent three hours choosing a lipstick. Peach Carnation, Peach Tango, Peach Please, Just Peachy. She counted more than thirty shades of peach.

When she decided she was presentable enough to face the day, she slid on a pair of black pants and a black sweater. Fumbling with the mammoth key, Marina closed the door behind her, and headed down the stairs to the restaurant. Meat and cheese platters were laid out alongside various sweet and savory breads. Nikola was sitting alone reading the paper, a cigarette perched on a saucer.

"Morning, *Mala*," her father said, glancing up over his glasses. "How did you sleep?"

Marina stifled a yawn. "Fine, you?"

"I only sleep well in my own bed. You know how I hate to travel," he said.

"I thought you liked it. You always did so much of it for Sirana. I remember the gifts you used to bring us."

"You do what you have to do, Marina," Nikola said, taking a sip of his coffee. "Anyway, there was nothing to complain about. I had a good job, our family had enough to eat. But the road does wear on you."

Marina flagged the waiter. "The same," she said, pointing at her father's cup. The waiter returned with a white coffee.

"Something different this morning, *ej*?" Nikola said, studying her.

Marina didn't know if her father was referring to her coffee order or her appearance.

Nikola's eyes focused behind her. She turned around and saw Luka. She felt a surge of warmth rise to her cheeks.

"*Jutro*," Luka said, with a touch of formality. He took a seat a couple of tables away from them.

Luka wore a fine blue coat, his white collared shirt crisply pressed. Nikola nodded in Luka's direction, smoothed his mustache, and went back to reading the paper. Marina wondered if her father was waiting for Josip to show up. Through the window, the naked trees appeared ghostly, suspended in a straining posture. Marina tried not to think of Luka sitting behind her, or the taste of *rakija* that lingered like last night's memory on her lips.

Nikola limped up Motovun's steep hill carrying a box of Sirana's cheese. Marina followed him with a stack of brochures, stepping carefully on the balls of her feet to avoid her heels getting stuck between cobblestones. Above them, the arched stone gate brought momentary shade from the weak December sun, which fought to be seen from behind the ceiling of clouds. Snow disintegrated under their footsteps, leaving the cobblestones shiny and slick.

The thick, earthy scent of truffles greeted her. It was early, hours before the fair was scheduled to begin, but vendors had already started to arrange their goods along the long wooden tables: jars of sliced white truffles in Istrian olive oil, minced black truffles, truffles in a paste the color of canned tuna. Whole truffles in glass cases were handled with white gloves and protected like precious jewels.

It was Josip's idea to make truffle cheese. Nikola had heard about it from one of Sirana's shepherds, whose wife's cousin worked at Janković. Everyone had been ordered to go home for the day, and all the workers were overjoyed. The wife's cousin, who'd dropped off his share of sheep's milk outside the factory in the refrigerated tank, discovered a strange odor coming from the Janković production room. Someone had left the door ajar, so he poked his head in and saw Josip himself cutting a bin of black lumps with a large knife, and the cousin had told the shepherd's wife, who told the shepherd, who then told Nikola, and it was in this way that rumors on Pag flew sideways and fast like rain caught in a strong *bura* wind.

When Nikola found out, he swore aloud and cursed Josip, who was once again ahead of him. The idea to create a Pag cheese made with truffles was innovative, combining two of Croatia's finest products. Marina knew her father felt he should have thought of it first. Like her father, she was hard on herself.

Nikola was on his third cigarette of the morning; it was an unusually stressful day already.

"Can I have one please, *Tata*?" Marina asked, surprising herself.

Nikola raised his eyebrow. "You don't smoke."

"Only occasionally," she said.

He opened his dented tin box and rolled her a fresh cigarette, then lit the tip.

"It's been a long time since I've been here," Nikola sighed.

Marina's eyes traveled over the stone wall and down Motovun's steep hill to the forest and fields below. On the drive up, Nikola had told her the last time he had been to Motovun was with Dragica, when their country was called Yugoslavia. Her parents had escaped for a romantic weekend in the height of a sweltering summer while Marina and Franko stayed with Grandma Badurina, who let them steal sweets from her pantry. Upon their return, Marina remembered her father describing the forest awash in emerald shades and farms plowed into neat herringbones, a veritable sea of green.

Before the war, weekends took her parents farther afield, not just to their cabin in the Lika forest that had been in Nikola's family since anyone could remember. Back then, there had been money to do such things. Now, *kunas* deducted from their diminishing paychecks all seemed to go to taxes or to the country's supermarket chain, Konzum, for expensive imported staple groceries and other goods. Marina was surprised how quickly her paycheck disappeared each month, after expenses were paid. If she didn't live with her parents, it would barely be enough to survive. Maybe her father was right. Maybe Yugoslavia had been better for everyone.

After the war, after Josip left, Sirana had been on a steady decline. Nikola stretched the money to cover salaries, often sacrificing his own. She knew he tried not to pay the workers late, even when money from vendors was delayed, and sometimes he paid them in trade, a bottle of homemade *rakija* or two, or some cheese, to make up for the missing *kunas*. Most workers didn't complain; to those who did, he told them it was the same as other jobs in Croatia which paid partial, late, or not enough. Yugoslavia used to take care of its people, and her father saw it as his duty to take care of his workers now that the country no longer did.

She heard a voice booming behind them. "We had a deal," the voice said.

Marina turned around and saw the back of Josip's looming figure.

"Low yield drives up the price," the vendor said, carefully placing his truffles for display on starched white cloths.

"Take your dogs out to hunt truffles at night!" Josip sputtered. "I have orders to fill. I need five kilos at the price you gave me before."

"I'll talk with the others. Maybe we can get you half at the original price, if together we have enough."

Josip slammed his giant hands on the table. "Five."

"Impossible," the vendor said. "We also had to ship some to Alba."

Josip spat on the stones. "Italians."

The vendor shrugged. "Truffles command a higher price in Italy."

"I'm sure they paid you handsomely."

"No one owns the forest," the vendor said, wiping his hands on his apron. "And no one can predict her bounty."

"I can predict what will happen if I don't get my five kilos," Josip said.

Marina watched as a wave of fear passed over the vendor's face. The man hadn't mentioned truffle poachers, who illegally took their dogs into the Istrian forests at night on land reserved for professional truffle hunters who had purchased permits. But he had mentioned the black market—those clever Italians who passed off Croatian truffles as Italian, because Croatian truffles were cheaper and *tartufo d'Alba* apparently had a better ring to it than *Istarski tartufi*. The soil composition and quality were so similar no one could tell the difference between them without lab testing. Italy's brand was well-known, a brand that Americans loved.

Marina found it funny that truffles that came from one side of a border were deemed more valuable, even though the fungi were essentially identical. It mattered where a truffle—or a person—came from.

"Since you're using them for cheese, I can maybe get you some damaged truffles," the vendor said. "Dogs sometimes get greedy and take a bite."

"Five kilos," Josip said, holding up his hand for emphasis and leaning in close to the man's face. "I don't care how you get them. And don't *you* be greedy like the dogs."

Josip turned around and faced Nikola, who stood just a few meters away from him. Her father appeared dwarfed in Josip's presence. Marina recalled Josip's piercing blue eyes from his days at Sirana, a color matching Luka's. As a girl, she imagined streams of lasers shooting out of his eyes, killing anyone unlucky enough to find themselves in his path.

Nikola stubbed out the butt on the ancient wall behind him. Unbeknownst to Josip, her father had been buying his own share of truffles for Sirana's batch of truffle cheese, for which Nikola had dug into their family savings to make the purchase; the money was slowly diminishing as he supplemented Sirana's growing costs, including their new specialty cheese. Marina felt guilty that she couldn't contribute, but she had little savings of her own.

Nikola told Marina not to worry. Uncle Horvat still had political connections in Zagreb, those who had survived the transition from socialism to capitalism. Some of them were the same men who helped her father get her out of the country near the end of the war. These men had a piece of most businesses, which made them wealthy and powerful. They could, for instance, call up truffle hunters in Istria and tell them to reserve a certain amount of truffles for Sirana. These men didn't have a stake in Janković. Given their investments in other businesses with Uncle Horvat, who co-owned Sirana, they would be pleased if Sirana succeeded.

Josip's icy blue eyes narrowed when they fell upon Nikola. The two men stared at each other from across the cobblestones. "I suppose you heard that," Josip said, coming over to their table.

"I'd already heard," Nikola said, smoothing his mustache.

Josip grimaced and folded his arms against his broad chest. "I shouldn't be surprised. Who told you?"

"You know, island rumors."

"How fast they travel," Josip said, glancing at Marina. He smirked.

Marina froze. Had the cleaning lady seen the kiss and gossiped? Or was Josip alluding to her separation from Marko?

"Good luck with your next truffle order," Nikola spat.

Luka entered through the archway. As he approached, Marina thought he looked tired. Nikola glared at Luka's tall, handsome figure, a carbon image of his father.

"Hello, Marina," he said with a touch of formality, nodding to her.

Marina nodded back in acknowledgment but didn't meet his gaze. Her heart fluttered. She cleared her throat.

"Marina, come," Nikola said, stubbing out his cigarette. "Let's get to work."

Names were scrawled in black ink and taped to tablecloths: Sirana and Janković. Their tables abutted each other.

"I can't believe I have to sit next to this viper," Nikola muttered.

Luka helped his father unload their cheese. Cutting boards, knives, toothpicks with little white flags. Luka glanced at Marina, who avoided eye contact. Josip fanned out a handful of brochures. Marina felt her hands tremble a little as she spread out Sirana's brochures. Their tables were like islands wedged too close together, a sandbar running beneath the sea, exposed in low tide. Years of connection built tiny grain by tiny grain, then washed away in an instant. The instant Josip left Sirana.

All around them people bustled to ready their tables for the day, to prepare for the locals and tourists who would flood through the ancient gates with their appetites and questions. Local camera crews milled about, there to cover the fair for the Croatian national news. In some twisted plot of the fair's organizer, who also apparently thought holding an outdoor festival in December was a good idea, Sirana and Janković were reluctant neighbors.

A stray black cat rubbed against Marina's leg. She shooed it away and it sprinted down the stones. Nikola leaned against the wall and lit a cigarette. His fourth—she was keeping count.

They all shivered, huddling inside their coats like turtles in their shells. Josip cursed under his breath. Marina was angry Franko wasn't there. He'd begged off to go to Zagreb to collect payments and play soccer, and Nikola had obliged, because they all knew it was impossible to make Franko do anything he didn't want to do. Anyway, had he come along, Franko would have likely just sulked about how bored he was. Nikola's strategy with Franko was to not push him, with the thought that, eventually, his son would take an interest in the cheese business. Marina didn't subscribe to her father's theory; she thought her brother had no interest in running the family business, ever. And it pained her to see her parents treating him like a child, supporting him and indulging his whims.

"*Tata?*" Marina said, pointing to the camera and tugging on his jacket sleeve. "They're asking you a question."

Nikola looked into the long lens. "I'm sorry, could you repeat it please?"

"You and Josip worked together at Sirana many years ago, correct?" The reporter tipped a microphone toward Nikola.

"Yes, that's right," Nikola said, glancing at Josip, who stood with his arms crossed.

"And now you both have family businesses on different sides of Pag," the reporter continued.

"Sirana is the oldest and largest creamery on the island," Nikola said.

"How is your cheese different, since it's made of the same milk?"

"We each have our own—" Nikola started.

"At Janković, we have a state-of-the-art production room, where milk from our hearty northern sheep is processed at lower heat levels to preserve the flavor of Pag Island herbs, which are more aromatic in the north," Josip cut in, with a gracious smile. He and Luka were the same; charm was like a light switch they could flick on with a finger.

The camera lens swiveled to Josip, and the reporter held out the microphone. Luka stood silently behind his father.

"Rubbish," Nikola muttered.

The reporter hesitated. "Did you have something to add?" he asked Nikola.

"In the south, we get wild herbs from Velebit because the *bura* blows seeds down the mountain," Nikola told the reporter. "Those potent herbs flavor our milk."

"The *bura* destroys so much of what grows in the south, on those naked parts," Josip said.

"Herbs have to fight to grow on our land, and that makes them stronger," Nikola shot back.

"Strong herbs grow everywhere on the island," Josip said, his face growing red.

"We don't have as much grass, which dilutes the potency," Nikola said.

The reporter frowned. "I'll circle back," he said, and went to talk to a truffle hunter.

Josip and Nikola looked like two bulls, red faces and puffs of smoke exhaling from their noses.

"You chased him away," Josip said. "Now neither of us will get the coverage."

Nikola glared up at Josip, who was more than a head taller. "I chased him away? You can never share. Especially not the spotlight."

Josip took a toothpick with a sample of Sirana's cheese and chewed deliberately. "Old Tomislav is still with you? I can see nothing has changed at Sirana, even after all these years," Josip said.

Nikola took a piece of Janković's cheese. "Ah, now I taste those strong northern herbs," he said sarcastically.

"I have nothing to prove to you. We already won the World Cheese Awards, so everyone in the world knows we're the best," Josip said.

Marina cringed. She glanced at Luka, whose eyes were downcast. Marina remembered fleeing the convention hall and Céline catching up with her. Their conversation about trying something new. Her heartbeat quickened.

"*Tata*," Luka said, a warning edge in his voice. He'd always been the peacemaker in his family.

"Luka, stay out of this," Josip said, his lips forming a snarl. "We've already made the headlines, and every newspaper in Croatia wrote about the World Cheese Awards."

"Did you pay them to write about you?" Nikola said, simmering. "Speaking about headlines, how about Gotovina's release? What a relief, *ej*? You should go to Zagreb to celebrate with him. After all, he's such a great friend of yours."

Josip's face turned ashen. Luka looked at his father questioningly.

"Our nation's hero, he deserves it," Josip said, crossing his arms.

"You're a hero, too," Nikola said, his voice curling like a viper ready to strike.

Tension rippled through the air. Josip broke the toothpick in half and let it drop on the cobblestones. His lips twitched.

"We should all be grateful he's been released," Marina said hastily.

"Your photo with Gotovina, shaking his hand at the end of Operation Storm, I'm sure you still have it on your wall," Nikola pressed, lighting another cigarette.

"Of course we do," Luka cut in, stiffening. "My father saved my life with that shot. He deserves to have been acknowledged by Gotovina for his bravery."

Josip's shoulders started to slump. Marina held her breath.

"*Doće maca na vratanca*," Nikola said to Josip.

Growing up, Marina was confused by that phrase. She didn't understand why a cat would come to a tiny door, but as she got older, she learned it wasn't literal, that the phrase really meant, "What goes around comes around."

The television reporter at the truffle fair never circled back to their cheese tables, much to Josip's chagrin. Apparently, a story about the truffle mafia was more interesting than an island rivalry.

Nikola had told Marina to get ready; he wanted to be on the road before dark. Marina walked downhill, past a green-shuttered house painted a cotton-candy shade, past a cream house with cobalt doors, through a sand-colored stone archway. She was about to turn the corner when she felt a hand on the nape of her neck.

She spun around. Luka smiled.

"Have you been following me?" Marina said.

"I was walking back to the hotel, same as you. Are you leaving?" Luka said.

"Soon," Marina said. She felt like running away but had no idea where she'd go.

"I'm sorry about my father," Luka said. "He gets competitive, and he's a proud man."

Luka's reality was based on his father's heroism, the man who he thought had saved his life. He'd been told a lie. She wanted to tell Luka it was her father who shot the Serb dead and saved his life, but she knew that truth would deeply wound him. Of course Luka would stand by his father. Family was family. And they were not family.

"This fight is between our fathers, not us," Luka said.

"Let's put 'us' in a drawer." Marina started walking towards the hotel.

"You don't mean that," Luka said, grabbing her arm. "You know, when you left for America, I was in love with you. I thought you'd come back after the war ended. I imagined after everything, it wouldn't matter to your father that I was northern, that maybe we could be together. And then my father left Sirana, and our families wouldn't forgive each other. I knew it was impossible, then. I accepted that."

"You never said anything," Marina said. Tears welled in her eyes.

"How, Marina? You only came for a couple weeks during the summers. I barely saw you, and I knew you would go back to your great life in New York. What did I have to offer you?"

"You should have told me," Marina said, feeling her face get damp and cold. "You should have said something."

"Would it have mattered?" Luka said, throwing his hands up to the sky.

"We'll never know," Marina murmured.

"And now you're back, and I can't get you out of my mind," he said, shaking his head.

Marina closed her eyes. She wanted things to be as they had been, but she knew it was impossible. She had to move forward.

"Goodbye, Luka," Marina said, turning away. She didn't want him to see her eyes filling with water.

She walked down the uneven path that millions of footsteps had shaped over centuries. How many people had shed blood, or tears? The cobblestones absorbed their fury and sadness; the rains washed the rocks clean for future footsteps. She remembered her father telling her about the giants of Motovun, and the legend that they used the forest's oak trees to sweep away their enemies, branches scraping debris from cracks between the stones. Marina wanted to sweep Luka and his family out of her mind, to scrub until the surface was smooth.

Packing her suitcase back in the room, Marina's phone rang. She looked at the caller ID and hesitated. Then she swept her finger across the screen and answered, wanting to talk to someone who wasn't a part of her family's—or her island's—feuds.

"Hi," she said.

"What are you up to?" Marko said casually, as if they had spoken yesterday and she was on a lunch break. His voice sounded far away.

"Working," Marina said.

"On the weekend?"

"There was a festival in Istria. Truffles," she said.

"Oh. Your father's there?"

"Yes."

"Just you and your father?"

Marina hesitated. "Yes." *And the man I loved before you.*

Silence on the line. For a moment, Marina thought maybe he had hung up.

"I felt like I should call," Marko finally said. "It's been almost half a year, Marina. We're still nowhere."

She swallowed hard. "Are you still with her? Is that why you're bringing this up?"

Marko paused. "What if I am?"

"I'm not going to keep doing this," Marina said.

"I don't even know what this is."

"I don't either, Marko."

"I'm paying for our apartment," Marko said, his voice rising. "And I don't want to live here, surrounded by your stuff when you're not even here."

"It's always about money with you. And what people might think."

"Don't start, Marina," Marko said.

"If I'm not going to start it, no one will."

Marriage was work; her father's words. *You can tell me*, she wanted him to say to her. *You can tell me anything.*

"I don't think we should speak again unless you're planning on coming home," Marko said. "We can't sort things out from a distance."

"Leave her, and then we'll talk."

"Just come back," Marko said.

Marina sucked in her breath. "What would be different?"

"We won't know unless you're here," he said.

"I need more time," she said, and hung up.

She thought about what it would mean to go home, if she wanted to go; if that place could be her home again or if it ever was her home in the first place. Would she find her belongings gone, erased? The place scrubbed clean of her?

Suddenly exhausted, Marina collapsed on the bed and curled up into a ball, clutching a pillow to her chest, her mind a dark horizon. When she closed her eyes, there was a tiny door with a black cat, its bright green eyes shining through a lonely universe.

Maybe she could go back to her husband, find another job in New York, resume her perfectly fine life. They could dance around the vacant space, the part of Marina their daughter had occupied. They could pretend because they had become experts. They could work harder on pretending to get back together and pretend to love each other again. They could pretend that losing a daughter didn't matter. She could pretend to be someone else. They could live that lie and perform it from the moment their eyes opened to when they shut them at night.

Marina didn't know where she was headed. But she knew Luka was going back to Zara and Kata, and that certainty was like a fine splinter wedged just underneath the surface of her skin.

The drive home felt longer without the stop in Rijeka. Nikola chain-smoked cigarettes while he drove. Marina wanted to return to a time when her life made sense, and she almost couldn't remember the texture of it, when it was arranged in a certain order, or at least in some way where the pieces didn't feel like they were stacked purposely to fall apart. She felt something in her let loose like those Jenga sets where every little piece depended on the others being in the right place and you couldn't just remove any little piece because you had to know which one you could remove or the whole thing would come tumbling down, down, down.

Marina's favorite Severina song, "Bože Moj"—"Oh My God" —echoed through the speakers. Its lyrics were fitting. *You're kissing me now like a stranger, you close your eyes; the golden chain broke, you're leaving me; No one has ever flown in the sky with you like I did; No one has ever broken my heart like you; There's a thick fog in front of us, a gray morning; The day has started as an empty wild storm.*

"You seem preoccupied, *Mala*," Nikola said.

"I'm tired of the fighting," Marina said.

"We have history. With history, there is fighting."

"Will it always be like this? We'll keep running into them, at festivals, for awards. People will always group us together because we both make Pag cheese."

"Luka's a good boy, and Branko was, too," Nikola said. "Too bad his father is such a bastard."

"I'm glad you didn't tell Luka the truth," Marina said.

Nikola exhaled a stream of smoke. "It wasn't my place. I shouldn't have even brought up Gotovina. But Josip makes my blood boil, and I lost my temper."

"What really happened, between you and Josip?" Marina said.

"It's not worth wasting breath."

"Please, *Tata*, the drive is long. Tell me what happened."

Nikola sighed. "You know most of it. Josip's business is built on Sirana's stolen milk. I was without a good dairy technologist for months. I kept having to fire people because they weren't as good as him, not even close. By the time I got to Tomislav, I was content with good enough. I needed the factory to run, not be the best."

"But why couldn't Josip have stayed at Sirana? You could have made it the best together."

"Josip is a selfish man. You see that in the way he runs his business, in the way he conducts himself. He is only out for himself. He doesn't understand loyalty." Nikola paused. "But I want to talk about you, Marina."

Marina's stomach lurched. "What is it, *Tata*?"

"You can't mean to stay here. Not forever. I know you, *Mala*. You were always destined to go away from this place. I don't think you're happy here."

"I wasn't happy in New York," Marina said. "So where does that leave me?"

"I think you should make a plan. By the time milking season's done, you should decide what to do," Nikola said.

Marina felt chilled. Was her father telling her to leave? She knew he wanted what was best for her, but she had nowhere else to go. Both he and Marko were forcing her to decide.

"I failed in America, *Tata*."

"You had a good job, a good salary. You had a husband."

"I never belonged. My work was good, but I didn't have the connections to get promoted. Sometimes, I felt it wasn't about the work at all, that it was more about how much your boss liked you, or if you stayed out late for drinks after work. Marko didn't like me doing that. He wanted me home. He was so controlling, I probably never should have married him. You were right about that."

"I was raised to believe a woman's place is in the home," Nikola said, tightening his grip on the steering wheel. "But you're different, Marina. I always saw great things for you."

"I'm sorry, *Tata*," Marina said, wiping away tears with the back of her hand. "You gave me every opportunity and I've made so many mistakes. It feels like it's too late to start over."

"It's never too late to begin again, *Mala*," Nikola said.

Her father's heavy hand rested on her shoulder. She wanted to believe him. She wished his palm would never leave her so she could carry that feeling of certainty forever.

Chapter Eight

Marina had come to Zadar to buy Christmas gifts, but she didn't have any idea what to buy for her family. Strolling around the People's Square on polished limestone slabs, past the clock tower of chalky rough-hewn stone, she thought about this year's Christmas, how different it would be spending the holiday without Marko and his parents in Queens. Every year, Marina would plan Christmas gifts for her family an entire month in advance to account for the lengthy time it would take to send them from New York to Pag. It was only a week before Christmas, and she hadn't even thought about presents.

Warm lights and festive displays beckoned Christmas shoppers. Above the canopied stores, brown shutters on buildings concealed life that pulsed inside. She walked past a *kavana* and ducked inside to have a coffee. A teenage couple chattered in a corner, the girl leaning into her boyfriend like his words were honey. After ordering, Marina wandered into the ancient church ruins tucked behind the café, gazing up at smooth stone columns, a skylight illuminating vast arches. "God," she started, and didn't know what else to say. She had long ago abandoned that relationship. During the war, she had prayed with her family in the Church of St. Mary's Assumption, all of them huddled on pews, old and young knees straining. She had prayed for their soldiers, for those souls who had perished, for peace. Now, she wanted to kneel on the hard stone and pray for her own salvation.

The waitress came with her coffee, and Marina took a seat. The café was mostly empty, with the exception of the teenagers and an elderly man who looked as if he had been sitting at the same table for hours—or maybe even years—reading the paper and smoking. She had asked her father for the day off, since business was slow the week before Christmas. They had already packed and delivered orders, and Sirana was not in the production cycle, which would begin again early in the new year.

As she sipped her coffee, she felt a wave of fatigue. For her, the holidays always brought on excitement paired with a sense of dread. All the decorations, presents to wrap, holiday cards to send. There would be no cards to mail this year signed *xx Marko and Marina*.

She allowed herself to wonder what would have happened if Luka had told her he loved her after the war ended, or if he had even told her some summer when she came back and visited, before he married Zara and she married Marko. Would she have accepted a proposal from him, despite the feud between their fathers? Or would she have refused him, owing to her newly acquired American attitudes?

And then she pushed away those thoughts because she couldn't be sad about the past, not like that, not anymore.

She sipped her coffee and turned her attention to gifts. She had thought about buying her parents a piece of Pag lace, to cover up the sun-faded spot in the living room where a photo of Josip and Nikola at Sirana had once hung. But her parents already owned a framed piece of ornamental Pag lace, and at hundreds of euros for a plate-sized piece it was out of her budget, so she decided to buy local artwork for them instead. Franko would want something to do with soccer; a new jersey, new cleats. Marina used to find vintage jerseys in New York and send them to her brother. Dragica always appreciated something for the kitchen—something useful, not too extravagant. One year, Marina had bought her a hand-hammered copper couscoussier, and her mother had thought it was so pretty she displayed it on a high shelf and almost never used it. Dragica preferred her old pots and worn cast-iron skillets and the dented Turkish beaker that had served coffee in their house since before Marina was born.

Marina finished her coffee and walked into the square. She pulled her coat tightly around her to keep out the chilly sea breeze. She was drawn to the window of an art gallery; propped on an easel was a landscape photograph of the edge of the sea at dawn, the bruised horizon indistinguishable from the water. She ducked into the shop to take a closer look. The photo seemed to glow from within, the white stone of Zadar's ethereal Sea Organ bathed in violet, blush, and cerulean hues. Marina could almost hear the whispers of sound from waves echoing underfoot, pushed through the tubes like a spell. She felt like running into the landscape, descending the stairs into the sea, feeling the saltwater cradle her body.

"How much?" she asked the shopkeeper.

"One fifty euros," he answered in English.

Marina bristled, knowing the price was too high. For larger-ticket items, everyone was already pricing in euros even though they hadn't yet joined the EU.

"I'll give you a hundred," she said.

"We don't bargain here."

"I know you don't have set prices." Marina felt heat rising to her face. "I used to come here all the time with my father," she said. "Nikola Maržić," she added.

The shopkeeper peered over his glasses. "You're Nikola's daughter, *ej*," he said, surveying her with a flicker of recognition. "You're all grown up now."

Marina immediately felt ashamed she'd used her father's name and the weight it held, but she was tired of being taken for a foreigner.

"I'd like to buy this as a gift for my parents," Marina said.

"We can give a small discount for Nikola, and Nikola's daughter, of course," the shopkeeper said. "How is your mother?"

"She's well, thank you," Marina said.

"You're spending the holidays here, *ej*? I thought you lived in America?"

Marina's cheeks burned. "This year I'm here."

"Nice to spend the holidays with family," he said.

He wrapped the photo in brown paper with twine. Marina took out some euros and counted out one hundred fifty, but the shopkeeper waved his hand and pushed the fifty back across the counter. "Merry Christmas to you and your family. Send us some Pag cheese," he said, winking.

Marina thanked him, tugged down her hat, and hurried onto the street holding the frame in front of her. Just then, she ran into Luka.

"Hello, beautiful," he said breezily, caressing her arm.

Luka always had been a flirt. Marina's eyes darted around the square to make sure no one had overheard, or glimpsed his intimate gesture. She could still feel his lips on hers.

"Hello," she said, shrugging him off.

"Buying presents?" Luka said, gesturing to the frame.

"Yes, and you? Where are Zara and Kata?"

"At home. I needed to buy a few last-minute things for Christmas," he said, holding up shopping bags.

"You're celebrating at your parents' place?" she said.

"Same as every year. Nothing much changes here."

For Marina, everything had changed.

She couldn't hold Luka's gaze; she didn't know what she wanted from him. He made her feel things she thought she had lost, and that somehow she couldn't access on her own.

"Listen, about Istra," Luka began.

"Let's not talk about it," she said, trying to close her stubborn heart chamber that refused.

"I care about you, Marina, I really do. But you're right, I've made decisions in my life," he said quietly.

"We both have," she said curtly. "We should keep the past in the past."

"*Ej!* Marina!" Ivana called, pushing a stroller towards them.

With relief, Marina waved at her friend, who hurried over to join them.

"How is little Ljubica?" Marina asked, kissing her friend on both cheeks and forcing a smile.

Ivana had given birth in early November. When Marina came to visit her, she watched as newborn Ljubica suckled at Ivana's breast, her tiny fingers curled around her mother's finger. Marina was happy for her friend, but it made her heart ache. And she couldn't hold Ljubica for too long because she feared she would want to hold onto her forever.

"She's beautiful," Luka said, peeking over the stroller hood. "How many weeks?"

"Seven," Ivana said, glancing at Luka, and then at Marina.

"We were just buying some gifts. Not together—I mean, Luka was buying gifts, I bought this for *Tata*, we ran into each other,"

Marina stumbled, feeling her face flush. She clutched the frame to her chest. The brown paper crinkled.

"I'm doing some last-minute shopping, too," Ivana said. "Don't worry, I won't tell anyone," she added in a whisper.

Marina wondered if Ivana was referring to the last-minute gifts, or seeing Marina and Luka together.

"What are you buying Darko this year?" Marina asked.

"Oh, just a bottle of Maraschino liqueur. You know how he loves cherries. We have a lot of extra expenses now, with number two," Ivana said, smiling down at Ljubica, who was fast asleep in a swaddled bundle.

"Maybe I'll pick up a bottle while I'm here, too. Zara loves that sweet stuff. See you," Luka said, giving a stiff wave.

"What was that all about?" Ivana asked, turning to Marina.

"We saw each other in Istra, at the truffle fair," Marina said, glancing down at the smooth white stones and feeling heat rise to her cheeks. "My father and Josip had a big fight."

"Nothing new," Ivana said.

"It's awkward."

"That's clear," Ivana said, raising an eyebrow.

"I didn't want to bother you with any of this. You're a new mother, and I'm sure Mia is also keeping you plenty busy."

"It was easier with one," Ivana said, sighing. "But you know you can always talk to me."

"My life's a mess. I need to make some decisions."

"You should stay. Not that you asked my opinion. You're working in the family business, and it's meaningful to you. And you're good at it. In America, you were always getting pulled into Marko's life, spending holidays with his family instead of yours."

Marina hadn't expected this from her friend who went to the Church of St. Mary's Assumption every Sunday and prayed like a good Catholic. And who had given up her nursing job to care for her family.

"Come, let's walk to the promenade and talk," Ivana said. "Are you alright carrying that?"

"I can drop it in the car, I got a spot nearby," Marina said.

They strolled around the edge of the Old Town peninsula, past whitewashed buildings with red-tiled roofs to Nikola's Yugo. Marina opened the trunk and set the wrapped photo carefully inside. As they rounded the corner and dusk settled over the sea, the circular Greeting to the Sun installation started to flicker, colored lights skittering across its surface, mirroring the sunset's hues. They walked over the solar glass panels as haunting notes from the Sea Organ pulsed with the waves.

"Can I be honest?" Ivana said.

"Always," Marina said.

"Every summer when you visited with Marko, you seemed more and more unhappy. You took your short vacation on Pag, and I felt that part of you didn't want to go back."

"That's probably true."

"He never really made you happy."

"I don't remember how happiness feels," Marina said, surprising herself with her own openness, realizing how American she had become. "Do you feel happy?"

Ivana hesitated. "Having another child is stressful, and I often wish I'd continued my nursing job, just to have something that is mine, outside of the house."

Ivana had been jealous when Marina left for college in New York. She was not often jealous, but the war had made them all weary, and everyone longed for an escape. In high school they had been the top students, competing against each other for first in class. Ivana wrote beautiful essays with Marina's Caran d'Ache pencil until it was simply a stub. Towards the end of that year, when Marina no longer thought of Ivana as a mainland refugee but a friend, she gave Ivana her last pencil. Ivana needed it more than her, and she knew Ivana shared with her four sisters. There was seemingly no end to her virtue.

Ivana was generous even when she had nothing to give. Marina often felt selfish in comparison. Ivana had volunteered her time after school at Caritas to help new refugee families who arrived on Pag throughout the war, searching for clothing and shoes, items to replace a life that had been left behind in haste. Despite not having much extra time to study, she managed to outdo Marina on exams. The teachers heaped praise on Ivana. When Ivana told Marina she planned to study in Zadar to become a nurse after receiving a full scholarship, Marina was not surprised. Marina knew she would be the best.

Ljubica's tiny lungs pierced the air. The sea sung her sad, familiar melody, whitecaps crashing against stone, waves ebbing in an endless cycle.

"Shhh, *draga*," Ivana hushed, stopping to offer Ljubica a pacifier. "I think you need love in your life, or it's not worth living."

"And you and Darko?" Marina said.

"I get my happiness from my kids now," Ivana said. "My life is theirs."

"You're lucky. You have two beautiful girls."

"But you're free, Marina, you can go anywhere. You still have time to find love."

Marina wondered if she would ever find love again. They walked back to the Yugo in silence, the Sea Organ howling at their backs.

On Christmas morning, Marina asked Nikola if she could accompany him to the upper pasture. It had been years since she'd been there; Nikola used to take her and Luka after school in spring-time, and they would play with limestone rocks and hide behind *suhozidi* walls—made with piles of stones the size of sheep's skulls—that reached higher than their heads.

They took Franko's Jeep, since the Yugo could never make it up the steep, moonscape terrain. The Jeep's wheels struggled and slipped on the sharp rocks. Patches of hearty shrubs dotted the bleached landscape like a rash. Marina felt the coffee jostle in her stomach. Out the window, the giant white wind turbines came into view; they appeared alien to the landscape, their red-tipped steel blades revolving faster and faster like a warning.

On top of the hill, Marina admired the panoramic blue-gray Velebit mountain range in the distance, clouds hovering above it like icing. Pag plummeted into the sea, lashing tongues of saltwater swallowing gulps of shoreline. The small stone hut, built by her late grandfather Maržić, was the only structure to provide shelter for the sheep, which huddled together under its rusted, corrugated tin roof. When Nikola retrieved a bag of corn from the trunk and poured it into the crude wooden trough, the flock bleated and moved as a skittish mass, their hooves delicately traversing loose limestones that clinked together like chimes. Mouths dipped into the feed with quick, jerky movements.

"Are you sure you want to stay?" Nikola said, taking out his tin and rolling a cigarette.

"I'm sure," Marina said.

Marina was no longer a girl who named lambs. Since return-ing to Pag she'd thought about their ancestors, whose bodies had been sustained by sheep and cheese, their bones buried beneath the island's hard limestone layers. In New York, she bought meat packaged in Styrofoam containers covered with shrink wrap. Marina felt she had become disconnected from her food; if she were going to eat it, she figured, she should see where it came from.

Meat was a small part of the business; Sirana sold lambs to local restaurants and to residents for holiday celebrations. She wanted to embrace her roots and the factory that supported them—even the parts of their business that were sometimes difficult to stomach. Accompanying her father felt like a rite of passage.

Nikola finished his cigarette and tossed it to the ground. He retrieved his sharp hunting knife from its scabbard and handed it to her. Her father had explained the importance of being merciful, to be assertive for the sake of the animal. "It's not that there isn't a tender spot in you, but you have to be decisive. You have to own it. It's no favor to the sheep to try to be polite," Nikola had said to his son before Franko had butchered his first lamb at thirteen. After Franko had repeated the story to Marina, Nikola's words had stayed with her all these years later. She often lacked conviction in her actions. It was time to change.

The sheep continued to munch on corn, their heads bobbing into the trough. A white lamb suckled at the mother's teat, its pale pink tongue hanging from the side of its mouth. When the lamb pulled away, Nikola wrapped one arm around its torso and supported its rump with his hand. He carried it around to the side of the hut, out of the flock's sight. The lamb's high-pitched bleats pulled at Marina's heart.

Nikola gently laid the lamb on its side, its neck facing the open sky. His right knee hovered over its shoulders. To Marina's amazement, under his sure grip, it surrendered and didn't shout. Marina made a clean cut across its throat with one firm stroke. Two crimson streams spurted out a few feet and seeped into the stone. She watched the lamb's pupils dilate.

She was surprised at the force it took to achieve a death. She didn't think she had it in her, not to look away. Franko hadn't been able to stomach it; he vomited that day her father showed him how to kill. But she had watched the life drain away from this beautiful animal, its pure white coat matted with blood. Her father would do the skinning later. Tender meat would turn and roast for Christmas dinner, the lamb's carcass rotating on a spit like the wind turbines, like the world on its axis and the relentless life cycle of birth and death.

Nikola lined the trunk with garbage bags and laid the lamb's limp body on the plastic, carefully covering it. The Jeep rumbled down the hill, its wheels occasionally slipping on stones. Marina stared out the window, lost in her thoughts. She wondered if the lamb's mother realized her offspring was gone. She closed her eyes, listening to the low hum of the engine. *The mother must know*, she thought. *She must.*

"Your mother made a feast," Nikola said to Marina, exhaling a stream of smoke and rubbing his hands from the cold. Outside, the lamb turned on the electric spit.

"We have God's bounty here on our table," Dragica said, wiping her wet hands on her red apron.

For a starter, Dragica prepared a fish soup with a fresh catch from their neighbor, which they had traded for some Pag cheese. Sheep, cow, and goat cheeses were surrounded by strips of smoked Dalmatian *pršut*, arranged on an olive-wood cutting board near a basket of her mother's crusty homemade bread. Potatoes from their garden were roasted in lamb fat Nikola had collected from the spit, alongside roast turkey on a bed of *mlinci*, flatbread squares soaked in the bird's juices. Marina's favorite, *sarme*—cabbage rolls stuffed with rice and minced meat—were nestled like siblings on a platter.

Dragica tucked a flaxen hank of hair behind her ear as she busied herself setting the last dishes on the table. Under the bright kitchen lights, Marina noticed a few strands of silver. Her mother appeared more youthful than her sixty years, her plump face virtually free of wrinkles. In many ways, Marina looked so different than her mother, her angular face in contrast with Dragica's round features, but she had inherited Dragica's bright-brown eyes, a nearly identical shade.

Marina and her mother had never been close. When Marina had finally gotten her period at fourteen, later than most girls, Dragica had shoved some sanitary pads at her wordlessly. Imported supplies were harder to come by during the war, and Marina felt her mother saw her menstrual cycle as an inconvenience. Her mother seemed perturbed at this aspect of womanhood and never explained to her that this monthly event meant a woman could have a child. Everything she learned about sex and bodies she learned from Ivana, who had her older sisters' experience to share.

Dragica was raised to believe a woman was accomplished if she married well, and Grandma Badurina had been pleased when Nikola, a southerner from a respectable family, had proposed. Dragica had made it her life's work to become a good Croatian wife, tending to their garden and slaving over the stove, preparing homemade meals for her husband and children. Marina did not understand how her mother was satisfied with domesticity, seemingly without any outside aspirations. Dragica had never once left their country, and seemed content to stay within the confines of the familiar. But maybe she knew best: Marina had returned without a husband, a child, or a career, as if all her years in America had been erased.

Marina finished setting their special occasion gold-rimmed plates, which shone under soft candlelight. "Franko's not back?" Marina called to her mother.

"Not yet," Dragica said.

Her brother's obsession with soccer bordered on fanatic, and Marina found herself jealous he was that passionate about something, even if it was a sport. She didn't know if she would ever be that passionate about anything, and the thought made her melancholy. Franko probably realized by now he wouldn't make the cut for Hajduk Split, but he played anyway, almost every day, including holidays.

"Can I get you anything, Mama? Some *rakija*?" Dragica asked her mother, who was lounging on Nikola's favorite reclining chair, her legs covered with an afghan.

"We should wait until after dinner," Grandma Badurina said, meaning that everyone should wait to have some until after dinner.

Marina's grandmother, a plump, formidable woman with an older version of Dragica's round face, did not feel the need to explain herself. After her husband died, she holed up in her house across the bay, on the other side of Pag Town. Grandma Badurina became a recluse and visited them only occasionally, when it suited her. She would take her favorite walking stick—made from the polished branch of an olive tree—and pass by the centuries-old salt warehouses, crossing the small stone bridge spanning across Tale Bay. At eighty, she no longer drove, yet insisted on being self-sufficient, rarely letting anyone drive her anywhere. She preferred to take the bus from Pag Town to Zadar on her own. Even Dr. Miletić made house calls for the stubborn old woman.

Franko burst through the door, his cheeks red from the cold. He removed his shoes and kissed Dragica and Grandma Badurina on the cheeks.

"I'm starving," Franko said.

"Nice of you to show up," Marina said.

Franko glared at her. "I'm going to shower."

"Be quick," Nikola said, squeezing Franko's shoulders.

Nikola opened a bottle of ruby Teran wine they had bought in Istria at the Motovun Truffle Festival. He filled their glasses. "Come, let's sit."

Nikola offered to help Grandma Badurina to one of the head seats, but she swatted his arm away. Dragica brought out a medley of roasted vegetables, hot from the oven.

"A little overdone," Grandma Badurina said to Dragica, surveying the vegetables.

Dragica frowned. "It's fine, Mama."

"*Ej*, you never did learn to cook very well, despite everything I tried to teach you," Grandma Badurina said, clucking her tongue.

Dragica sat quietly next to her mother. Marina took a sip of Teran.

"Wait to toast," Dragica scolded.

Marina set down her glass. On this holy day, she vowed not to fight with her mother.

Nikola emerged from the backyard with a plate of steaming lamb. He set it on the table.

"Beautiful," Grandma Badurina said, clasping her hands together.

"Go get Franko," Dragica instructed Marina. "Dinner will get cold."

Marina walked down the hall and pounded on the bathroom door. "Hurry up!"

"Coming, coming," Franko shouted.

Franko emerged with slicked, still-wet hair. "Mmmm," he said, surveying the food.

"Let's say grace," Nikola said, holding out his hands. "We thank God for this good food and pray for a blessed year. Amen."

Silently, Marina thanked the lamb. They broke hands.

"*Živjeli!*" Nikola said, raising his glass.

To life, Marina thought, raising her glass. But she didn't feel it. What life? Her miscarriage, Marko's affair. It seemed like someone else's life.

Dragica played a *klapa* CD on low volume. She passed each heaping plate to Grandma Badurina, who took the first serving.

"Dragica says you're having some French girl come to Sirana, to help with the cheese?" Grandma Badurina said, helping herself to a slice of lamb.

"It was Marina's idea," Nikola said. "We need some fresh blood in the factory. And the French know cheese."

"What does this girl get out of it?" Grandma Badurina said. Her generation was especially skeptical of outsiders.

"Céline and her father are very interested in Croatia, and our cheese," Marina said.

"Did their cheese win any awards?" Grandma Badurina said, raising an eyebrow.

"They placed second in the Best Western European Sheep's Milk Cheese category at the World Cheese Awards," Marina said.

"Not bad, not bad," Grandma Badurina said, chewing a piece of meat.

Nikola had been the one to tell Grandma Badurina about Sirana's loss at the World Cheese Awards. Marina had been afraid of her grandmother's reaction. Grandma Badurina immediately asked about Janković, and when she learned Josip's cheese had won, she'd pursed her lips, indicating immense disapproval.

"Did you give it any more thought, if Céline can stay in your apartment upstairs?" Nikola said, heaping his plate with glistening potatoes.

Grandma Badurina transferred a cabbage roll to her plate. "I suppose, since it's the off-season and I won't be renting it out," she said. "As long as she's quiet."

"I'm sure she's quiet, Mama," Dragica said. "It would really help us out, since we don't really have the space, now that Marina is home."

Marina grimaced. She wanted to tell her mother that she had never planned to stay so long, to be a burden on them. But it was Christmas, and she told herself to be grateful she had somewhere to go, grateful that she had a family.

"Who will feed her? I only cook for myself now," Grandma Badurina said.

"I'll take care of the food. We promised her room and board," Dragica said.

"When does she arrive?" Grandma Badurina said.

"Just after the new year. We'll pick her up from the airport," Nikola said.

"I'll send her home with something she can heat up on the stove," Dragica said.

"As long as she takes care of herself," Grandma Badurina said.

"Good, that's settled, then," Nikola said.

Franko took another slice of lamb and passed the plate to Marina.

"*Ne, hvala*," Marina said, surprising herself.

"What?" Dragica said. "You love our lamb. Don't tell me you're becoming a *vegetarijanka* like your American friend."

Nikola glanced at Marina. She could feel her cheeks becoming hot.

"I don't feel like it today," Marina said.

"I told you she shouldn't go," Dragica said to Nikola.

"I'm a grown woman, Mama. Please don't," Marina said.

"You're missing out," Franko said, holding up his fork with a piece of meat and wiggling it.

"Shut up, Franko," Marina said.

"Did you name another one *snijeg*? Your little snowy lamb?" Franko taunted.

"Did you vomit again at the sight of blood?" Marina shot back.

"That's enough," Nikola said, frowning at them.

They ate in silence. The candles flickered.

"So Marina, any news from Marko?" Grandma Badurina said.

Marina swallowed. "We're not really speaking, Grandma."

"*Ej*, he's your husband, you have to speak to him. I still speak to mine, and he's dead!" she said, chuckling.

"Mama!" Dragica exclaimed.

"Oh Dragica, don't be so serious," Grandma Badurina said, taking a sip of wine.

"When was the last time you talked?" Dragica said.

Even though divorce was becoming increasingly common, they were staunch Catholics, and it was a reluctant conclusion. Dragica was mortified that Marina was living in limbo under their roof, bringing shame to the family.

"Mama, do we really need to discuss this now?" Marina said.

"Leave the girl alone, it's Christmas," Grandma Badurina said.

"She needs to learn to live with the choices she's made. She's no longer a girl," Dragica said, sounding a lot like the priests at church.

"I heard Marina's found someone new," Franko said.

Everyone turned to Marina. Her cheeks burned. She felt her father studying her, and knew he could read her face.

"What, now?" Grandma Badurina said, squinting at Franko with her hawk-like gaze.

"People say she's been hanging around with Luka in Zadar," Franko said.

Marina's stomach lurched. Nikola placed his fork and knife neatly on the sides of his plate and smoothed his mustache.

"Josip's boy?" Grandma Badurina said, pursing her lips.

Grandma Badurina disliked northerners, but none as much as the Janković family. Everyone knew Grandma Badurina held it against Nikola that he had courted Sanja, when she and Josip had briefly broken up during university in Zadar. It caused a wedge in his friendship with Josip, but eventually, Josip reunited with Sanja some weeks later, and shortly after, they married. Marina couldn't be sure if her grandmother was more upset that he had chosen someone else before Dragica, or that he had chosen a northerner.

And then there was the gossip; at the wedding, people looked for a bump in Sanja's belly beneath her wedding gown. Sanja convinced Josip to forgive Nikola and mend their friendship, and as a gesture, to make Nikola his best man, despite the disapproval they'd face from other northerners. Months later, she gave birth to Branko, and everything between the two men seemed for a time to be forgiven, but not forgotten. By the time Luka was born, Nikola, Josip, and Sanja were all working together at Sirana in a country called Yugoslavia.

"I ran into Luka in Zadar, with Ivana," Marina said. It wasn't entirely a lie.

"Franko, it's not nice to spread rumors," Grandma Badurina said.

"I'm just saying, people are talking," Franko said.

Marina felt heat rising in her cheeks. Her throat squeezed like a vise, quick and furious, something ground against her organs, in her mouth there was a foul taste like bile. She speared a piece of lamb, put it on her plate, and cut a bite. She chewed quickly and swallowed, swallowing, too, her anger at Franko and the words she wanted to say to him.

"People are always talking about something or the other on Pag," Nikola said, with a note of finality that ended the discussion.

"I'll make *fritule*," Dragica said, pushing back her chair and heading into the kitchen.

They finished eating in silence. Marina couldn't wait for the meal to end. Out of politeness to Grandma Badurina she would stay and eat *fritule*, little balls of fried dough sprinkled with powdered sugar. She would swallow the sweetness to suffocate any thorny memories that crept up the stairs, puncturing the walls of her throat.

She realized she didn't belong here, at this table, in this house. She was no longer a child, even though she was still being treated like one. Marina had left when she was on the cusp of adulthood, and now that she was a grown woman, she was living with her family as if nothing had changed. Her father was right; she had to make a decision. She couldn't stay in her parents' home forever.

Chapter Nine

From Pag Town, Marina watched dazzling northern fireworks light up the midnight sky, bursts of color dotting the black canvas like fluorescent sea urchins. "Showing off as always," Nikola grimaced. The large fireworks, which reached high above the northern hill that hugged Pag Town, were from Zrće, the party beach in the north that her father despised. He saw Zrće as a cash cow that attracted summer revelers, lining northerners' pockets with heaps of excess *kunas*.

In the forefront, a few modest starbursts glittered over Tale Bay, their rippled reflections blurry like an Impressionist painting. Southerners did not like to spend on frivolous extravagances like fireworks that burned money for brief moments of beauty. Marina knotted her scarf tighter in an attempt to keep out the cold, and took a sip of prosecco. Her head was starting to become light, the alcohol and revelry eliciting an effervescent feeling.

On New Year's Eve, people made an unstated pact to let go of grievances, even if they would, inevitably, reappear later that year. The baker's son raised a glass to the butcher's son, though they had bitterly fought over the same girl. Grandmothers who made Pag lace, and had stolen each other's summer customers with price wars, ceased their quarrels and embraced like friends. Nikola presided over the festivities like a king, shaking everyone's hand, filling glasses, and passing platters of Sirana's cheese. Her father's generosity was legendary, but it was also, in part, why Sirana was in trouble.

Even Grandma Badurina had crossed the pedestrian stone bridge to ring in 2013. She sat on a bench near the water, watching lights shatter against the dark sky. People milled around, glasses clinked, children played on swings and slides near the bay. Above the hum of voices, Marina heard her father's hearty laugh. A crackling blast made her jump; all these years later, sniper fire from the war in the mainland still echoed in her cells.

Ivana and her friends had already retired for the evening, returning to their homes carrying small yawning children. *Teta* Marina did not have a reason to return home. Most of the husbands stayed in the square, drinking and loitering by the edge of the bay, talking and occasionally throwing stones into the water. They stole glances in her direction. Under their impertinent gazes, Marina felt reduced to her mother's finely ground Turkish coffee.

After the episode at Christmas, Franko had apologized to her. Marina had asked him if there really were rumors about her and Luka, what exactly had he heard and from whom. Of course people saw them in Zadar that day on the People's Square—half the island was out shopping—and someone had probably seen his caress. Gossip was impossible to trace back to a single source; it echoed through the island like a Greek chorus. She even wondered if the rumors were created by northerners, designed to hurt Sirana's business. What if Josip had started them?

Marina joined Grandma Badurina on her bench. "*Sretna Nova Godina*," Marina said, kissing her on the cheek.

"Dear, after all the years I've lived, this is just another," sighed Grandma Badurina.

"I hope this year will be a happy one," Marina said.

Grandma Badurina balanced her palm on her cane. Her gnarled hands looked like branches of the northern olive trees, from which the cane was made. Marina wondered if she would ever have the opportunity to speak to her own granddaughter, on the eve before a new year, and what she'd say. She had not lived the life she'd envisioned until now, and couldn't begin to imagine what the next years would hold.

"What will this year bring for you, Marina?" Grandma Badurina said, raising her voice over the pop and hiss of fireworks.

"I wish I knew," Marina said.

"Wishing won't get you anywhere," Grandma Badurina said, straightening her spine.

Marina lowered her eyes. "It isn't only up to me."

"Heaven helps those who help themselves. You want a divorce? Your father will disagree, but I say go and get one. Life is too short for a heavy heart."

Her grandmother surprised her, but then, Grandma Badurina had always been progressive, urging Nikola to hire women in the factory, which he did at her insistence after he took over Sirana. Even her father had to admit that most of the female cheese packers were better than their male counterparts.

Earlier, Marko had texted, "Happy New Year." Marina had texted the same back to him, but she felt nothing. She was numb, vacant, swirling in the unhappiness that was her fractured marriage, a flurry of flakes in a snow globe turned upside down.

"Hey, we're going to the triangle, then to Zrće," Franko interjected, already on his way to drunk. "Wanna come?"

"Not if you're driving," Marina said.

"Mate's driving," Franko said, elbowing his sober friend, who had approached from behind.

Mate was one of Franko's more sensible friends. He had a sense of humor, often introducing himself to British tourists as "Mate, rhymes with latte," just to get a laugh. He was lean and tall, with a boyish smile.

"I don't feel like hiking. Or partying," Marina said.

"It will be fun," Franko said, grabbing her by the arm.

"I'm not going to Zrće."

"Then come to the triangle, let's see some aliens! We'll stop and get our boots. I'll drop you home after."

Ever since Christmas dinner, Franko had been trying to befriend her, apologizing in his way with small gestures. He brought Marina coffee from the machine at Sirana; he washed the Jeep after she took it into their muddy pastures. Marina had nowhere else to be besides home in bed, alone on her faded, flowered sheets, so she agreed to join them.

Summers, when she returned to Pag for those two fleeting weeks of vacation, first alone and later with Marko, she had avoided going to Zrće. The beach's crescent stretch of sand held too many memories of stolen moments with Luka. Zrće was a place for young lovers, for people who wanted to be free and had the future in front of them. She wanted to go back to that place, but she was afraid that—like everything else—it had changed.

"See you," Marina said, hastily kissing Grandma Badurina on the cheek.

Franko pulled Marina up from the bench and waved goodbye to Grandma Badurina, who shook her head.

They picked up a case of Karlovačko from the garage and Marina, Franko, and Stjepan piled into Franko's Jeep. Mate started the engine. Marina had not been up north since the summer.

The Jeep careened around a hairpin turn and up the hill. Driving past the entrance to Zrće with her brother and his friends recalled languid summers with Ivana on the beach, before it became full of nightclubs and foreigners. The beach then was pristine and nearly deserted, with smooth white pebbles that tortured their feet, which had been snug in shoes all winter. In those days, teenagers escaped the watchful eyes of their conservative families, and northerners met southerners for illicit romantic rendezvous that took place in the hush of night amid chirping cicadas.

Janković's black sign with bright white lettering came into view. Franko and his friends jeered with ugly language and gestures as they passed the enormous, modern factory with ostentatious windows—a stark contrast to Sirana's communist concrete bunker, built after the Second World War. She knew Josip had received EU funds to purchase new equipment, but it was apparent from the extra money he'd spent on his new factory that business was booming. Marina stared at the glowing heart. Illuminated from behind, it seemed to pulse.

Mate drove to the entrance to *Paški trokut*, which sat high on a hill near Novalja. Marina recalled how, years before, over the long-distance line, Franko had breathlessly explained that the triangle was accidentally discovered by a Croatian geodesist, who was monitoring the island to further understand the Earth's orientation in space. It was big news on Pag. Marina was in New York, preparing to graduate from college. She'd found an entry-level marketing position and an affordable extra room in an Astoria apartment share. She decided to stay in New York City, forever changing her destiny.

Then, Marina had silently scoffed at the people back home, at the revelatory discovery of a pile of stones in the shape of a triangle, its footprint roughly the square footage of a suburban house. She was living in a big city, with big dreams, far away from petty island discoveries and divisions. Now, she saw that city through her father's eyes: a churning mess of limbs and fists, people endeavoring to climb on top of each other while pulling others down, reaching up, up, up to the peak of a triangle from which they would inevitably fall. And so, she felt inextricably connected with the triangle, an unknown force that beckoned.

Rumors started to circulate about the unusual formation. There was talk of aliens, UFOs, and the intergalactic origin of the strange isosceles triangle, which was made from rock unlike any of the other surrounding rock and had holes on each side of the triangle, as if a spaceship had landed and anchored itself to the earth. Over the years there had been many reports of strange sightings above the island, shining objects seen by hundreds of people in the north. Nikola dismissed the northerners and their stories, calling them superstitious.

Marina had visited the spot once before with Luka, the summer after it was discovered—before she met Marko. Each summer she visited, in those two short weeks, Marina dipped her toes into her former life, just long enough to ease into the slower pulse of Pag before she had to leave, accosted by the hustle of New York City soon after the plane touched down. Marina had felt Luka had wanted to tell her something, but she'd left, and they had gone on separately with their summers.

Franko, who was obsessed with the triangle and the idea of aliens, sent her emails with updates on new findings. He told her experts had concluded that the lighter-colored rocks inside the triangle had been exposed to extreme temperatures in the Neolithic era. Some said it was a random pattern of geological faults, but Marina, like Franko and many others, preferred to believe a spaceship had landed on their island. She hoped there was life beyond their world's trivial grievances, that their island had been touched by something greater. She hoped for something greater for herself.

When Franko opened the Jeep's passenger side door, Marina immediately regretted agreeing to come. Strong winds tumbled down Velebit and rushed into the car, slamming the door shut with force. "Come on, let's meet some aliens," Franko said, turning on a flashlight. He passed flashlights and beer to Marina, Mate, and Stjepan.

They followed signs and red arrows spray-painted on *suhozidi*, combing flashlights over pale rocks. Marina had forgotten the unforgiving terrain, sharp spikes of limestone that made walking difficult, even in boots. Rocky needles protruded from the wild landscape. Marina stumbled. The *bura* whipped across her face, pushing against her body like a thousand icy fingers. They walked in silence. The furious wind screamed, and she pulled her hat over her ears. She concentrated on the treacherous ground. Her steps felt grueling, heavy, the cold intolerable.

She cursed the weather, she cursed the wind, she cursed the new year, which seemed, all of a sudden, ominous. Back in the city, Marko was probably snug indoors, celebrating and drinking with their friends, like they used to do together. Each year, approaching midnight, on the big-screen television that occupied a wall of their living room in Astoria, they would all watch the ball drop in Times Square.

Last year, when they watched the ball drop, Marina had sat on their couch, a glass of Champagne numbing her hand. Marko toasted with their friends, and as she clinked her glass and heard that hollow sound, she hoped her emotions wouldn't overflow like foam gushing over the lip of her glass. She couldn't push the image of her baby's tiny, purple body out of her mind. During the two endless days she delivered her daughter, who she knew would never breathe, Marina cried when anyone touched her. Marko tried to hold her hand, but she pushed him away. Even a gentle caress felt painful.

Doctors told her that if she wanted to become pregnant again after a second-term loss, it was better to deliver. She tried to prepare herself for the delivery and all it would entail, the panoply of emotions on the labor and delivery floor, screams of pain and joy. "Don't worry, it's not like a normal birth," the nurse said briskly before they started inducing her, as if that was somehow supposed to be reassuring. It only made her feel more terrified and alone.

After the delivery, after the endless pushing and screaming, the nurse had said it would be better to see her daughter's body sooner than later because the color would continue to change. Shaking, she'd held her still, silent baby, swaddled snugly in a striped hospital blanket. Her daughter's tiny eyelids were closed.

She wanted to go to Zrće, to feel free, like she'd felt on that beach as a teenager.

"Let's go to Zrće," Marina said, fighting back tears. "I don't know what I was thinking, agreeing to come up here after midnight. We won't even be able to see the triangle."

"We're halfway there," Stjepan said.

Franko laughed, bringing the flashlight under his face, making it appear ghoulish. "See, Mate? I told you."

"Told him what?" Marina said.

"Your brother said you'd go to Zrće if we hiked up here first," Mate said.

Marina hit Franko on the shoulder. "Ouch," Franko said, feigning injury.

"He knows you well," Mate said, laughing.

"Too well," Marina said, forcing a laugh. But Mate was wrong. Her brother didn't know her at all.

It was a short drive from the triangle to Zrće. Marina surveyed the beach, which hugged the crescent shoreline. Walking across the white pebbles in her thick-soled boots, she recalled the sensation of irregular shapes imprinting on her bare feet. A roaring bonfire rimmed the waves with touches of gold. Palm trees guarded the beach like sentinels. Someone had brought speakers to one of the open-air clubs, which were packed during summers. Gone were the sweaty foreign revelers; the stages were boarded up with protective planks for winter. Huddled figures stood around the fire, creating leaping shadows across the pebbles.

The fireworks startled Marina. Even though it was nearly one o'clock in the morning, unpredictable stragglers burst and rained above them. Her father was right; northerners did like to show off. Wealth generated from Zrće's summer revelers lit up the sky, burning *kunas* in a flaunty spectacle. Light from the explosions and the bonfire flickered on dozens of upturned faces. Marina was surprised so many people were out braving the cold, but then, the northerners always knew how to party.

An international playlist pounded through the speakers. People started to sway to the music. Franko and his friends threw back beers. And then, across the fire, she saw him. Luka had his arm draped around Zara, who was smoking a cigarette, her red nails flashing as she flicked the ash. Her cheeks were rosy, her lips full and pouty. They were with some friends Marina didn't recognize. Luka laughed heartily, his head tilting back.

Marina's chest tightened. She should have anticipated Luka and Zara might be here, but she had reasoned they'd be at Josip and Sanja's, or home with Kata. Marina wanted to look away but couldn't stop staring at them.

"Drop me home, please?" she said to Mate, raising her voice over the booming music.

"We just got here," Franko said, popping open the cap of another bottle, which landed on the stones.

Mate looked confused. "I can take her," he said. He was never one to take sides in an argument. Of all Franko's friends, Marina liked Mate the most.

"Not yet," Franko said. "We're just starting to have fun."

Marina glanced across the fire at Luka. He hadn't seen her yet, or if he had, he was ignoring her. Seeing him with his wife conjured a feeling she couldn't name. It was part jealousy, part rage, and something else that felt like black tar clogging her throat.

"Oh look, it's Prince Janković," Franko said, following Marina's gaze.

"Franko, don't start," Marina said, grabbing his arm.

"The big cheese is here," Franko shouted, twisting free. Her brother's eyes narrowed into slits.

Luka heard him this time, and his gaze settled on Franko, and then on Marina. She couldn't read his expression. Zara was oblivious, laughing with her friends. Marina held her breath. Luka turned away.

Alcohol made Franko expand into a more obnoxious version of himself, ready to pick a fight. And the Janković rivalry really got him going. Her brother could never forgive Josip for what he did to Nikola, especially since they'd all fought together during the war, on the same side.

"Come on, Franko, leave him be," Mate said.

Franko ignored Mate. "Just because you won the World Cheese Awards, you think you're better than us?" Franko taunted.

"Franko!" Marina hissed.

"You coward, you can't even face us!" Franko slurred.

Stjepan and Mate backed up their friend, hurling insults and making obscene gestures across the fire. Marina felt chilled. Franko had Nikola's stocky build, and like her father, Franko's face turned red when he started to lose his temper.

After the war, her brother had changed. He didn't share much about what he'd seen on the battlefield, but she knew he had witnessed Branko's death, the moment when Branko had leapt in front of Luka to save his life. Franko had been just a boy of fifteen. After Nikola knocked him to the ground to protect him, Franko had watched his father get shot in the leg, resulting in a painful limp that would last a lifetime. Nikola had wanted Franko to become a man, to fight as a patriot for their country and bring their family honor. But the war, like everything, had consequences. "You can't unsee the dying," Franko had told her. In the years following the war, Franko was irascible, with uncontrolled out-bursts—especially when he drank.

"Franko, please," Marina said, this time grabbing her brother by the shoulder.

Franko shrugged off her hand. His gaze was fixed on Luka. Marina watched as her brother's face twisted into an ugly shape; the words he hurled were even uglier. Luka's friends returned insults, but Luka's back remained turned to them.

Zara stood clustered in a tight circle with her friends, and across the fire, Marina caught her gaze and quickly looked away.

"Slut!" Zara shouted at Marina across the fire.

"*Kurva, kurva, kurva!*" Zara's friends echoed in a mount-ing chorus.

So they had heard the rumors, too.

Franko threw a half-empty beer bottle into the fire. It landed on the edge of the flames, close to the group of clustered north-erners, spraying embers in their direction. Everyone jumped back.

"Get out of here," Luka boomed, turning around and drawing himself up to his full height.

"Make us," Franko shouted.

Luka strode in their direction, followed by his friends. Seeing the rage in Franko's eyes from across the fire, Zara tried to stop Luka, but he wrenched away from her grip. Luka rounded the fire, the two men facing each other, Luka a head taller than Franko, just like their fathers. Marina was rooted to the ground, her heart beating uncontrollably.

"You should leave," Luka said, his voice deep with threat.

"*Jebo ti pas mater*," Franko spat. *May the dog fuck your mother.*

It happened in an instant: Franko punched Luka squarely in the face. Luka stumbled backwards, bringing his hand to his nose. Then, fists and blood and broken bottles. Marina watched the scene helplessly, dark figures clashing under bursts of fire. Franko swung in all directions, and amid the chaos, on the opposite side of the fire, the northern women huddled together like sheep. Marina watched the spectacle as if removed from the reality, the blood and flames surreal.

"Stop it!" she screamed, but no one listened.

It was the same scene replaying itself in a different generation, boys fighting over turf and women, everyone taking the sides they were born into, adhering to allegiances from an island division that was decided by men centuries before.

At some point the fighting stopped. Luka and his friends, bloodied and bruised, retreated to the opposite side of the fire. Franko wiped his face on his sleeve, spat, and turned on his heel towards the parking lot. Marina followed. Mate drove home with steady hands, down the hill and hairpin turn, across the thin bridge that spanned Tale Bay. In the early morning hours, most Pag Town residents were snug in their beds, dreaming peacefully into the new year. Already, Marina knew she wouldn't sleep.

Chapter Ten

On New Year's Day, Dragica made *palačinke* for breakfast, rolled with fresh, creamy *skuta* and homemade jam. Marina had attempted to make the crepes in New York, but the flour was different, the butter was different, or maybe it was the milk. She could never replicate the recipe with American ingredients, it just didn't taste right. Besides, *skuta* was impossible to find, even in the city. How was it that she could find burrata from Italy in specialty stores, but not her beloved sheep's milk ricotta?

Nikola was immersed in the newspaper, reading about the former prime minister's corruption scandal that broke the day before New Year's Eve. Franko emerged from his bedroom and sat down at the dining table. He picked at a thread coming loose from Grandma Maržić's crocheted tablecloth. Marina glanced at him and quickly averted her eyes. Last night's brawl was written across his face.

Dragica emerged from the kitchen. "*Bože moj!*" she exclaimed, almost dropping the plate of *palačinke*.

Franko's left eye was different shades of purple. Her brother looked almost clown-like with his swollen, red nose, the eye patch-shaped bruise. Nikola lowered the newspaper and stared calmly at his son. Franko had had his share of scuffles in the schoolyard, and after the war, his aggression intensified. He was a reckless boy, and the war had unleashed something inside him, or maybe the conflict itself was the root. He carried the fury everywhere, ready to boil over at any slight.

"What happened?" Dragica said, setting down the plate in front of him and caressing his hair. "Let's get you some ice."

Marina hated how her mother babied her brother.

"It's nothing, Mama," Franko said.

"Your eye says otherwise," Dragica said, frowning.

"We ran into that Janković bastard," Franko said.

"He made a problem?" Nikola asked, smoothing his mustache. He lit a new cigarette, which was ready, resting on the edge of the almost-full ashtray.

"He thinks he's better than us just because they won the World Cheese Awards, and his wife disrespected Marina," Franko said.

"We really shouldn't have gone there," Marina said, taking a bite of crepe.

She wished she could take back the night.

"Now we can't go to Zrće because of your boyfriend?" Franko said, his eyes narrowing.

Marina stopped chewing. Her temples pulsed. So much for the truce with her brother. More than anything, she wanted to call Luka, to ask if he was okay. But seeing him with his arm around his wife—glimpsing that small window into his life—had left her bereft.

"He's not my boyfriend, and there's nothing going on between us," Marina said, narrowing her eyes. "But you had to start something, didn't you? You couldn't help yourself."

"He's not going to disrespect our family," Franko said.

"There's no disrespect. Why do you have to make everything a fight?" Marina said, raising her voice.

"What did he say?" Dragica said.

"His wife called Marina a slut," Franko said.

Marina looked down at her plate, feeling her mother's gaze. A long moment of silence passed. Nikola smoothed his mustache.

"Marina, I've heard the rumors," Nikola said, his voice heavy.

"It's not what you think," she said. "Nothing is going on."

Marina's cheeks burned. She felt like crawling under the table.

"I have a strong standing in this community," Nikola continued. "You know how things are here. You have to be careful about how people might interpret what they see."

Exhausted and overwhelmed by emotion, she was tired of feeling scrutinized and judged by everyone. "And what about you and Sanja?" Marina snapped, the words escaping her mouth before she could swallow them. She clasped her hand over her mouth. The last thing she wanted to do was hurt her father.

A look of shock registered on Nikola's face, his eyebrows like two floating parentheses. Marina couldn't look at her mother. Nikola cleared his throat.

"You're out of line," Nikola said, his face growing red. "And anyway, the situation was completely different back then. I have nothing to hide."

Marina stayed silent. She had heard the rumors when she was a teenager, and, unable to defend her father, thought he'd had an affair. Marina had so many unanswered questions. Had Nikola loved Sanja, and if so, why did he let her go? Why did Josip and Sanja get back together? Did Josip betray her father and Sirana partially out of revenge?

"Now, let's have a nice breakfast. It's a new year," Dragica said, smoothing her apron.

Leave it to her mother to act like nothing happened, glossing over difficult subjects.

"Your mother's right," Nikola said.

Marina ate the last few bites of *palačinke* and excused herself from the table, glaring at her brother on the way to the kitchen. She rinsed the plate and put it in the dishwasher.

Her phone dinged. *Meet in Zadar in an hour?*

The text was from Luka's number. Her heart raced. She quickly gave a thumbs-up and shoved her phone into her jeans' pocket.

"Where are you off to so early?" Dragica said.

"Meeting Ivana for coffee," Marina lied, grabbing her coat and the keys to Franko's Jeep.

Luka stood facing the Adriatic on the edge of Zadar's Sea Organ. The winter wind howled, kicking up seafoam onto the Sea Organ's large white steps. Cresting waves produced a rim of whitecaps in an expanse of moody grays that met the cloudy horizon.

Marina approached from behind, bringing her hand to his arm. Luka flinched; his shoulders relaxed as he turned around to face her. Marina dropped her hand and gasped. Luka's face was swollen, his lip split. Like Franko, he had a formidable black eye, which had blossomed into a dark-purple color overnight, shadowing his bloodshot eyes. It was clear he hadn't slept much, either. His gaze was cold.

"I'm sorry," Marina said, looking away. "We shouldn't have come up north."

"You have a right to go where you want," Luka said.

His voice was detached. Marina felt chilled. She pulled the zipper of her coat tighter around her throat.

"I didn't mean for there to be trouble. My brother was out of line."

"Zara insulted you. Frankly, in his place, I would have done the same," Luka said.

"Did you speak to her about the rumors?"

"I told her it was just a kiss," he sighed. "She told me to grow up, to stop chasing some girl I loved once."

Marina inhaled sharply. It was just a kiss, she reminded herself. But for her, it wasn't just a kiss, and it wasn't just about the kiss. It rekindled something deeper, a reservoir of memories. What was she holding on to?

Suddenly, she didn't know why she had come to meet him, or what she had hoped she would hear him say. What she really wanted was to rewrite their history, but that was impossible. The thought of Luka's beautiful, wild-eyed child, who had comforted her in the olive groves all those months before, filled Marina with envy. Perhaps she wanted to dispel the life that could have been hers, if circumstances had been different.

The sea air was misty, enveloping them in a thick fog. Marina couldn't see the horizon clearly. She was chasing ghosts. They couldn't return to how things had been; they couldn't repeat their past. They couldn't feign innocence, or recapture that feeling of endless possibility when Luka's hands had cupped her face on Zrće, sun-warmed pebbles pressing into their feet, on an island that belonged to a country called Yugoslavia. None of it existed anymore. Everything had changed.

Marina sighed. "I'm a different person now. You're different."

"We all change, Marina. But it doesn't change what's in our hearts."

"I'll always love you, but it's too late for us," she said. "We both need to move on. My family needs me, and yours does, too."

"I know you're right," he said. "I want to be your friend, but I don't know how."

"Remember Sirana's cheese castle?" Marina said. "We were friends first. We can be friends again."

"We'll always have those memories," Luka said softly.

"I should go," Marina said, willing herself to turn away.

Marina walked towards the Jeep. She felt the *bura* wind whipping past her ears and pushing hard on her back, quickening her return to Pag, as if the elements were conspiring in their separation. As she flung open the Jeep's driver's side door, the *bura* brushed tears off her face as soon as they fell, carrying them in the sea air, dispersing her sadness into the atmosphere.

Coffee at Zec? Marina texted Ivana as she drove, glancing at Zadar becoming miniature in her rearview mirror. Marina realized too late that she'd texted the name of a café that no longer existed, but she knew Ivana would understand. A few seconds later Ivana texted a thumbs-up. Marina collected herself on the drive, pulling over to put in moistening eyedrops. Thankfully, the café was empty. She ordered a white coffee and waited at a table for Ivana, who entered with Ljubica in a covered stroller. Marina was never so grateful to see her friend.

"Sorry, it took me longer to get out of the house—you know," Ivana said, hugging Marina and gesturing to the stroller. "*Sretna Nova Godina!*"

"Happy New Year," Marina echoed. She motioned to the waiter for another coffee.

"I heard about New Year's Eve," Ivana said, pushing the stroller back and forth.

Marina almost spit out her coffee. She attempted to regain her composure. "You're joking."

"My cousin was at the beach last night. Everyone is talking about it. He said Luka looked terrible."

"People are talking already?" Marina said, attempting to keep her voice calm.

Ivana nodded and rolled her eyes. "You know how people are. Anyway, what caused the fight?"

Marina hesitated. "You know about the feud between our families."

"If you don't want to talk about it, I understand," Ivana said, her eyes searching.

"Too much family drama," Marina said, taking a sip of coffee. "I'd rather talk about you. And Ljubica."

Marina recalled how they used to play with dolls together even when they should have been too old for such childish play, dreaming up stories about the dolls' families and wondering aloud how many children they themselves would have when they grew up. Neither of them ever imagined a life without children.

"Oh, that's boring," Ivana said. "Once you have kids you don't have any time for yourself. Everything is about what they need, what they want, now or in a few minutes, or what they'll need tomorrow. Half the time I can't even think!"

"I think too much," Marina said.

"Well, at least you can," Ivana said. "All I do these days is feed these kids, cook for them, clean up their messes. This one is sucking the life out of me," she said, gesturing to sleeping Ljubica, who looked like a small cherub fallen from heaven.

"Breastfeeding is difficult?" Marina asked. Early on in her pregnancy, she had imagined what that sensation would be like, the soft suckling she had witnessed in spring when Pag lambs pulled at their mothers' teats.

"It's harder with this one—she has trouble with latching. Of course my husband thinks it's something wrong with me," Ivana said, rolling her eyes.

Marina felt her throat tighten. "I know that feeling," she said. Tears fell onto her cheeks.

"*Ej*, what's wrong?" Ivana said, clasping her hands around Marina's.

"Marko made me feel defective," Marina said. "Like I was unworthy of being a mother—incapable. And maybe I am."

"I'm sorry," Ivana said, handing Marina some tissues from her purse. Of course Ivana had tissues: She was always prepared for the needs of her children.

"I gave birth," Marina said, starting to sob. "She had already died inside me, in my second trimester. I carried her corpse and she felt heavy, so heavy, I couldn't bear it. I wanted to keep her, and at the same time I wanted to release her. I wanted her to breathe but I knew it was impossible."

"*Bože moj!*" Ivana said. "When? Why didn't you tell me?"

"I didn't tell anyone. I only recently told *Tata*. Mama doesn't know."

"How could they ask you to do that, to give birth? To a child that had passed, for the love of God?" Ivana made the sign of the cross, pressed her fingers to her lips and then to the sky.

"The doctors, they said if I were going to try to get pregnant again, I should deliver the baby. I thought that getting pregnant again was the only way to save my marriage, that it would be the only thing that would make my sadness go away. I thought if I could bring a life into this world, it would make us whole again. Make me whole."

Ivana looked into Marina's eyes, pressing her hands together. "I'm not sure any of us are ever really whole. Having a child won't change that."

"After I left, there was a part of me that felt so broken," Marina said. "I've been searching for answers. I think I stayed here to try to find them."

"We were all broken after the war," Ivana said. "If I think too much about the past, I feel like things could fall apart."

"Being back here, I can't not think about it. We're surrounded by ghosts."

"If you'd stayed, you would probably be living a life like mine. Would you be happy then?"

Marina hesitated. "I don't know."

Ljubica, as if on cue, started to wail. Ivana swept her daughter from the stroller in a familiar, fluid movement that was so natural it filled Marina with envy. Ivana flipped up her shirt and brought the baby's tiny head to her pale breast; Ljubica rooted, and became instantly pacified after finding her mother's milk. Marina watched in awe while her friend took a sip of coffee and acted as if nothing had happened.

"How does it feel?" Marina asked.

"Like I'm a cow," Ivana said, bursting out laughing.

"Or a sheep!" Marina said, simultaneously laughing and crying, wiping the tears from her eyes with the back of her hand.

As they walked along Tale Bay, Marina was grateful for her friend. She couldn't remember the last time she'd laughed that hard. Marina dropped Ivana off at her house, kissing her on both cheeks, and felt momentarily lighter. Maybe this was what it felt like to start to move on.

Chapter Eleven

*C*éline's plane was scheduled to arrive at 3:30 p.m., but the flight from France was delayed. Marina and Nikola had driven an hour to Zadar Airport to pick her up, and now, they waited in uncomfortable chairs near the arrivals area. Nikola retrieved his dented tin box from his pocket and rolled a cigarette.

"*Tata,* you remember you can't smoke in here now, right?" Marina said.

Nikola fiddled with the tin. "This is crazy, not being able to smoke," he huffed.

"When was the last time you came to the airport?"

"Your graduation," Nikola said.

"Was that really the last time?"

"I've had no reason to get on a plane." Nikola shifted in his seat.

Marina wondered if Dragica was keeping her father home, if he otherwise would be traveling for work or pleasure.

Every year, Marina looked forward to returning to Pag, a welcome respite from her hectic New York City life. She felt herself slow down as the thick Mediterranean climate permeated her bones. There was something that felt safe in the smaller scale of everything, the familiar scents and sounds—their clear Slavic language filling her eardrums.

Franko's ugly words from two nights before were lodged in her memory. The fight by the fire still seemed surreal. She couldn't get Zara's painted face out of her mind, lush eyelashes thick with mascara. Marina wondered what Zara looked like under the makeup, after they went home and Luka climbed into bed with her. She wondered if Luka loved Zara's naked face. And then she stopped herself. She needed to let him go.

"You shouldn't have let Franko off so easily. He always gets away with everything," Marina said suddenly.

Nikola started rolling another cigarette, arranging the tobacco neatly on the paper. "Boys come to blows sometimes," he said.

"He's not a boy anymore, *Tata*. And we were on their side of the island."

"*Ej.*" Her father shrugged, licking the paper and sealing the cigarette.

"Franko is reckless and immature. I don't think he even wants to take over Sirana."

"He'll be ready, eventually."

"Can't you see his heart is on the soccer field?"

"Don't fault him for loving something, Marina. Commitment takes passion."

"I'm just not sure he's committed to our cheese."

Nikola flipped the lid of the tin open and shut. "I hope this girl knows something about cheese," he said finally.

Marina knew not to push him.

"Her father taught her everything he knows. She's taking over the business from him," Marina said, feeling suddenly defensive.

Marina hoped that her father might be inspired after seeing a French girl a decade younger than his own daughter whose expertise surpassed his own. Céline's father had trained her in the art of cheesemaking and chosen her over her brothers. Céline would take the temperature of the curds, fretting over any variation; she would measure the salinity of the *salamura* like a scientist, tracking any fluctuation in the brine. Marina yearned to immerse herself in the craft.

Over the loudspeaker, Céline's flight number was announced. Marina's heart leapt in anticipation. It had only been a couple months since she'd seen Céline at the World Cheese Awards, but so much had happened since then. Marina told herself not to hope too much, not to have high expectations, but still, she couldn't help imagining Céline as Sirana's savior.

Céline emerged from baggage claim rolling an oversized suitcase made all the more giant in comparison with her petite frame. She wore a red jacket with a tie at the waist, low black boots, and a stylish, geometric-patterned scarf. She looked like she was coming from Paris, not rural Basque. Marina worried about her father's first reaction to the posh girl.

Marina waved and smiled. Céline headed over to them, her brown eyes bright with anticipation.

"*Bonjour!*" she said, kissing Marina on both cheeks. "Or, how do you say it here?"

"*Bok*," Nikola said, shaking her hand. "Welcome to Croatia," he said in halting English.

"Welcome," Marina said. "How was your flight?"

"With exception of the delay, *parfait!*" she said.

Céline's walnut-colored hair was cut into a neat bob, and her lips had just the right amount of pink lip gloss. Marina wondered how French women could always look so chic, even after a flight.

Nikola, at a loss for the English words, gestured to take Céline's suitcase.

"Oh, how do you say 'thank you'?" she said.

"*Hvala*," Marina said. "Don't worry, I'll translate everything for you. My father doesn't speak English very well, and neither of us speaks French."

"Of course, we will manage in English," Céline said, smiling. "But there will be some technical words in cheesemaking I won't know for the English."

"*Nema problema*," Marina said. "It means, no problem. That's an important Croatian phrase to learn."

Céline's laughter sounded like a teaspoon clinking against a fine Champagne glass.

Nikola wheeled Céline's suitcase out to the parking lot. Marina had convinced her father to drive Franko's Jeep to the airport; she was embarrassed by his old Yugo and wanted to make a good first impression. Already, everyone on the island had heard of the visiting French cheesemaker's daughter. Marina was nervous about showing Céline Sirana's humble facilities.

"Please take the front seat. I've seen this drive so many times before," Marina said.

Céline chattered on unprompted about her father's cheesemaking business; about Petit Agour, their beloved sheep's milk cheese; and about the Basque people, who, she said, have always been fiercely independent, with their discrete language and culture.

"But, you speak French?" Marina asked.

"We speak both Basque *and* French," Céline said over her shoulder. "We are very different people from our French neighbors. We have more in common with our Spanish Basque neighbors."

Marina translated for her father.

"We are not as well-known as the Spanish part of Basque, but our land is just as beautiful," Céline said, a note of pride in her voice.

Marina wondered if Céline felt defensive, like her province was the less pretty sister, trailing behind Spain's alluring Basque Country and the rest of beloved France. It reminded her of Pag's northern and southern people, each constantly claiming themselves superior.

"Our history dates back to pre-Roman times," Céline added.

"Ours, too," Marina said. "And so does our cheese."

Marina remembered sitting with Ivana in European history class, learning about all the influences on Pag over the centuries: the ancient Illyrians in the Bronze Age; the Romans; the Croats; and the division that occurred as a result of two kingdoms quarreling over their island. Always a pyramid of limbs and fists fighting to reach the pinnacle. It's the story of so many places, this battle to reign, to push out the other. Marina wondered how many wars could have been avoided if factions just decided to share.

As they drove over Pag Bridge, Marina pointed out Fortica, the small fortress that guarded the island in the Middle Ages, a steadfast sentinel on the narrow straight called *Ljubačka vrata*—the Love Door—separating Pag and the mainland. There was a time in the not-so-distant past when there was no bridge, only ferries and boats that deposited people and goods from one shore to the other. The bridge had been built before she was born, during the time of Yugoslavia. Nikola had told Marina stories about taking a ferry to the mainland with his father to get supplies, and also to make Sirana's cheese deliveries to stores.

"How bald it looks, like an old man who lost his hair!" Céline exclaimed.

"Our northern wind, the *bura*, is so strong that nothing can grow where it blows. It is one of the reasons our island isn't like any of the others," Marina explained.

They followed the curving road above Pag's steep cliffs, which plummeted into the crystal sea.

"But look at your beautiful sea—even around Brittany's islands, it doesn't look so clear as this, like ice," Céline said.

"In summer, you can see so far down," Marina said.

"Oh, look!" Céline said, pointing at a craggy hill, a handful of sheep lining its steep peak. "They remind me of home."

Céline had just arrived and she was thinking of home, Marina mused. But then, Marina had mourned aspects of her New York City life soon after she decided to stay on Pag. She missed going to packed bars with interesting, well-dressed people; museums that offered glimpses of genius; restaurants with cuisines from around the world, made by immigrants like her. She found herself craving authentic Thai food, but there was nowhere on Pag or even in Zadar that served that type of cuisine. For the most part, Croatians didn't like spicy food. But Marina was different; she always had been different.

When they pulled into the driveway, Dragica was waiting in the doorway, wearing her flowered apron and holding a basket of food. Marina wondered how long she had been waiting there; they'd called from the airport, but didn't give an exact arrival time. Dragica brought the basket over to the car and Céline opened the passenger door.

"Welcome, welcome!" Dragica said, handing her the basket.

"*Hvala*," Céline said.

"*Brava*!" Dragica said, beaming and clapping her hands together. "She already speaks Croatian!" she said in Croatian.

"Does she need anything? Tell her, if she needs anything, only to ask."

"We should get her settled at Grandma Badurina's," Marina told her mother in Croatian. "I'm sure she's tired and wants to unpack."

"Of course, there's plenty of time for introductions later," Dragica said.

"*Tata*, let's go," Marina said with a note of impatience. Her mother never fussed over her arrival.

The Jeep crossed the narrow bridge over Tale Bay to Grandma Badurina's house. Céline took photos on her iPhone, marveling at the wild landscape.

Nikola knocked on Grandma Badurina's door. Marina heard her grandmother's walking stick clicking across the tile floor, punctuated by the shuffling of her house slippers.

"*Bok!*" Céline chirped, as soon as the door opened.

"Isn't she a perky one," Grandma Badurina said in Croatian, her lips curving into a wry smile.

"What did she say?" Céline said, a look of confusion crossing her face.

"She said, she's happy to have you stay with her," Marina said.

Céline beamed. "Please tell her I have some of our cheese for her, and for you also. And tell her I am so happy to be here."

"She has some cheese for you," Marina told Grandma Badurina.

"She thinks we need more cheese?" Grandma Badurina said, raising an eyebrow.

Marina stifled a laugh. "Thank you," Marina said to Céline. "My grandmother will show you to your room."

Grandma Badurina led the way up the cement stairs on the side of the house to the separate apartment entrance, leaning on her cane and holding the railing with her left hand. During the high season, she rented the apartment to tourists, but every summer, she complained about their noise overhead. It was good money, and her meager pension wasn't enough to cover her annual expenses, so it had to be done; still, she lamented, wishing the entire summer for a return to peace and quiet.

Grandma Badurina fished an old-fashioned key out of her housecoat pocket and opened the door. The room had a bed with a bright-orange wool blanket, a two-burner stove, a beige Formica sink, a bathroom with a handheld shower, and a small balcony with glass doors overlooking the bay.

Céline parted the balcony curtains. "A view of the water," she sighed.

"It's more beautiful in summer," Marina said. "You'll see."

"It is lovely to have a water view in any season," Céline said.

Nikola placed Céline's heavy suitcase on the wooden bench at the base of the bed. Céline unzipped it and gave Nikola and Grandma Badurina each a wheel of cheese.

"A gift from Basque Country to you," she said, smiling.

Marina showed Céline the stove, which needed to be lit with matches to ignite; the shower heater geyser, which needed to be turned on from an inconvenient switch high above the toilet before showering; the drain that often became clogged, forcing shorter showers for guests, since water would overflow the shallow plastic rim, drenching the tiled floor. Despite the complaints, Grandma Badurina never got around to fixing the drain, since she saved on her water bills with shorter showers. She told guests it was an old building, and what could you do, old buildings are like old people with clogged, hardened arteries, and she'd laugh one of her belly laughs.

Marina gave Céline the small portable heater from Yugoslav days, which sounded like a loud car motor revving. Marina was familiar with showing guests this apartment; growing up,

Grandma Badurina had enlisted her to speak English to visitors, answer all their questions, and acquaint them with the studio. They'd found her a charming young girl, with her halting, elementary school English, and tipped her generously with their foreign currencies.

"Will she come to dinner tonight?" Nikola said.

"My father asks if you'll come to dinner tonight. My mother will cook," Marina said.

"I would love to, but I don't want to intrude," Céline said.

"*Nema problema.* We'll pick you up in a couple hours. I'll call you," Marina said.

"Wonderful," she said.

"Is there anything you don't eat?" Marina asked Céline. "I think my mother's making lamb."

"I eat everything," Céline said. "Especially lamb!"

When Nikola and Marina returned home, Dragica was at the stove, her back turned to them. Her mother was wearing house slippers, like they all did; Dragica never allowed shoes in the house and insisted on slippers in all seasons, for fear of catching cold.

"*Ej*, she seems like a nice girl," Dragica said, turning around and tasting something from a spoon.

"Mama, you barely met her," Marina said, leaving her shoes near the door and slipping her feet into wool cocoons.

"She's coming to dinner?" Dragica said.

"Yes. We'll pick her up in an hour or so. She seems happy to be invited," Nikola said, shrugging off his jacket and taking the tin from his pocket. "Where's Franko?"

"He'll be home in time for dinner," Dragica said, stirring.

Marina wished she had something like her brother's soccer, where the hours passed by effortlessly. Sometimes her life felt like Sirana's old Soviet equipment that ached and groaned every morning when the production line commenced.

"What is she like?" Dragica said.

"She's sophisticated," Marina said quickly, hoping her father wouldn't disregard Céline based on her chic appearance.

"We'll know more about her when we see her work," Nikola said. "Cheesemaking always leaves fingerprints."

"When I met her at the World Cheese Awards, she seemed to have a lot of ideas. I hope she has ideas about how we can improve our cheese," Marina said.

"That's why she is here," Nikola said, picking up the newspaper.

Franko entered with a gust of cold air. He discarded his muddy cleats on the mat outside and put on slippers.

"Nice of you to show up," Marina said, pouring herself a glass of water.

Franko glared at her. "Did you pick her up?"

"Just dropped her off at Grandma's," Marina said.

"Grandma's coming to dinner?" Franko said.

"She's staying home, she's in one of her moods. I'll pick up Céline soon."

"Is she hot?" Franko said.

"Franko!" Dragica said, clucking her tongue. Her mother didn't like hearing such things. She pretended Franko didn't have sex, even when he had girlfriends.

Franko smiled sheepishly.

"God, how old are you?" Marina said, rolling her eyes.

"Well?" Franko said.

"She's pretty."

"Do you know much about her family?" Dragica asked.

"Not much. Just that their cheese is one of the best in their region. She brought some for us," Marina said.

"We can serve it with our cheese tonight," Dragica said, returning to the stove and checking the oven.

"I'm going to stop at the pasture before I get her for dinner," Marina said, glancing at her watch.

Marina removed her coat from the hanger near the entryway and kicked off the wool slippers. She slid her socks into her Nine West boots. They did not have a Nine West store in Croatia, or at least not in Zadar. She remembered when foreign shoe stores like Camper came to Zagreb, and slowly to the coast, and how people marveled at them and whispered about the high prices. In New York, on her way to the office after emerging from the subway, Marina gawked at the expensive stores lining Fifth and Madison Avenues. Sometimes she would walk by the window displays and imagine herself in shoes that cost a month's rent, sometimes two. Marina wondered if Marko bought his girlfriend designer shoes. He'd always criticized Marina's expensive taste.

She looked down at her boots: The tips were covered in a thin layer of dried mud from walking in Sirana's pastures, as she was apt to do lately when she needed time and space to think, away from her meddling family. She had offered to help Nikola after work, unloading feed and refilling the troughs, work that felt useful, unlike anything else she was doing in the dead of winter.

She started the ignition and drove up the steep, rocky slope. The sheep skittered when the Jeep first arrived but timidly approached once they recognized her and realized she was bringing food. As she poured feed into the troughs, the sheep bleated and the wind howled. She entertained the hope that 2013 would bring welcome changes for herself and for Sirana. She let herself miss Luka and what they might have been.

Marina looked forward to getting back to work after the holidays. She needed Céline's help for the upcoming SIAL Global Food Marketplace in Paris; Céline would translate Sirana's marketing materials from English to French, and use her contacts to help them introduce Pag cheese to the French market. In the new year, Marina wanted to get her mind off Luka and Marko. She wanted to focus on production. Cheese would distract her from her life.

She glanced at her watch and quickly drove to Grandma Badurina's. Céline opened the door, dressed in jeans and a cream cowl-neck sweater that skimmed her bob.

"Did you get settled?" Marina said.

"Oh, yes. Your mom's basket was so thoughtful, it has everything," Céline said.

"I'm sure she'll love to hear that," Marina said.

They crossed the narrow bridge across the bay.

"What are those mountains?" Céline said, pointing at the moody blue peaks.

"Velebit," Marina said. "The largest mountain range in Croatia."

"I read that Pag is also famous for salt production?" Céline said.

"Yes, there is a long history of salt in our town especially. Actually, that is the reason Pag Town was built in the fifteenth century. I should have pointed out the salt flats on our drive in. Don't worry, there will be plenty of time for you to see everything."

Marina pulled into the driveway. "Is your area famous for anything besides Petit Agour?"

"The rural part, we are most famous for our cheese," Céline said. "On the coast, they make some good sandals, espadrilles, and people holiday in places like Biarritz."

Marina opened the door for Céline. The thick scent of roasting meat greeted them. Nikola was sitting in his favorite chair reading the paper with a half-finished cigarette; her mother was plating the lamb, fresh off the spit. Marina removed her shoes and Céline followed, revealing her wool socks.

"Hello, Céline, welcome," Dragica said in effortful English, removing her apron and kissing her on both cheeks.

"*Hvala*," Céline said, tentatively sounding out the syllables.

Dragica clapped her hands in excitement, as if Céline were a toddler who had just learned a new word.

"Please also tell your mother thank you for the basket, I love it," Céline added in English.

Marina translated for Dragica.

"*Ništa, ništa*," Dragica said, letting her hand flop in the air in a gesture that indicated it was, in fact, nothing—but Marina knew her mother had stayed up late cooking a medley of dishes to make sure Céline would not want for variety.

"You've met my father, and this is my brother, Franko," Marina said.

Franko had dressed up, trading in his track pants and T-shirt for a navy blue button-down dress shirt and dark jeans. He'd shaved and put on cologne. Her brother, with his mop of hair and bangs that fell into his eyes, looked undeniably handsome.

"Nice to meet you," Franko said in halting English. Unlike Marina, he had never been good in school, and English was his least favorite subject.

Céline blushed. "It's a pleasure," she said.

Marina wondered if her parents noticed the flicker of chemistry between their son and the French girl.

"Sit, sit," Dragica said, relishing her role of hostess. She opened the lid of the steaming platter with a flourish. "We have tonight some of our famous Pag lamb with potatoes—Marina, can you translate?"

"Mama, I think she can see it's lamb," Marina said in Croatian.

"But tell her why ours is special," Dragica pressed.

"My mother wants you to know that our lamb is special here, just like the sheep's milk, because of the salty herbs they graze on, which flavors it uniquely," Marina said.

"I cannot wait to try it," Céline said, glancing at Franko, who ran his fingers through his hair, brushing his long bangs out of his eyes.

"Here, Mama, from Céline," Marina said, handing Dragica the wheel of Petit Agour.

"*Hvala*," Dragica said, stepping into the kitchen to cut it as they took their seats.

Nikola poured ruby *Plavac mali* from a bottle. Marina knew Céline wouldn't understand that having a bottle of wine meant a special occasion dinner, but on Pag, they usually drank home-made wine, which was made by their neighbors and stored in old plastic jugs. This was quality wine to accompany a special meal, for a special guest. The "black" grape variety—*crno vino*, as Croatians called red wine—came from further south in Dalmatia, from vines that struggled to survive on steep slopes under scorching sun, which produced a tannic, complex wine bursting with rich red fruit that announced itself on your palate. Marina often thought how struggle brought out the best—in vines, in sheep, in people.

Nikola sat at the head of the table. Marina sat next to Franko, who sat across from Céline. Nikola held out his hands to Marina and Céline. Dragica sat at the end of the table and joined hands with Céline and Franko. They bowed their heads while Nikola closed his eyes and said grace in Croatian. Marina didn't know if Céline was religious, and she hoped Nikola hadn't offended her by saying a blessing.

Nikola opened his eyes. "Are you Catholic?" he asked, nodding to Marina to translate.

"Yes, almost all of us Basques are," Céline said, nodding, her bob swinging back and forth.

Nikola nodded in approval, passing the platter of lamb to her. Her father had never been a staunch Catholic, but ever since the war—during which Catholics, Orthodox, and Muslims clashed—he seemed more aware of religion.

"What is like there?" Franko asked in his bad English, spearing a piece of lamb. His eyes met Céline's briefly.

Marina studied Franko, the way he looked at her shyly, as he spoke. She'd never seen her brother so smitten.

"Our Pyrenees mountains are magnificent, our land has many white farmhouses with red shutters. My family's *basseri* is large," Céline said, her voice becoming wistful.

"A *basseri* is a farmhouse?" Marina said.

"It is more than a house," Céline said. "In old times, it contained stables, kitchens, bedrooms, living rooms, hay and produce storage in the attic, spread over three floors. We made our cheese at home, and the *basseri* allowed families to be completely self-sufficient. In our language, *basseri* means 'home.' We have a big attachment to our *basseri* because they represent our origins."

"We also made our cheese at home in the old days," Marina said, translating for her family. "Some people here still do."

"Do you have brothers and sisters?" Nikola asked in Croatian, indicating to Marina to translate for him.

"Five older brothers," Céline responded. "They are all shepherds. I was the only one who went to university, in Paris, to study dairy sciences, so my father wants to train me to work as our dairy technologist."

Paris explained the clothes. Marina glanced at her father, who quietly took in the facts as she translated. She wondered if he made the connection that Céline's father was entrusting their family business to his only daughter, his youngest child. Marina wanted Nikola to teach her the business of cheese, as he had taught her the geography of their land as a girl.

"We are going to SIAL in Paris, in April. You should come with us, especially since you speak French," Nikola said.

Marina's mouth fell open. It was supposed to be their trip, a father-daughter team effort that would make up for the World Cheese Awards—the possibility of entering a new market with this year's cheese production, which they held hope would be much better. It made sense to take Céline for translation, but the girl had only just arrived and Marina felt Nikola had already invited her into their family. It was not like her father to be so welcoming to foreigners.

"I would love to come, thank you," Céline said. "It has been a couple years since I've seen Paris."

"Do you have a boyfriend?" Franko blurted. ·

Dragica and Nikola exchanged a glance. Céline blushed. "Not right now," she said.

Franko blushed at his outburst, too. An uncomfortable, lengthy silence passed. Marina chewed a piece of meat and took a sip of wine. She savored seductive black cherry, smoke, pepper, and spice.

"Your father must be happy to train you," Marina said, glancing at Nikola.

"Oh, he is," Céline said. "He is happy to have the business stay in our family's hands. We have a concept in Basque called *indarra*, a spiritual energy that fuels life changes, from pregnancy to the process of wine aging to curdling milk with rennet. The master of the house keeps the *indarra* intact, and parents choose only one child to take over the cheesemaking operations. This inheritance preserves our tradition."

Marina translated, watching her father's expressions carefully. When translating, she always felt the language to be slightly stilted, as if the literal translation was never quite right, deficient of nuance. Nikola smoothed his mustache and took a sip of wine.

"Tradition is the most important," Nikola said.

Dragica excused herself and returned with two platters of triangle-shaped slices. Her mother offered Céline a slice of Sirana's cheese and passed the Petit Agour to the rest of her family.

Marina bit into the smooth cheese. The sheep's milk had a clean, sweet flavor, with grassy notes; she was at once transported to the Basque countryside—a place she had never been—its fields and pastures rimmed by the Pyrenees Mountains, flocks of local breeds roaming the craggy foothills. The lingering finish on her tongue hinted of hazelnuts, meaty and satisfying.

Céline took a bite of Sirana's cheese. Marina watched her chew. A blank expression crossed Céline's face, her eyebrows pinching into a barely discernable frown. Marina knew Sirana's cheese lacked the richness of its potential. After Josip left Sirana to create Janković, Tomislav was never able to get the cheesemaking process exactly right, a combination of the failings of their old Soviet equipment and his lack of technical acumen. It might have had something to do with the shepherds, too, who sometimes watered down their sheep's milk, thus diluting its potency, or fed their sheep too much corn, which dulled the strength of the milk's herbal flavor.

"The mark of a great cheese is to taste the land," Nikola said, chewing thoughtfully. "I can feel your earth, the rich dirt beneath my fingernails."

Marina translated for Céline, observing her carefully. Céline had said nothing about Sirana's cheese.

"Your father is very poetic," Céline said, finally. "I look forward to seeing your facilities tomorrow."

"I'll come tomorrow, too," Franko said.

Nikola and Dragica exchanged glances across the table. Franko had come to Sirana only a handful of times in the months since Marina had returned to Pag, and he only came to pick up cheese for distribution after badgering from Nikola, who threatened Franko's paycheck if he didn't contribute his share to the family business. Franko was too old to punish like a child, but since he was still dependent on Nikola for money, arguments always ended in fights over *kunas* and Nikola's threats to withhold them.

Marina caught Céline discreetly stifling a yawn.

"She's tired. I'm taking her home," Marina translated for her family.

"I should get some sleep," Céline admitted, "since you will start production early."

"We start at seven. I'll pick you up a little early and we can have a coffee before work," Marina said.

"Thank you so much for the lovely dinner, *hvala*," Céline said, pushing back her chair and setting the napkin on it.

"Thank you for come, for help," Nikola said in his halting English.

Céline smiled. "I hope to learn things here, too," she said.

The platter of Petit Agour was almost finished. Céline had only taken one slice of Pag cheese.

On the drive back to Grandma Badurina's, the Jeep's headlights illuminated the narrow bridge over the bay. Marina waved goodbye to Céline, who climbed the steep concrete stairs with the ease of youth. Marina tried to remember herself at that age, a decade ago, but that vague version of herself conjured a ghostly outline. She tried to imagine herself single and carefree.

"See you tomorrow, sleep well," Marina called into the darkness.

"Thanks again to you and your family. We'll make beautiful cheese tomorrow," Céline said, waving and disappearing up the stairs.

Marina prayed this girl would be the answer to their problems. Marina's family—and Sirana—had struggled enough.

Chapter Twelve

arina picked up Céline early so they could have a coffee at the former Café Zec, Marina's favorite hangout as a teenager. On the café's rickety chairs, she and her girlfriends would sit for hours and lament over crushes and boyfriends. They'd share secrets and dreams, problems at home. The café had changed under the new owners. Gone were the beat-up wooden tables with lovers' names with hearts and arrows carved into the worn wood, the grain forever marked with coffee spills and rings, imprinted with memories. Marina remembered sitting with Ivana at their usual table, telling her that her father was sending her away to America, both girls crying and hugging, knowing their destinies were being put on separate paths, with no idea if they'd find their way back to one another. Now, coffees were placed on a shiny stainless steel bar, the assortment of milks and sugars housed in sleek pitchers and jars.

Céline and Marina both ordered milky white coffees without sugar, preferring to savor the bitterness of the strong grounds blended with the natural sweetness of the milk. Céline talked about how she was eager to see the workings of production in the bowels of the factory. She wore jeans and an old sweatshirt with sneakers, no makeup today. She looked ready to work.

"Does your brother help with the production?" Céline asked.

Marina hesitated. "He helps more with distribution."

"But he is learning the ropes, no? Will he take over Sirana after your father?"

Marina sighed deeply. "It is traditional here that the son takes over the business."

She felt Céline's eyes on her. Marina stirred her coffee with the small spoon, diluting the remaining foam.

"And you, you have always known you will participate in your family's business of cheese?" Céline asked.

Marina laughed. A look of surprise filled Céline's eyes.

"Oh, I'm sorry, I forgot you don't know. Up until a few months ago, my life was completely different. I lived in New York, I was married, I had a job in marketing."

"You are divorced?" Céline said, glancing at Marina's ring finger.

"Separated. We are … in between."

"In between what?"

Marina thought for a minute. "I mean that we are in between being married and not being married. We don't know what we are right now, and we don't know what we are going to be in the future."

"I see," Céline said. "That must be difficult."

"It is. There's the uncertainty that eats away at you, not knowing how we will end up," Marina said, taking a sip of coffee. "But the harder part is trying to figure out what I really want or how I feel about him. Especially being so far away. I haven't seen him in six months."

"Have you spoken?" Céline asked.

"We speak on the phone from time to time, but it's not the same. And it usually ends in a fight."

"I know that feeling," Céline said. "My mother left us when I was small. My parents were always fighting. Even though I was the youngest, I helped with everything, I had to become the woman of the house early on. I think that's why my father is training me to take over the business. In a way, I have been training for it my entire life."

"That is hard," Marina said. "So much responsibility at such a young age. And you didn't even have a choice, from what it sounds like."

"The truth is, I feel lucky I was chosen. I like the cheese business, and it means something to carry on the work of my family. When my mother left, our *basseri* was broken. But we have become stronger now with her absence. Like with our sheep: The more they have to eat, the fatter they become, the less they have to struggle, and their milk suffers. They need to fight for the difficult grasses, and then their milk becomes stronger and more flavorful."

"My father often says the same thing. The best quality milk comes from seasons of adverse conditions."

"That's probably true," Céline said, avoiding Marina's eyes and taking a deep sip from her cup.

Marina looked at her watch. "We should probably get going."

She wondered what this season had in store for them.

Nikola was waiting for them in the hallway, wearing a white lab coat and a gauzy white shower cap that covered his balding head. He gave Marina and Céline white coats, caps, and booties, so they could join him in the production room. He pushed open the heavy metal door. A primal smell resembling a blend of wet socks and refrigerator mold greeted them. Marina held the back of her hand over her nose. Men and women in white suits and boots were busy hand-packing blocks of cheese curds into plastic cylinders. The old Soviet machinery hummed. Sheets of cut curd slid down the production line to workers who crammed the curd into cake-sized molds with their hands and fists.

Céline's eyes traveled over the room, landing on its tiled floors. Errant curds littered the surface. She took a step forward, careful to avoid stepping in puddles of cheese runoff.

"After the cheese is packed and pressed, it goes into brine?" Céline asked.

"Yes. We call it the *salamura*," Marina said, gesturing to the large stainless steel saline tank. "We use salt from our island."

"Here is where we pasteurize the milk," Nikola said, indicating for Marina to translate.

Céline walked over to the thermometer and frowned. "Is this correct?"

Marina translated for Nikola, who looked at the thermometer. He nodded. Céline's eyebrows shot up.

"He's absolutely sure?" Céline asked Marina.

"Is something wrong?" Marina said.

"These are very high temperatures for processing," Céline said. "You kill the taste with this level of heat."

Marina recalled Céline's blank look from the night before after sampling Sirana's latest batch of cheese. Nikola looked questioningly at Marina. After she translated, a shadow crossed Nikola's face. He smoothed his mustache.

"The temperature sometimes fluctuates," he said gruffly. "Old machines."

"He says our machines are old and the temperature isn't always consistent," Marina told Céline.

"I can give you the name of the man who sold us our machines, when you're ready to buy new ones," Céline offered.

Josip had complained about Sirana's poor machines before he left, before he stole Sirana's milk and made his own garage batch of cheese. Sirana couldn't afford new machinery, not then or now. That is, not without foreign investors, which would dilute Nikola and Uncle Horvat's ownership shares in the company. Nikola refused to consider it. "Sirana must always stay Croatian-owned. Enough has been taken from us," he often said.

"We're waiting for EU funds," Marina said.

"And if you don't receive them?" Céline said.

Marina questioned her father, raising her eyebrows.

"We'll manage, like we always have," Nikola said, turning away from them and limping towards the aging room, indicating that they should follow.

"He says we'll make do," Marina told Céline.

"What about the rennet? You use local rennet, I assume?" Céline asked, trailing behind him.

"We use imported rennet," Marina said.

"Why not Croatian rennet?" Céline asked, giving Marina a look of confusion.

Yugoslavia used to manufacture many things, but all that had stopped during the war and never really started again. It seemed everything in Croatia was imported.

"We used rennet from what is now Serbia until 1991, when Croatia declared its independence from Yugoslavia," Marina said, glancing at her father. She knew he didn't like it when she brought up the war, especially with outsiders.

"What are you saying?" Nikola asked in Croatian, not understanding her English but recognizing the words "Serbia" and "Yugoslavia."

"I told her we used Serbian rennet until Croatia became independent," Marina told him in Croatian.

"No need to go into all that," he said. "Tell her why we use Italian rennet now."

"I thought it was because Italians bought our cheese during the war, to support Croatia," Marina said in Croatian.

"That's true, but just tell her it produces better results," he said. "Go ahead."

Céline nodded thoughtfully as Marina spoke.

"So you use microbial rennet?" Céline said.

"No, animal rennet," Marina said.

Céline looked horrified. Animal rennet was obtained from the stomachs of unweaned baby calves, lambs, and goats—and although the animals were not killed for the making of the rennet these days, it was not vegetarian, and an unpopular choice in some cheesemaking circles. But Nikola insisted on maintaining tradition, and microbial rennet—derived from a fungus—was not traditional.

The production door heaved open and Franko sauntered in, wearing Sirana's white uniform. It had been many years since Marina had seen her brother dressed in their production room clothing. Usually when he came to Sirana, he only stopped by the packing room to pick up cheese for delivery at the behest of Nikola. She resented him for wearing the uniform now; it was all for show.

"You're late," Nikola said in Croatian, looking over his shoulder.

"Sorry, *Tata*," Franko said, following them into the production room.

Céline gave him a shy smile. He grinned back at her.

Wheels of maturing cheese were stacked on wooden planks two dozen high. Women on ladders were wiping the developing rinds with oil, flipping them on opposite sides for their next days of rest, during which they would continue to change and grow in complexity. Marina often thought how different batches of cheese could be, even in the most controlled environments—microbes and enzymes transforming texture and intensifying flavor, a mysterious process that took place beneath the waxy surface.

"Is your aging room as big as ours?" Franko said, jerking his head towards his sister to translate.

Céline smiled politely. "Ours is maybe ten times this size. We no longer make cheese out of our *basseri.*"

Franko looked surprised. "That is big."

"How many tons of cheese does your island produce every year?" Céline asked.

"Two hundred," Marina said.

"And how many people on this island?" Céline asked.

"Eight thousand," Marina said.

"Well, you see, even in our small French Basque, we have nearly a quarter million people. So, many more people to produce cheese," she said, smiling.

"Are people leaving their family cheese businesses to do other things? That is a problem here," Marina said.

"Yes, it is unfortunately a problem for us as well," Céline sighed.

"Do you hire foreigners to work in your factory?" Marina asked.

"We have not had to do that yet, but maybe the next generation will face this problem," Céline said, frowning.

Marina translated for Nikola and Franko.

"There will always be our cheese, and our people here to make it," Nikola said, with a note of finality that ended the conversation. She knew he could not imagine a world without Sirana or Pag cheese. It was in the marrow of their bones.

Marina did not share her father's confidence. Many Croatians were taking jobs abroad, and with their country becoming part of the European Union, she feared the ability to work across borders would lure many from the younger generation away from home, away from a life close to the land and sheep. Even in her father's generation, there was a departure from agrarian life.

They ended the tour in the packing room. Wedges of cheese were vacuum-packed and branded with Sirana's sky-blue label, the web of Pag lace in the background under gold lettering.

"Will you ever increase production?" Céline asked.

Nikola's face pinched into a frown. Marina explained, "It would have been possible once, but now, we fight for the milk from the border area."

"Ah, that makes sense. There is that other factory in the north—what was it called? I imagine they take all the milk from up there to use for their cheese. I remember the son from the World Cheese Awards. Luka was his name?"

Marina's stomach flipped. Nikola looked at her questioningly, after hearing Luka's name. Marina tried not to picture his bloody face, illuminated by the fire.

"She wants to know about Janković," Marina said.

Marina translated for Nikola. "The factory in the north dominates the milk supply there, and that is why we cannot grow our production very much."

Marina could see her father becoming increasingly agitated talking about Josip's factory.

"And the shepherds in the border area?" Céline asked.

"They are like pirates! They sell to whoever offers the highest price," Nikola said, crossing his arms. "I need a cigarette," he said, limping and pushing open the heavy metal door in the back of the factory with all his weight, which flung open and let in a blast of cold air and light.

Marina felt the chill. The *bura* was ramping up, stewing over Velebit and tumbling down its slopes, a pressure valve releasing on the sea like God's giant, angry fist. Nikola had always told her that their northerly wind was meant to clear the mind, but Marina's thoughts were scattered. She had hoped that Céline's arrival would signal a new beginning for Sirana, and for her, but she felt instead an ominous portent carried down the mountain by the *bura*'s violent gusts.

Chapter Thirteen

Céline was often the first to arrive to Sirana every morning. She came before six o'clock, which meant leaving Grandma Badurina's apartment at least a half hour earlier. She didn't mind walking in all weather conditions. One day she arrived to work, breathless, explaining that the strong *bura* almost knocked her off her feet, nearly catapulting her petite frame from the narrow footpath bridge into frigid Tale Bay. Marina, who had a shorter walk to work, couldn't seem to beat her, and in the weeks that followed, the question of who would arrive first became a friendly competition between them.

The French girl was a hard worker and cared for the cheese like a mother doting over a small child, taking the temperature of the curds and speaking to them during the process as if coaxing a plant to grow. Sometimes, she spoke in her own Basque language, and sometimes she used French, especially for cursing, and Marina came to know the meaning of *merde*, which Céline would exclaim when a step in the process had gone awry.

Other times, she used the few Croatian words she had picked up in her weeks on the island: "*Dobro, dobro,*" she said in her funny accent, when she was satisfied with a particular batch.

She sat with the workers during her break, preferring to eat in the lunchroom instead of upstairs with management. Sometimes, Marina would invite Céline home to lunch, and Dragica would busy herself preparing a heavy home-cooked meal that would easily carry them until dinner.

In what seemed like no time at all, Céline had mastered all aspects of production. She found a way to work with Sirana's old Soviet machinery, learning its quirks and constantly monitoring fluctuating temperatures to ensure consistency. She learned each of the shepherds' names and, with Marina's help translating, chatted with them about their wives and the weather while they deposited their sheep's milk into Sirana's refrigerated tank every morning, surreptitiously checking to see if they'd watered down their milk and casually making a mild remark if the milk looked too thin. At future drop-offs, the milk looked as it should, a testament to her keen eyes and charming smile.

She built a strong camaraderie with the workers, and in an effort to impress and please her, they picked up their speed and packed curds faster than ever before. Nikola told Marina he had never seen Sirana run so smoothly, except for when... and then he trailed off. They both knew he didn't want to say the name Josip Janković.

In the evenings, her father would have an additional glass of *rakija.* Marina knew Sirana's sales were down, and money was tight. The new cheese Céline had helped them make in January wouldn't be ready until March, fresh out of the aging room and just in time for the SIAL competition in Paris in April. Nikola was consumed with worry. What if their new cheese wasn't good enough?

Marina struggled to keep her mind on her work like Céline. Local rumors circulated furiously like wildfire through grape-vines, leaving a path of destruction in their wake. People in Pag Town looked at her sideways on the narrow cobblestone lanes and bent their heads in whispers over cups of coffee at the café. Everywhere she went, she felt eyes staring, boring holes into her back. On Pag, reputations were everything.

Ivana had been upset to learn about the rumors. When Marina finally told her what happened, Ivana took it as a personal affront that Marina hadn't told her about the kiss and her con-fused feelings for Luka, since she had considered them to be close friends, even with the physical distance separating them for so many years, even despite their vast gaps in experience. Now, when Marina needed a friend the most, Ivana was aloof and distant, cit-ing childcare responsibilities as the reason she couldn't meet for coffee. When Marina offered to come over to her house, she often made excuses, some of which were real (her colicky baby, catch-ing a cold) and some of which seemed not.

In February, Céline had finally asked her about Luka, timidly broaching the subject—she'd heard the rumors from Franko, and suspected something was amiss at the World Cheese Awards. In a burst of intimacy, Marina told her everything, and finally, for the first in a long time, she didn't feel quite so alone.

Céline had listened intently, as if being told a fable, where the exiled woman became a banished, lone wolf because she frater-nized with the son from a rival pack. She listened without com-ment, nodding. Finally she said, "Sometimes living in a place where people care so much about what happens to each other can be a good thing, but it has its downsides."

Céline herself had quickly become entrenched in island life, from the politics at the factory to the personal. She started see-ing Franko, who had become her guide, showing her the island's surrounding environs on weekends. To an onlooker, it seemed Franko had finally found an occupation other than soccer to consume him, and even Nikola made a comment that he should make some money in the summer guiding tourists around Pag and Zadar. Franko took care to hide that his enthusiasm was really directed at Céline, and even discussed the idea of studying to become a historical tour guide in his spare time, in addition to helping out at Sirana.

The cheesemaking season would end in July and production would shut down until January, when the milking would begin again—ushering in a new season of cheese. Céline would not stay to rub wheels with oil, or clean machines, or pack cheese. That July, Céline would return to Basque, and Marina knew her brother's heart would be broken. She wanted to warn him, but she knew it wouldn't do any good. The heart doesn't listen to reason.

One Sunday in late March, after Mass at the Church of St. Mary's Assumption, Dragica invited Céline to lunch so Nikola could discuss their plans for the SIAL exhibition. Marina picked up Grandma Badurina and Céline. The landscape was beginning to awaken out of its winter slumber; brave herbs were sprouting through crevices in the rocky ground, taking a stand against the *bura*, which flexed its strength at unexpected times, hurling gusts of salty sea air through Pag Town.

Céline had become a regular fixture at Dragica's table. She took her usual seat across from Franko, next to Grandma Badurina, whom she helped ease into her chair. The old woman let Céline take her elbow, a gesture that indicated a rarely allowed intimacy.

"So, Céline, we will soon go to your country together," Nikola said, passing her the potatoes and nodding to Marina to translate.

"I love Paris," Céline said, taking the platter. "I have such fond memories there from school. And I will look forward to introducing you to my father."

"It will be our pleasure to meet him," Nikola said.

Franko glanced at Céline. "*Tata*, why don't I come with you to Paris?" Franko offered.

Nikola studied his son. Marina knew her father was pleased that Franko was finally taking an interest in Sirana, no matter the reason. Nikola smoothed his mustache and speared a potato. "Marina is coming with me," he said.

"But I could come and help. If there's no money, I can do some tours this summer, and pay you back later," Franko pressed.

Céline's ears perked up at "no money." Since Franko's English was so poor, he had been teaching her some Croatian, and she was becoming increasingly adept at recognizing simple phrases.

Marina glared at her brother. He knew better than to talk about money in front of Céline.

Nikola balanced his fork and knife on the edges of the plate. "Franko, it's not possible now," he said.

Marina wondered if Franko had discussed his plan to try to go to Paris with Céline beforehand.

"I could borrow some money from Uncle Horvat," Franko said.

Marina drew in a sharp breath. Their rich uncle in Zagreb was the main reason Nikola had political connections in the capital. After the war, Uncle Horvat had helped Nikola privatize Sirana, when Croatia's economy was in turmoil, its future uncertain. Uncle Horvat transitioned Yugoslav companies from state-owned to privately-owned, and that had made him a very wealthy man. But Nikola hated asking his older brother for help out of a sense of pride. Uncle Horvat could be a ruthless businessman, concerned only with his own profit—not unlike Josip.

"*Ne!*" Nikola said, slamming his fist against the table, his face flushing red.

Franko hung his head like a beaten dog. Marina couldn't tell if Céline fully understood what had just transpired. However, she certainly understood the word "no".

Grandma Badurina, unfazed, took a sip of wine. "You should discuss the plan for Paris," she said calmly. "It's a great opportunity for Sirana. And I heard there's a new batch almost ready?"

Marina glanced at her father. "Should I translate?" she asked.

"Ask Céline to speak about the batch that will be coming out of the aging room," Nikola said, regaining his composure. "I have a wheel here that we can sample. It is a little early still, but I pulled one out so we can taste its potential."

Dragica excused herself to the kitchen to cut slices.

"I have faith in this new batch," Céline said. "I pasteurized the milk at a lower temperature and tweaked a few other things in the process. Cheese always transforms as it ages, however. Nature keeps some mystery."

"Will it be ready by SIAL?" Grandma Badurina asked.

"I hope so."

Dragica returned with a platter. They each took a triangle. Marina bit into the smooth slice of young cheese, concentrated with rich herbal flavors, seasoned with sea salt from the water surrounding their island. Marina was at once transported to when Josip made cheese for Sirana, to the days after school when he used to give her and Luka slices of his newest batch to taste, the rind like a soft cocoon. This was the cheese of her childhood.

"Céline, it's beautiful," Marina said, her eyes welling with tears.

Marina's eyes met her father's; he was altogether somewhere else, chewing thoughtfully. Franko looked stunned, holding a piece of cheese midair, as if he'd forgotten what to do with it. Her mother looked ready to cry. Grandma Badurina turned to the girl and, having no English words to express herself, put her hand tenderly on Céline's shoulder.

"You have resurrected the cheese of our past," Nikola said, his voice breaking. He coughed and cleared his throat. "Just in time for Easter," he joked, to lighten the mood. Marina translated for Céline, who joined in the laughter.

The feeling was too good to last. The next day, Nikola received news that Sirana didn't receive the EU funds he'd expected, which would have allowed them to purchase new machines and invest in a well-trained dairy technologist for the following cheese-making season. The funds were meant to help develop Croatia's agricultural sectors and rural areas in preparation for joining the European Union, but like everything, the decision was political, and Nikola had been too proud to ask for help from Uncle Horvat, whose powerful friends could have influenced the decision.

The committee cited Sirana's lack of awards as one factor in the judgement, since they wanted to invest in the country's best dairy producers, the candidates that had the best chance of being profitable and well-known throughout Europe. When Nikola opened the inky pages of *Free Dalmatia* later that morning, he learned the winner from Croatia was a celebrated cheesemaker from the mainland, who had won the Cheesemaker's Innovation Award for his blend of goat's milk and donkey's milk cheese, and had been given the funds to develop a new hybrid cheese with camel milk, in partnership with Morocco—one of the EU's leading trade partners.

Nikola shut himself in his office and focused on preparing materials for SIAL. Marina left her father alone to allow him to deal with the failure privately and decided to visit Céline in the production room instead of hiding in her office upstairs. The workers whispered in hushed voices, which Marina could hear between groans emitted from Sirana's ancient machinery. When Marina saw Céline's face, she knew Céline was aware of their loss. The workers, with whom she'd become very friendly, had already told her. They had read the headline.

"Want to take a walk?" Céline said.

"Yes. Coffee?" Marina suggested.

Céline nodded. That was another thing they had in common: Coffee was the answer to everything.

"I heard and I'm very sorry," Céline said, as the heavy production room door slammed behind them.

"My father was counting on that money," Marina said, sighing.

"Is there any other way?" Céline asked.

"The cheese you produced is extraordinary, and I have great hope for SIAL," Marina said. "But in the process, so much raw material was wasted. We threw out many batches that weren't right, for one reason or the other. Sirana can't be profitable if we continue that way."

"I'm sorry for that. Your machinery is old and unpredictable, and I did my best with what I had to work with."

"I understand," Marina said, turning her gaze to Tale Bay, which glittered under the morning sunlight. "But we can't throw out half our milk and curds to make the perfect cheese."

"You will need better equipment if you want to become better, and bigger," Céline said. "Couldn't he borrow some money to buy new production machinery?"

"My father doesn't want to take on any more debt," Marina said.

"Maybe he could sell some shares to get money to invest in new equipment?"

"He would never do that," Marina said. "He wants to remain the majority shareholder."

"Who else owns Sirana?" Céline asked.

It was a natural question, but something made Marina pause before answering. Marina had shared so many intimate stories with Céline, and in the short span of a couple months, she had become like family. Still, talking about Sirana's business and anything related to money matters made Marina uneasy, given they were in such a vulnerable position.

"I'm sure my brother told you about Uncle Horvat," Marina said slowly.

"Your uncle who lives in Zagreb," Céline said.

"Yes, my father's elder brother. Uncle Horvat helped my father transition the company to become privately owned after the war."

"Maybe Uncle Horvat could sell some of his shares? I am sure buyers from the European Union would be interested, now that Croatia will join."

Marina knew Uncle Horvat had agreed to a minority position in Sirana for visibility reasons, ceding control of the company to Nikola by 1 percent. Uncle Horvat, who owned 49 percent of Sirana, did not want to be the face of the company, preferring to remain anonymous due to his other holdings, which required discretion. Marina suspected some of Uncle Horvat's other business dealings were not entirely aboveboard, residing somewhere in the murky ex-Yugoslav market, which had persisted long past the end of the war.

"My father would not ask Uncle Horvat for anything, and definitely not to sell shares to foreigners," Marina said flatly. "He wants Sirana to remain Croatian-owned."

"I can understand that," Céline said. "Still, there must be a way. You have beautiful raw materials here, but not a way to use their full potential."

They sat at their usual table in the corner. Marina flagged down the waitress, who by now didn't even ask for their order.

Marina sighed. "We'll have to find a way to make do with what we have."

Chapter Fourteen

Céline suggested a weekend trip to Basque in an effort to cheer up Marina. "My family misses me, and besides, it will be a nice escape for us," she said. They found cheap flights, and Marina agreed. She needed to get her mind off Sirana. There was still so much work to do before SIAL, but they needed a break.

After they landed in Biarritz, it was an hour's drive to reach the Pyrenees. Across the valley, snow-covered peaks marked the border with Spain. White houses with red shutters were named, not numbered. Céline told Marina that the names of Basque houses, defined by the landscape, often reached back centuries.

"Ours means 'edge of the valley,'" Céline said, pointing to a large stone-and-oak house perched on a hillside.

Her father, Aitor, was waiting by the door. "My Céline," he said, embracing her. He had a stocky build and a thin mustache. "And you must be Marina."

"Nice to meet you," Marina said, shaking his hand.

"Welcome, welcome," Aitor said, taking their bags and ushering them in.

Marina took her shoes off in the entryway. Inside, the house was not what Marina had expected. It was modern, with tasteful rustic elements, including original oak beams. The marble floors were heated, and through the large sliding doors, she saw a covered pool and a hot tub. High ceilings gave the living room an airy feel. Everything seemed to be white. It was pristine, like a photo from a luxury-homes magazine.

"You have a beautiful home," Marina said.

"Thank you," Aitor said. "We did a renovation recently, the house needed an update. Why don't you settle in, and then we'll have a drink before dinner."

"Come," Céline said, grabbing Marina's hand and leading her upstairs.

The house was even larger than Marina first imagined, at least ten bedrooms. She knew Céline had five brothers and wondered if they all still lived at home. Even so, there was ample space for everyone.

"I hope you'll be comfortable," Céline said, opening the door to a large, well-appointed bedroom. It had an ensuite marble bathroom with fancy fixtures. Marina suddenly felt embarrassed for Grandma Badurina's humble apartment, with its clogged drain.

"It's lovely," Marina said.

"Come down when you're ready. We'll have a drink and some tapas."

After she unpacked and freshened up, Marina descended the stairs. A fire was roaring. Céline spoke in hushed tones with her father and brothers. They sat on white leather couches draped with sheepskin.

"Wine?" Aitor asked, holding up a glass.

"Thank you," Marina said, joining them.

"These are my brothers, Antton and Ander," Céline said, gesturing to the two dark-haired men sitting opposite.

"Nice to meet you," Marina said. "Where are your other brothers?" she asked, turning to Céline.

"They're away on business," Aitor said.

"All of our family's names begin with 'A,'" Céline said, rolling her eyes.

"Except yours," Marina said.

Céline grew quiet. "The boys all have Basque names. But my mother loved French names."

"We've heard wonderful things about your island from Céline," Aitor said, glancing at Céline and taking a sip of wine.

"I'm happy to hear. We're so grateful for Céline's help. It was kismet we met at the World Cheese Awards."

"What is this word, 'kismet'?" Aitor asked, crossing his legs and setting down his glass.

"It's like fate," Marina said.

"Yes, fate," Aitor said, swirling his glass.

"And Tomislav is still here? I hope he's been able to provide some help to you?"

Aitor's mustache twitched. "Tomislav is a kind man," he said. "So, I hear we will see you at SIAL? I'm looking forward to meeting your father in Paris as well."

"He'll be there," Marina said. "We still have a lot to prepare, but I think Céline's cheese will draw positive attention to Sirana."

"What she's learned, she's learned well," Aitor said.

"I'll take that as a compliment," Céline said.

"You still have a lot to learn," Aitor said, frowning.

"Don't be so hard on her, Dad," Ander said.

"Was I talking to you?" Aitor asked, his eyes narrowing.

A woman emerged from the kitchen and said something in Basque that Marina couldn't understand.

"Dinner's ready. I smell fish stew," Céline said.

They sat down at the table. With no mother to do the cooking, Marina had wondered how Céline's father managed. How nice must it be to have a housemaid. Marina wondered if Céline had grown up this way, or if the family cheese business had only recently made enough money to indulge in such luxuries.

Antton's phone rang. As he spoke to the person on the other end of the line, his brow furrowed. "Dad, it's Andone. It's about the *Eslovenia* acquisition," Antton said in Basque, handing him the phone.

Eslovenia. Did he mean Slovenia?

"Slovenia?" Marina said, turning to Céline.

"Just one of Dad's business things," Céline whispered.

"Later," Aitor said, waving away the phone.

"It's urgent," Antton said.

"Excuse me for a minute," Aitor said, taking the phone into the family room and closing the door.

"Sorry for that," Antton said. "We're in the middle of a deal."

"Céline had told me your family was interested in exploring some investments in Eastern Europe," Marina said. "So, you're doing business in Slovenia?"

"We're expanding the portfolio," Antton said.

"Let's not talk business at dinner," Céline said, shooting her brother a look and smoothing her napkin. "She's here to relax."

On Sunday, Céline suggested they go to a tavern in a neighboring village. She ordered tapas and two bottles of Basque wine. Marina tasted red fruits and minerality, elemental earth. She imagined Basque land in summer, awakened in all its pastoral glory, sheep grazing near rivers, vineyards sprawled across limestone slopes. In many ways, it reminded her of Pag.

The afternoon slipped by, fueled by copious amounts of wine. She couldn't remember the last time she'd laughed so much. A weekend away with a friend was just what she'd needed.

"In June, we have an ancestral practice called transhumance," Céline said, taking a sip of wine. "We should come again then. The weather will be much better."

"What happens during transhumance?" Marina asked.

"It's like a seasonal migration. The shepherds move our flocks from the valley to the mountains." Céline swirled her glass. "Sometimes, my mother would take me into the mountains. I don't remember much of her, but I remember that."

"How young were you when she left?"

Céline took a long sip of wine. "Five."

"Why did she leave?" Marina asked, and then immediately regretted it. "I'm sorry, I understand if you don't want to talk about it."

"No, it's an obvious question," Céline said. "She had six children, and I think she was just done with being a mother in a small town. She felt trapped in tradition and didn't love her role, which was in many ways thrust upon her. She wanted a different life."

"Where did she go?"

"Paris," Céline said. "She's an artist there now. She lives a very bohemian existence. I see her sometimes, when I visit. I studied dairy sciences there, just to be close to her. I wanted her to see what I'd become."

"She must be proud of you," Marina said.

Céline shrugged. "She doesn't care much about money, or our business. We're very different people."

"Was your business always so successful?"

"We always did well, but in recent years, we have been blessed. Enough about me. How is your situation?"

Marina sighed. "There's not much to add."

"What do you want?"

It was the first time someone had asked her the question so directly. What *did* she want?

"I don't know," Marina said. "But I need to decide. Maybe I need to spend some time alone."

"That takes courage," Céline said, raising her glass.

"And you and Franko?"

"Your brother is a charmer," Céline said, smiling.

"That's all I get?" Marina teased, pouring more wine.

"It's a little weird to talk about it with you, no?"

"I mean, how serious is it? You're coming back here in July, after finishing work with us at Sirana. Long-distance relationships are tough, take it from me."

"Let's see where things are by the beginning of summer," Céline said.

"With your father grooming you to take over, I'm guessing we couldn't convince you to take a dairy technologist position at Sirana," Marina said.

"I belong in Basque," Céline said, draining her glass.

Marina was jealous of Céline's certainty in knowing where she belonged. Would Marina know when she discovered what it was she really wanted? And what did belonging even mean for Marina anymore?

Chapter Fifteen

In a blink, it was April. Céline had helped Nikola and Marina find a cheap rental apartment on the outskirts of Paris, since the centrally located hotels were too expensive. Céline insisted on staying with her father, who was coming up from Basque for the SIAL exhibition and staying in a hotel near the event venue. Nikola had offered to pay for a separate apartment for her, but Céline insisted she missed her father and wanted to stay with him. Marina wondered if Céline was trying to save them money, now that she was aware of Sirana's financial situation.

Paris was a different world from London. Colorful, energetic. Maybe because it was springtime, Marina felt like it was a place rife with possibility. Well-heeled people sat in cafés drinking coffee—or wine—in the middle of the day as if they had nothing to worry about, everything was going to be okay. And maybe it was.

She regretted they wouldn't have time for sightseeing—she would have loved to see the Louvre and go up the Eiffel Tower. She would have loved to take long walks on the Seine, sit in cafés for hours. Something in this city brought her back to life.

The SIAL event hall was gilded, built in an earlier, grander era. Marina wondered what other events had taken place in the giant ballroom, which had an elaborate ceiling made of curved glass panes, creating a dome of sky.

Marina and Nikola asked for directions to the Croatia table. Marina had prepared herself to see Luka, and she was sure her father had steeled himself to encounter Josip again. She hoped neither Josip nor Luka would mention the EU funds; surely they had read the paper or heard Sirana didn't receive them.

As they approached, her father suddenly stopped, nearly running into a passerby. Marina followed her father's gaze: Josip's wife, Sanja, stood next to her husband and son. She was sticking toothpicks into slices of cheese, stopping for a moment to wipe her forehead with the back of her hand. The event hall was stuffy and overly warm with crowded bodies and tendrils of auburn hair clung to her cheekbones. Marina glanced at her father. He looked as if he'd seen a ghost.

"*Tata*?" she said.

"Come, Marina," Nikola said, straightening himself and walking towards the table.

Josip, seeing Nikola approach, drew himself up to his full height.

"Josip," Nikola said cordially.

"Nikola," Josip said, with a sharp nod.

Marina glanced at Luka, who lowered his eyes.

"Nikola," Sanja said softly.

Marina watched the way Sanja looked at her father. She had not seen Luka's mother since the days when she kept records for Sirana, ledgers of milk and money. Sanja used to drive Luka down to Pag Town after school, and now Marina recalled hearing Sanja's laughter fill her father's office, the two of them chuckling like old friends. Marina wondered why Sanja was here now; she was

Janković's bookkeeper and had a reputation for efficiency when it came to extracting money from distributors who owed them. Maybe Sanja was here to use her considerable charms to push Janković's cheese over Sirana's.

Nikola busied himself with helping Marina set up their side of the table. The surrounding hum of activity helped to distract from the awkward silence. Marina focused on displaying Sirana's pamphlets, cutting slices of cheese for sampling. Nikola pulled out the SIAL program and studied the list of distributors, glancing up to see if he could recognize any name tags and wave them over to sample Sirana's cheese.

Marina had to admit, she was excited for people to taste their cheese. The new batch had matured into magnificence. When they had tasted Céline's cheese at Dragica's table, Marina knew it had potential; with just an additional month of aging, the flavors had ripened, developing complexity and strength. As if it knew it must be ready, the cheese had come into its own just in time for the SIAL competition.

A man came over to their table, stopping to shake Josip's hand. Marina glanced up and read the man's name tag. John: Dissa, Borough Market, London. John was not a judge, but he was almost as influential. He had determined the fate of Pag cheese in London after the World Cheese Awards, giving Janković exposure that had catapulted the brand in Western Europe and made Janković famous, placing their cheese on the cheesemonger map.

"Good to see you, my friend," Josip said, clapping John on the back. "Try our new batch. I think we'll do well with it here."

John took a toothpick and chewed thoughtfully.

"I think you have a winner," he said. "Your cheese has been doing very well in London."

"Could I offer you a taste of Sirana's Pag cheese?" Marina said, raising her voice to be heard above the din.

John turned to Marina. "I remember you, from the World Cheese Awards. Cheese is a small world," he said, smiling amiably.

Nikola looked confused upon hearing "World Cheese Awards," the only English words he recognized. Marina didn't have time to translate what was happening for her father.

"Yes, we did meet there. I remember. But our cheese has changed, we've been doing some things differently. Please try it. You won't regret it." Marina was surprised by her own persuasiveness.

Luka looked impressed. Josip, at first registering shock at Marina's forwardness, shrugged and gestured with an open hand, as if he couldn't care less about their London distributor sampling Sirana's cheese. Marina understood now why her father thought Josip was arrogant; he obviously doubted Sirana could achieve anything other than mediocrity without himself at the helm.

John accepted a sample of Céline's latest batch of Sirana's cheese, and as he chewed, Marina felt herself starting to perspire, trickles of sweat threatening to travel down the nape of her neck. She watched his face transform into an expression of surprise, and then, pure delight.

"This is... quite different," he said slowly.

Josip frowned, reaching over to take a piece of Sirana's cheese. He popped it in his mouth whole and chewed. His eyes started to bulge, and a vein in his forehead swelled as he swallowed.

"That French girl made this cheese?" Josip said in Croatian, his voice thick with malice. "Surely it wasn't Tomislav. He didn't ever make cheese this good."

"Yes, it's Céline's—and Sirana's," Marina said in Croatian, before her father could answer.

"You let a girl make your cheese?" Josip said, taunting Nikola.

Sanja's eyes lowered. Luka stood motionless behind his father, his eyes on Marina. She felt ready for anything.

Nikola looked up squarely at Josip, who towered above him. "I've always recognized talent," Nikola said.

John appeared lost in thought. Marina saw the gears turning in Josip's mind, calculating how to turn the situation to his advantage. For once, Marina didn't feel she had to sell anything to anyone; the cheese spoke for itself.

"Let's go out to coffee, John," Josip said, smiling in his charming manner. "I've brought along my wife—I haven't introduced you to her properly—and my son has some exciting news to share with you."

"Yes, let's have a coffee," Sanja said, smiling.

"I suppose I could duck out for a bit," John said, looking distracted and fanning himself with a brochure. "It's a sauna in here, isn't it? Besides, much as I love cheese, even *I* need a break from it."

Before John could say goodbye, Josip ushered him out of the ballroom, his large hand on John's back. Nikola put his hand on her shoulder and she realized she was shaking.

"Marina!" Céline said, approaching her. She was wearing a smart black dress and a string of pearls, her hair pulled neatly into a bun. "It took us some time to find you, this place is so large. Nikola, please, let me introduce you to my father, Aitor."

Nikola extended his hand to Aitor, who was smaller than Nikola, but of the same stocky build, with a thinner mustache. Marina noticed his designer shoes, his tailored jacket, his crisp dress shirt with embroidered initials. Petit Agour must be doing well.

"Since neither of you speak English, we can translate," Céline said.

"Your daughter has quite a talent," Nikola said, nodding to Céline.

Aitor smiled. "I saw it in her since she was a girl."

"I saw Marina's talent early, too," Nikola said. Marina turned to her father in surprise.

"I hope Céline has been helpful to you during her time on Pag," Aitor said.

"She made our best cheese in two decades," Nikola said. "We owe her a debt of gratitude."

Aitor paused, taking a sample of Sirana's cheese, nodding in approval as he chewed. "It's your first time to Paris?"

"Yes. Unfortunately, we will probably only have time to see the inside of this place," Nikola said.

Aitor dabbed his forehead with a handkerchief. "If we don't all melt in here first."

"Not the ideal temperature for cheese—or for people," Nikola said, chuckling.

"So, how is business?" Aitor said.

"Hopefully it will be better now, with this new cheese," Nikola said.

"Céline mentioned you didn't receive the EU funds," Aitor said. Nikola frowned. "No."

"Maybe we can help," Aitor said.

Nikola's frown deepened. "Thank you, but no, we will manage on our own."

"We could begin a profitable partnership," Aitor said. "Please think about it. Our support would make Sirana stronger, more appealing in Europe."

"I have no desire to sell any of my shares in Sirana," Nikola said, his face starting to flush.

"That's unfortunate," Aitor said, sighing. "I hoped you would feel otherwise. But you see, I have spoken to Horvat, and he has already agreed to sell me his shares in Sirana." As Céline translated for her father, the English words sounded harsh on her tongue.

"You told your father about Uncle Horvat?" Marina said to Céline, her heart beginning to race.

"Translate for your father, please, he needs to understand," Céline said calmly.

"What do you want me to translate? That you're forcing your way into Sirana?"

"Sirana will thrive under our leadership," Céline said.

"You traitor," Marina said to Céline, before translating the message for her father. She imagined reaching out and strangling the girl's narrow throat.

When Nikola spoke, his words were slow and steady. "I am still the majority shareholder in Sirana."

"That is technically true, by one percent," Aitor said. "However, when Horvat converted Sirana from state-owned to privately-owned after the war, and split the shares between you, he added a drag-along clause that states that the purchaser of his shares can force the majority shareholder to sell his shares to the buyer."

Nikola's face turned red. "That is impossible. Drag-along clauses are designed for majority shareholders. Horvat is a minority shareholder in Sirana. He can't do that. Why would he do that?"

Aitor shrugged. "It is possible. You signed the paperwork. So, once I purchase his shares, I can buy your shares at the same price as I will pay him and take full control of the company. I will own Sirana in its entirety."

Marina's mouth fell open. She searched her mind for how to break this devastating news to Nikola. With every word she spoke, his face slowly drained of the blood that had filled it.

"*Jebi ga*," Nikola cursed under his breath.

"Nikola, it's a good plan," Aitor said. "You would still be Sirana's CEO, if you will agree to our terms. With your strong ties to the community and familiarity with the way things are done, you are valuable to the company. But now I worry that you don't like this plan, and this might not work."

"You're damn right, I don't like this plan!" Nikola sputtered.

"We recently did a similar deal in Slovenia, and it's working out quite well for us," Aitor said.

"It's a shame, that your father is so stubborn and won't accept our help," Céline added, crossing her thin arms.

Marina wanted to slap the smugness off her placid face.

"Did you plan this all out, even before you even came to Pag?" Marina hissed.

"We had our sights set on Sirana, Marina," Céline said. "I told you we wanted to invest in Croatia. I hoped you would grow to understand how much we could help you, after I was able to make such a beautiful cheese with Sirana's subpar equipment."

"We don't want your goddamn help," Marina said, without translating for her father.

"You won't have a choice," Céline retorted.

Marina stared at her. She couldn't believe this was the same girl she'd laughed and cried with on Pag.

"But you don't have Horvat's shares yet," Marina said. "And my father will convince my uncle not to sell them to you."

"Horvat has agreed to a price already," Céline said. "Everybody has a price."

As Céline and her father walked away, their fine heels clicking on the elegant inlaid floor, Marina felt ill. The air was claustrophobic. Sweat beaded on her skin. She threw her arms around her father and wept. She cried for Nikola, who had been betrayed by his best friend who was like his brother, and now, by his older blood brother who had always put his own interests first. She cried for Franko, who would be devastated by Céline's deception. She cried for the friend she thought she had.

Later, at the awards ceremony, Marina felt as if she were floating through a dream. Janković's name was announced in third place for the Eastern European sheep's milk cheese category, and Josip approached the stage to accept the bronze trophy. "In second place, Sirana, from the island of Pag," the woman announced in a thick French accent. Nikola limped to the stage to accept the silver trophy. Marina stared at her father and Josip standing next to each other under the bright stage lights, Josip a head taller than her father, Nikola's balding head shining. In any other circumstance, this would be a triumph for her father, who had waited for so long to upstage Josip. She glanced across the row to Luka and Sanja, who were politely clapping, their faces tight with worry. Marina knew they were concerned about placing below Sirana, and possibly losing Dissa as a distributor. Without Céline to make their cheese, Marina had no idea how Sirana would survive the season. And if Aitor succeeded, Sirana would no longer be theirs.

Dazed, Marina made her way out of the awards ceremony room, brushing past people who stopped to congratulate her. As she exited the building, Marina noticed Luka leaning on a wall near the entrance. He took a long drag on his cigarette, staring blankly into the passing traffic. She hesitated, then walked over to him.

"That's a bad habit," Marina said in Croatian, startling him.

Luka blew out a stream of smoke. "I keep saying I'm going to quit."

"Can I have one?"

"Sure," he said, handing her one and lighting it. "Congratulations, by the way."

"Thanks," Marina said, exhaling.

"You really impressed John with your cheese. My father couldn't stop talking about it."

"Yeah, well, it might be the last of its kind," Marina said, taking a deep drag.

"Why?" he asked.

"I need to get some air," she said, stubbing out the cigarette. Smoking wasn't helping her nerves.

They made their way to the Seine. The weather was mild, the river a murky greenish gray. Boats filled with people taking photographs passed under bridges.

"What's going on, Marina?" Luka said, breaking the silence.

He gestured to her hands. She realized she was pressing her nails into her palms.

"I've known you since we were children," he said. "I know when something's wrong."

"I thought I knew her," Marina said.

"Who?"

"Céline. I don't know who to trust anymore."

"You can trust me."

Marina stopped and looked into his eyes, searching. She wanted to believe him. At this point, what difference would it make if she told him? No one else would understand.

"Promise not to say anything to your father," she said.

"I promise."

Marina sighed. "Céline played me."

"How?"

"They were planning to take over Sirana all along. Her father wants to buy Horvat's shares, which would give them control of the company."

"What happens to your father?"

"They said they'd keep him on as CEO."

"It doesn't sound like such a bad deal."

"My father would never work for them. He doesn't trust foreigners, and he wouldn't want to be a figurehead."

"Why doesn't your dad buy Horvat's shares?"

Marina grew quiet. "He can't."

"I'm sorry," Luka said. "I know what Sirana means to your family."

"I brought her in. I trusted her. I don't know what we're going to do."

"You'll figure it out," he said.

But Marina wasn't so sure.

Craving solitude, she left Luka and walked the city until dark, letting her mind unspool. For now, she didn't mind being lost in this enchanting city, roaming its streets without any direction. When she returned home, she knew that had to change, too. She needed to find her compass.

Chapter Sixteen

Pag Town was abuzz with the news of Sirana's victory over Janković, and Céline's latest batch of Sirana's cheese had nearly sold out on the island. All anyone could talk about was the flavor, which took them back to when Sirana was the best cheese factory in all of Yugoslavia, when Josip and Nikola were a team—before the war, before their country fell apart.

No one besides Luka and Marina's immediate family knew about the French business deal, not yet. Céline wouldn't be returning to Pag to finish the cheesemaking season, and people would eventually find out about the scandal. She could already imagine people gossiping about her family's financial problems and about Uncle Horvat. She could envision the headline confirming the rumor: FRENCH CHEESEMAKER TAKES OVER SIRANA.

The night Marina and Nikola returned from Paris, Dragica cooked needle macaroni with goulash for dinner, knowing everyone would need some comfort food. She shaved young Pag cheese on top—a blanket of salty, herbal flavor. Growing up, Marina had watched her mother wrap dough around knitting needles to shape the pasta, treating each like a miniature sculpture. Marina would attempt to form the dough with her small fingers, but she was never able to shape it like her mother's perfect, uniform pieces.

Nikola had barely spoken to Marina since the competition. On the plane ride home, he busied himself with preparing a list of talking points for what was sure to be a difficult conversation with his brother.

"Pass the salad," Nikola said.

Marina passed her father the bowl of finely cut green cabbage, heavy with vinegar, oil, salt, and pepper. Franko slumped over his plate, picking at Dragica's goulash. Ever since he heard Céline wasn't returning, he hadn't said a word. She had never seen her brother so wounded over a woman.

"Enough of this," Grandma Badurina said, tapping her cane on the floor to break the silence. "The girl was a snake and we didn't see it, not even me. The viper blends into its surroundings, biting quick and deep."

"I still can't believe it," Franko said quietly.

Marina felt a pang of empathy for her brother. This was the first time someone had really betrayed him. People could betray you every day, little by little, chipping away at the unseen foundation of your relationship until one day you wake up and realize the beams are rotting and unstable, and you are left balancing precariously on a ledge. That was her marriage.

Marina also felt bereft. She had divulged her life to Céline. She had been so desperate to trust someone, to share that warm, safe space of intimacy she had lost with Marko. She had unwittingly opened up about all her family's troubles, including her own, and Céline had betrayed her confidence. She wondered if it had been a mistake to open up to Luka. Would he betray her confidence, too?

Ever since they'd come home, she hadn't slept more than a few hours, lying in bed semi-awake, worrying about what tomorrow would bring. The last time she remembered feeling this way was during the war, when her father and Franko went off to fight on the mainland. She fretted about their fates from a distance during Operation Storm, tossing and turning in her aunt's spare room in Queens. When she found out later that Branko had died—not Franko or her father—she felt guilty about the relief that washed over her.

"Nikola, did you speak to your brother?" Grandma Badurina said.

Nikola lit a cigarette and took a deep drag. The smoke curled up to the ceiling like a snake. "I'm still trying to convince him not to sell."

"Can't he at least wait until Sirana recoups some funds?" Grandma Badurina said.

"Horvat said some of his other business holdings are devaluing," Nikola said. "He's nervous."

Grandma Badurina shook her head, anxiously rubbing her palm on her cane.

"But *Tata*, why does Uncle Horvat want out of Sirana now?" Franko said.

Nikola's face darkened. "The tides are turning politically. We will join the European Union in just a few months, and people who operate in the gray—well, they need clean cash to balance the black money. He's worried about the authorities taking a closer look at his finances."

When Marina returned home for summer visits after college, she had overheard her mother's hushed whispers with Grandma Badurina about Uncle Horvat's questionable business dealings, but paid them no attention. After the war ended, a mighty few had grabbed power and divided the country's spoils among friends.

Until now, she hadn't considered who might have lost while others won. And now, her family could lose everything.

"I can't control what Horvat will do with his shares," Nikola said. "But as long as I'm still CEO, I'm going to finish this cheesemaking season, one way or another. Our workers need us. We need money to keep Sirana afloat, and to make money, we need cheese. Good cheese."

Her father was intent on doing right by everyone, even as he was losing his grip on the company that had defined his life. Sirana had literally given them sustenance. They all feared losing it.

Marina took a sip of wine. "*Tata*, I have an idea," she said.

"I've had enough of your ideas," Nikola snapped.

Marina winced.

"Nikola," Dragica said firmly. "This is not Marina's fault. Hear her out."

Marina was startled. Her mother almost never defended her, and rarely spoke out against her father. Her poor father. With his unshaven stubble, large circles under his eyes, and deep worry lines creasing his forehead, Nikola looked as if he'd aged years in a few days. Marina deeply regretted introducing Céline into their lives.

"I'm sorry, *Tata*. I thought she could help us."

"*I'm* sorry, Marina," Nikola said, sighing. "How could we have known her true intentions? How could I have known Horvat tricked me all those years ago? You know, I didn't even read through the paperwork. I trusted him, and I signed. After all, he is my brother. But it was my fault. I should have hired my own lawyer." Nikola tapped his cigarette on the edge of the ashtray. "Anyhow, tell me, what is your idea?"

"For the months she was here," Marina started, not even wanting to speak Céline's name at their table, "I had to translate everything for her. I shadowed her every day, and I watched her every move. I know the shepherds as well as she does—I know the names of their wives and who I need to watch to make sure they don't water down their milk. I know how to operate our machines, to monitor the temperature of the cheese for optimal pasteurization. *Tata*, you know the entire process from when you supervised Josip in the production room before the war. We can finish the season together."

Nikola sat back in his chair and took a drag. "It has been a long time since I've made cheese."

"I've been in the production room every day. I know the workers. If we all pull together, I know we can do it."

"It would be good not to hire a new dairy technologist now," Nikola said, stubbing out his cigarette in the ashtray. "Money is so tight. All these people owe us from selling our cheese, and they haven't paid yet. They say they will pay, but everyone is keeping cash reserves. They are afraid of what will happen after we join the European Union. You saw what happened with Slovenia."

Marina shuddered. Their ex-Yugoslav neighbor to the north had joined the European Union nearly a decade before. The *tolar* was replaced by the euro, and with the introduction of a new currency, regular working people had trouble affording basic items like clothing, which became too expensive overnight. Croatians were holding onto their *kunas* and collecting euros for the rainy day that might come.

"But now, at least, we have everyone's attention because of our high placement at SIAL," Marina said. "If we can make cheese of the same quality, people will buy it."

"That girl wasted so much material, I don't know how we'll make enough of a profit if we work that way," Nikola said.

"Maybe we can raise the prices," Marina said.

"People won't be able to afford it."

"They afford Janković's cheese. And ours is as good or better than his now."

Nikola paused and lit another cigarette. "I'd hate to raise our prices."

"It can be temporary, until next season," Marina said. "If we sell the cheese directly to consumers, instead of through our local distributors who already owe us money anyway, we can make sure we get the money. All of it."

Nikola raised his eyebrows. Marina knew the stores took a sizeable cut of Sirana's profits, but Nikola felt they needed a presence in the local stores alongside Janković. Besides, it was tradition: That was how business in Croatia was done.

"Instead of driving to deliver our cheese to the stores, I can take orders for delivery," Franko said, perking up. "We can put a note on our website, and I can tell some of my friends to spread the word that we are starting direct deliveries to customers."

"We have a relationship with our distributors," Nikola said. "They've sold our cheese for many years and promoted Sirana in their stores."

"Right now, Sirana's cheese is in demand," Grandma Badurina said. "Tell them they can have more of Sirana's cheese only if they pay for what we've already supplied to them."

"It sounds fair to me," Dragica said, clearing the plates.

"And what will you do if Horvat sells his shares?" Grandma Badurina said. "Will the Basques come here and take over Sirana?"

"*Polako*," Nikola said in a measured voice. "One step at a time."

The next day, Nikola surprised the workers with his presence in the production room. He was there before they arrived, inspecting the machinery, making sure the salinity levels in the *salamura*

were correct. The last time they had seen Nikola in the production room was when he gave Céline a tour back in January.

Her father glanced at the clock: 7 a.m.

"Good morning, everyone," Nikola said. "I wanted to personally congratulate you on the cheese you made for SIAL. We are so pleased with our silver medal, and it was all thanks to you." He clapped, and Marina joined in, urging the workers to give a round of applause for themselves.

"I want to stress that it was you who made that cheese," Nikola said. "Your hands shaped it, your palms bathed it in oil, you turned it gently as it aged. You cared for Sirana's cheese, and that meticulous attention was recognized." He paused. "I say this, because Céline will not be returning to finish the season."

Someone gasped. Workers whispered among themselves.

"She is needed in Basque to help her father. Tomislav will be retiring as planned in Slavonia. But the good news is that Marina has been watching all aspects of production for the last few months, and between all of us, I have confidence that we can continue to make superior cheese."

Marina glanced around at the workers' faces. Some seemed to have skeptical looks, while others, she was fairly sure, looked relieved to hear the news that Tomislav wouldn't be returning. During lunches with Céline in the bowels of Sirana, Marina had gotten to know the minds of many of the workers. They thought Tomislav was a kind man, but a little lazy and stuck in his old ways. Sometimes, they even spoke openly about Nikola, forgetting he was her father. They worried he had distanced himself too much from the production process over the years.

"We will need the same diligence Céline required of you," Marina said. "I will be overseeing all aspects of production, along with my father. Everything else will continue on as before. We have almost sold out of our last batch of cheese, and we need to continue to make as much as we can, especially now that people have heard about our success at SIAL."

One of the cheese packers timidly raised her hand. "Is it possible to have one additional break for coffee?"

Marina smiled. "Of course."

"Let's get to work!" Nikola said, clapping his hands.

Nikola and Marina had supervised that morning's milk drop-off, casually chatting with the shepherds, who asked about Céline. Nikola had told them that she was called back to help her father with the end of their cheesemaking season, and they nodded and seemed to accept this. Marina wondered how much longer they could contain the secret. If Uncle Horvat decided to sell his shares, Céline and her father would take over Sirana, and share their version of the story. What if they brought new machinery and imported workers from France? Or chose not to work with the local vendors? Her father's legacy and the pride of their town would be lost. Sirana anchored them. They had to fight for it.

The following weeks passed in a blur. During long hours at Sirana, Marina didn't have time to think about Céline or Luka or Marko. The French business proposal threw them all into a spiral, and she was even more focused on work, not on resolving things with her husband. She wondered if that meant something.

Cheese production dominated her life now. She dreamed about stacked wheels and breathed in their earthy, primal aroma. Nikola had to throw out the first couple of batches, which frustrated him and Marina both. Céline had made it all look so easy, but when they tried to get all the components just right, the process required skills Nikola had forgotten and Marina was just coming to possess.

Their third batch was a success. All the workers were visibly relieved, having put their faith into Nikola and his daughter to guide them. With practice and timing, the cheese improved. Marina ended her days satisfied and exhausted, often going straight to bed so she could get up early to start her day at 6 a.m. Sometimes, she woke up before daybreak and went into the pastures to check on the shepherds, who grew to expect her and welcomed her with smiles and offerings of coffee from a thermos. Even the sheep seemed to skitter less when she approached.

Franko had joined the effort as well. If he was not out on the field playing soccer, he was driving to make deliveries and finding ways to take new orders. Marina admired her brother's new initiative, but he was running—anyone could see that. She wanted to tell him that he wouldn't be able to outrun his emotions, that one day, when he was least suspecting, they would creep up his back and close around his throat.

In May, blossoms emerged in Dragica's garden. The Adriatic Sea traded its dark, winter blues for vibrant hues of turquoise and cerulean. Birds chirped and twittered. The landscape yawned.

Nikola stood outside Sirana's production room door smoking. He wore rubber boots, wet from cheese runoff, his lab coat unbuttoned.

"*Jutro, Tata*," Marina said, squinting to shield her eyes from the early morning sun. "I've just checked on the shepherds. They said the milk yield this morning was good."

"*Dobro*," Nikola said, exhaling a stream of smoke. He coughed, pressing a handkerchief to his mouth. Before he placed it back in the breast pocket of his shirt, Marina glimpsed a bright-red stain.

"*Tata*, is that blood?" Marina said.

"It's nothing," Nikola said, tucking the handkerchief down further.

"It doesn't look like nothing," Marina said, frowning. "You should visit Dr. Miletić."

"I don't need a doctor," Nikola said, stubbing out the cigarette with the heel of his boot. He coughed into the handkerchief again.

"When was the last time you saw him?" Marina said. She knew her father hated going to the doctor.

"A few years, I suppose."

"A few *years*? You don't have annual physicals?"

"Last time, Miletić wanted me to do some stupid exercises for this old injury," he said, gesturing to his leg. "I told him there is nothing that will make this kind of pain go away."

"But *Tata*, you should be seen every year. It's important."

"What else will he tell me, that I'm getting old and breaking down?" Nikola said, his cough turning into a laugh.

Marina frowned.

"Oh fine, if it's that important to you, I'll go. But you should also see him. It's been almost a year since you arrived, and if you're going to stay here, you should get reacquainted. He hasn't seen you since you were a teenager."

Marina remembered Dr. Miletić giving her creamy Bajadera chocolates after her childhood checkups. He was a kind, bespectacled man, the town's family doctor who could address most common ailments. For special cases, people from the island would drive to Zadar or Split, Dalmatian cities that had more facilities and specialists.

"Okay then, I'm making appointments for us both," Marina said. "We'll see him later today, if he is available."

"Fine," Nikola said reluctantly, heaving open the production room door.

Marina's eyes wandered up to Sirana's neglected sign, cracked and sun-faded. They never had enough money to replace it, always sinking profits into the cheese, repaying its debts and the workers who made it. For many years, it felt as if they were always trying to dig out of a hole, only to look up and find themselves deeper.

The machines had been breaking more often than usual, resulting in expensive repair visits. First, it was the machine that filtered and pasteurized milk from the tank outside the factory, where shepherds deposited their milk to Sirana every morning. The filter hadn't been cleaned properly by one of the workers, an avoidable mistake that frustrated Nikola. He had calmly explained that there was no room for careless errors, and paid the repairman from Zadar a hefty sum out of his own pocket. Marina knew her father didn't have an endless supply of *kunas*, and he couldn't keep covering Sirana's expenses forever.

Next to die was the *salamura*, the machine that submerged fresh wheels of cheese in brine. After the curds had been drained and pressed into cylindrical molds, the *salamura* helped to pre-serve the cheese and form rinds by lowering the wheels into the giant saltwater tank. Like a stubborn donkey, the long metal tray, which lifted cheese up and down from the saltwater, refused to move. For a few batches, until the machine could be fixed, the workers had to improvise by lowering the cheese into the brine using fishing nets, which left unsightly rope marks on the rind. Marina named that batch *mornar*, scrambling to create a special label with a sailor on a boat holding a net full of fish, to make a clever story out of their misfortune. The taste of the cheese was what mattered, but still, people cared about appearances.

That very afternoon, another machine broke. It was a crucial element of the assembly line, whose function was to form the curds into neatly cut blocks, ready for the workers to hand-pack into molds. Instead, the workers had to reach into the large vat with their gloved hands and scoop out the unformed curds, manually draining them, which created a mess and wasted more raw material than they could afford. They had to brainstorm creative solutions to collect the remaining curds from the stainless steel vat and created a giant ladle.

No machine can tell you when the cheese is done. The meter can measure pH levels and temperature, but can't replace instinct and years of experience. It can't substitute an understanding of the seasonality of the milk, or how Pag's severe and shifting climate conditions affect the flavor. "I just know. I listen to the cheese," Céline had said, when Marina asked her how she knew a particular batch was ready. No timer or formula could help. So Marina whispered to the cheese, pleaded with it. Some of the workers thought she was losing her mind.

Marina watched her father's cheesemaking skills resurface slowly, information lodged in the back of his brain like wheels of cheese lifted out of brine after a submerged slumber, sipping their first breath of air. Together, they fell into a rhythm. Nikola's years of working alongside Josip at Sirana, coupled with Marina's observance of Céline's techniques, resulted in a singular creative process. Later that day, when the mechanized agitator broke—a machine that resembled a gigantic mixer—Marina had the idea to sanitize an old wooden oar in saltwater and manually agitate the milk to help it curdle. Stirring the milk with the oar, Igor looked like a mythical chef hovering over a cauldron fit for the giant Klek.

Marina and Nikola were both relieved to finish that challenging week, clocking out at 3 p.m., their usual time—but these days had not been usual, and twelve or fourteen hours had become standard. Ending work at the regular time, even on a Friday, felt like playing hooky.

"Now we go to the doctor," Marina said, tucking her white rainboots under the bench and hanging her crumpled white coat on the hook. "He's agreed to fit us in before the weekend."

"*Ej*, Marina, it's been such a long day already," Nikola said. "Can't it wait?"

"*Tata*, you promised," Marina said.

Nikola sighed. "Let's get it over with, then."

Fortunately, there was no one in the waiting room. It was one of the benefits of living in a small town, on an island with eight thousand people, less people than on her city block in Astoria. Marina remembered the day she visited the clinic in the bustling city, vulnerable and pregnant and facing a room full of strangers. She waited for over an hour to see a doctor, who took one casual look at the sonogram and pronounced her baby dead. Marina had stopped feeling the baby's small swells of movement which she sometimes thought she only imagined. She wanted to believe her baby was resting, floating on her back in amniotic fluid like Marina did on the sea in summer. She would have given anything to keep that tiny heart beating.

The nurse called Nikola's name almost as soon as they sat down. Marina perused a Croatian tabloid magazine. How many times she had sat in this waiting room, on these fraying brown chairs. Dr. Miletić had seen her through countless fevers as a child, when Dragica would call on him late at night, fretting over Marina's rivers of sweat. He had given her her first gynecology exam, she thought uncomfortably.

Nikola emerged with furrowed brows. "You're next," he said.

"What did he say, *Tata*?"

"I have to go to Zadar for some tests."

Marina frowned. "What for?"

"My lungs. They need me to see a specialist. It's probably nothing."

Marina sucked in her breath. "It's your smoking, *Tata*."

"Don't worry, Marina. You worry too much."

"When are the tests?"

"They can wait until the season is over. We have too much work to do."

"No, we need to have the tests done now," Marina said.

"Marina, we only have a couple months left to finish the season. It can wait."

"No, *Tata*," Marina said firmly. "Your health is more important than cheese."

Nikola sighed. "Fine, I'll call them and see if I can go next week."

"Marina?" the old doctor called, poking his head out the waiting room door.

"I'll wait for you," Nikola said, picking up a newspaper.

"Please make the call to schedule the tests," Marina said over her shoulder, following the doctor into the exam room.

"Well," Dr. Miletić said, opening up a yellowed file. "It's been, let's see, eighteen years since I've last seen you? Can that be right?"

"Yes. I left Pag when I was seventeen," Marina said. She could hardly believe so many years had passed.

"I suppose we should start from the beginning, then," Dr. Miletić said. "Any new allergies?"

"No."

"Surgeries?"

Marina winced. "Yes."

"What for?"

"Fibroids. And, an ectopic pregnancy." She instinctively covered her abdomen with her hand.

"When?"

"Five years ago for the fibroids, four for the ectopic pregnancy."

In tears, Marina had told Marko that the embryo had implanted itself outside her uterus, in her fallopian tubes—a place it couldn't survive. It would never be a viable pregnancy. She was further devastated to learn she needed surgery, and that the abnormal pregnancy could be life-threatening. The operation left one of her fallopian tubes damaged. If she'd only known then that it was just the beginning, that more losses were to come.

"Any other pregnancies or miscarriages?"

"Yes."

And with that, and the lack of sleep and long workdays that had worn her nerves to the ground, she couldn't stop the tears that tumbled down her cheeks.

"When?"

"Last year. A second trimester miscarriage. I delivered the baby."

Marina released the torrent that had been pent up inside her, everything she had been holding onto. She sobbed so hard her body shook. She clutched the arms of the chair as if she might fall off.

Dr. Miletić paused his scribbling, took off his glasses, and sighed. "Oh Marina, I'm sorry. That must have been unbearable." He put his hand on her shoulder. She remembered when he had given her the news that she needed to get her tonsils out before the start of kindergarten, his reassuring hand that made her feel like everything was going to be fine.

When Marina finally regained her breath enough to speak, she said, "It was unbearable."

"Have you spoken about it to anyone, professionally?" he said.

Marina was shocked her provincial town doctor was recommending a therapist. Croatians were known for their stoicism in the face of trouble.

"No. I've barely spoken to anyone about it. Only three people besides my husband know. And, I'm sure you've heard, we are separated."

"I can give you the name of someone to speak to in Zadar, about your miscarriage and your marriage. When you're ready."

"Cheese is my therapy," Marina said. "Maybe after the season ends, I'll look into it," she added, to mollify the doctor.

"Maybe it is better to reschedule the exam for a later time, too?"

"No, I can do it."

"There is no rush."

"I am overdue for my annual exam, and my doctor in New York wanted to keep an eye on the fibroids. Let's just do it now."

He hesitated. "Given your history of miscarriages, I will probably need to send you to a specialist in Zadar anyway."

"I want to know what you think, and I can also see a specialist. You've known me my whole life here," she said, beginning to tear up again.

"I think it's better if we reschedule," Dr. Miletić said, handing her a tissue. "You've been through enough this year already."

Marina wiped her tears. "I don't have time. We are in full production, and I need to be at Sirana. I need to do it now."

Legs splayed open on the exam table, Marina felt the cold metal speculum click and stretch her vaginal cavity open. The doctor's latex fingers probed inside. Tears continued to slide out the sides of her eyes. Her baby's body had traveled through that dark tunnel, her soul already departed.

Emerging into the bright waiting room, Marina told her father she also needed to see a specialist. Even though Dr. Miletić was a family doctor also trained as a gynecologist, Marina's complicated issues were outside his scope, and he didn't have the necessary equipment to execute a complete evaluation. Her fibroids had grown and, like her New York doctor, Dr. Miletić was concerned about their potential negative effects on her fertility. She called to make an appointment with the OBGYN the following week, on the same day as Nikola's appointment with the pulmonologist, so they could make the trip together.

Exactly a week later, after clocking out of Sirana following another stressful, grueling week, Nikola and Marina departed for Zadar. They had to leave around lunchtime, but not before ensuring the last of the cheese was resting safely in molds, tall stacks of cylinders pressed like coins in a sorter, draining runoff onto the tiles. They would work together over the weekend, transitioning the batch to brine.

Marina had barely spoken to her father about anything other than cheesemaking, which seemed to keep the peace. But Céline and her father each had reached out to them repeatedly, also regularly calling Uncle Horvat to try to convince him to sell his shares. Nikola phoned Horvat almost daily, pleading with him and asking for more time. *"Molim te, brate,"* Marina heard Nikola say over the phone before they left Sirana. *Please, brother.* Nikola could not hide the desperation in his voice. Horvat had finally agreed to wait to sell his shares in Sirana until Croatia joined the European Union on July 1; he would give them until the day before. After that, he said, he needed the money to "balance the books."

Nikola lit a cigarette and eased himself into the driver's seat. The Yugo's engine rumbled to a start. Marina opened the passenger door; a rush of hot air escaped. This May, the entire region was experiencing a heat wave. Pag felt like a naked planet on fire.

Driving past the salt flats, Nikola coughed into his handkerchief.

"*Tata*, has it become worse?" Marina said, eyeing the splatter of droplets that stained the handkerchief red.

"Same as before," he said, stuffing the handkerchief in his breast pocket. His thinning hair was slicked to his scalp, his mustache moist from perspiration.

"Does Mama suspect anything?" Marina asked.

"She's concerned about my coughing. I've been careful to rinse my handkerchiefs to get out the stains, before I put them in the wash. No need to worry her prematurely," Nikola said.

"And your coughing at night, is it worse?"

"Marina, let me see the specialist first and I'll tell you what he says about my symptoms," Nikola said, flicking ash out the window.

They drove in silence past the salt flats, on the snaking road that bordered the sea, passing roadside restaurants with skinned lambs on mechanical spits that rotated slowly over leaping flames.

"Have you spoken to Marko?" Nikola asked.

As they crossed Pag Bridge, Marina felt her stomach lurch. Even with the windows open, the heat felt unbearable.

"Not recently. Why?" Marina asked.

"You left almost a year ago," Nikola said.

"I know."

"And? Have you decided what you're doing?"

"After I moved to America, I thought I was done with starting over," Marina said.

"I did what I thought was best then," Nikola said quietly.

"I know you sent me away because you wanted me to be safe, to have opportunities in America," Marina said, her vision becoming blurry. "At the time, I thought it was for the best, too. It's just that I've always wondered how things would have turned out if I'd stayed."

"We will never know our unlived lives, Marina," Nikola said.

"*Tata*, I don't blame you. It's just that I don't think I realized what leaving home would mean. I didn't know how it would change me."

"You're still young enough. There's a point in life where the decisions you've made close some paths forever."

"Are you talking about Sanja?" Marina said quietly.

Nikola looked straight ahead at the road. "Some things are not meant to be. I will always love Sanja, but your mother and I have been through a lot of life together. We've grown together, and our love has strengthened over time. Maybe that will be true for you and Marko."

Marina had the urge to tell her father about Marko's affair, but that would only make Nikola hate Marko more than he already did.

Marina fought back tears. "Let's just get through the season first. We're so close," she said, quickly wiping her eyes.

"You've done well, Marina," Nikola said, softening. "With these direct deliveries to our customers, we've made up some of the money owed to us by distributors, and I think we just might make payroll for everyone, which I thought was impossible."

"But what happens after, *Tata*? How will we manage if Horvat sells his shares?"

Nikola grew solemn. "I hope Horvat will act decently," he began. "On the other hand, I don't want him apprehended by the European Union authorities. They could make life very difficult for him, and he is, after all, my brother. Horvat has enemies from when he used his political influence to help overturn Gotovina's convictions."

"Why should we suffer for Horvat's illegal dealings? And why should Sirana?" Marina said, her voice rising.

"It is complicated, Marina," Nikola sighed.

The powers that be shielded themselves in smoke, disappearing into their stashed wealth and barricading in fortresses, leaving others in impossible, vulnerable positions. After four years on the run, even Gotovina, who had been hiding in the Canary Islands, was ultimately caught. His powerful friends couldn't protect him from charges for crimes against humanity, but they eventually helped to broker his release. Marina didn't want to see her uncle in jail for his financial crimes, but she didn't want her father to suffer the fallout, either. On Pag—their beautiful, bald island—there was nowhere to hide.

"You will not have children," the doctor in Zadar said in a harsh Slavic staccato, removing her latex gloves with a snap. Marina felt herself go cold. In advance of her appointment, Marina had asked the clinic in New York to fax their notes and scans, her formidable file that told the story of her miscarriages and struggles with infertility, the birthing of her breathless daughter and resulting complications. The fibroids had grown considerably since her exam in New York, blocking her uterine cavity. Although they were not the sole cause of her infertility, they were symbolic, a wall of benign tumors that had reappeared after surgery, obstructing her fallopian tubes, one of which was irrevocably damaged.

Returning shakily to her father in the waiting room, Marina took a few steps and then collapsed into his arms, crying uncontrollably. Her dream of creating a biological family was gone. That door leading to future generations was closed forever. Nikola's strong arms enveloped her and he stroked her back, over and over, repeating, "It will all be fine, *Mala*, it will all be fine." They stood there for what seemed like hours, until she finally lifted her head and let her father escort her outside. The clear, sunny day laughed at her, chiding her agony. Marina's tears continued to flow as they made their way down the sidewalk.

"What did they tell you, *Mala*?" Nikola said softly.

"I can't have children, *Tata*," Marina said finally, choking out the words.

Nikola wrapped an arm around her tightly, as they walked. "I'm sorry," he said.

"No man will want me now."

"You don't need a man," Nikola said. "You have two feet, and you are standing on them."

Marina looked over at her father, wiping her tear-streaked cheeks with the back of her hand. "I love you, *Tata*," she said. He smiled at her, but something was wrong. He looked pale, his mouth drawn into a thin line. She had burst out of the office so consumed with her own despair that she hadn't noticed the red circles rimming his eyes, tears trembling at the edges.

"*Tata*, what's wrong?" she said, her voice rising like a little girl's.

"Ah, Marina," he sighed, exhaling a stream of smoke. "*Mala*, I'm dying."

"What?" Marina choked. In the thick heat, she felt faint. "What?" she repeated, as if she hadn't heard herself.

"Lung cancer," Nikola said. "Your mother was right about the smoking, after all."

"You can't leave us," Marina said, wrapping her arms tightly around her father's thick girth, burying her head into his chest.

She wanted to stop time.

"They said a couple months," Nikola said, tossing the cigarette butt to the ground. "It's far progressed. Damn tumors are all over the place."

"We'll get a second opinion."

"I saw the X-rays, Marina."

"We can fly to New York. We can see doctors there. They have some of the best in the world."

"What would they do? Give me a slower death? I don't want to die on foreign soil. I want to die here, at home."

"*Tata*, you can't die," Marina sobbed.

"Let's take a walk," Nikola said, linking arms with her.

They strolled through Zadar's Old Town, through the bustling People's Square, over smooth white cobblestones. Marina felt as if she was in a waking dream, her eyes falling on familiar sights that appeared distorted, forming a reality she couldn't fathom—a life without her father. Her feet guided her to the promenade, towards the Sea Organ at the end of the peninsula. The Adriatic Sea glittered. They sat together on the stairs listening to the longing, ephemeral tones interrupt waves lapping and receding in an endless ebb and flow.

"I wasn't planning to have this discussion now," Nikola said, taking the dented tin from his pocket and rolling a cigarette. "But in light of what the doctor said today, I need to get my affairs in order. I don't know how much time I have left."

Marina swallowed. Her throat was dry. "*Tata*, I'm staying."

"Don't make your decision because of this. Because of me," Nikola said.

"I had already decided. This is my home."

Her father lit a cigarette and took a drag, gazing out at the sea, at the hazy line where it kissed the blue horizon. "Sirana is also my home, *Mala*. Those people are like my family. I need to make sure they will be in good hands. Those hands will be yours."

Marina turned to her father. "You want me to run Sirana?"

"You've made me so proud over these last few months," Nikola said. "I hope Franko will continue to help you with the business, but I have faith in you, Marina. You are the one who can lead Sirana in these times."

Marina felt a swell of emotion rise in her chest. "*Tata*, how will I do it without you? I don't want to do it without you. I don't know how."

"You will be just fine, *Mala*. You already know so much of what I know. I'll need to show you Sirana's books. I'm afraid the numbers do not tell a happy story, and I'm sorry you'll inherit this disaster."

"Don't be sorry. It's not your fault the distributors didn't pay."

"I should have hired an accountant, but we never had the money. It used to work so well at Sirana, when Sanja managed the books and Josip made the cheese. It has never been the same without them." Nikola's voice was brimming with nostalgia.

"We don't need them, *Tata*," Marina said. "We can make it on our own."

Chapter Seventeen

That night, when Dragica served dinner, no one at the table spoke. They sat together in silence, heavy in their collective grief. The old fan spun above, rotating on its axis, pushing hot air from one place to another. Dragica refused to turn on the air conditioner, for fear they would all catch a cold. Now, Marina believed wholeheartedly in her mother's superstitions. Drafts can kill you. So can smoke.

"It isn't fair," Franko said finally. He twisted his napkin into a rope.

"Life isn't fair," Nikola said. "But we must accept what is."

Dragica picked at her goulash. Marina's mother had cried so much her eyes were bloodshot. She stared blankly at the food.

Marina took a sip of homemade wine, which tasted like vinegar. Everything tasted sour. She had made her father promise not to tell Dragica about her infertility—her mother would already have an unconscionable burden with Nikola's diagnosis. They all faced the impossible challenge of trying to savor their remaining days with Nikola, and at the same time, preparing in their own ways to let him go.

The doctor had said, "a couple months." How was that measured in days, or hours? Time felt indeterminate; Nikola had been given an estimate for his remaining life, but it could be any day. It could be tomorrow. They could lose him any day now.

"How do we go on without you?" Dragica wailed, pressing her napkin to her mouth, as if she wanted to swallow back the words so that none of them had to confront the reality facing them.

"Together, you will find a way," Nikola said, patting her hand.

Franko clenched his fists and twisted the napkin harder. Marina's parade of salty tears seemed bottomless, like clouds absorbing the sea in a cycle of perpetual release.

"I need you all to work together," Nikola continued, assuming a businesslike voice to overcome his emotion, which was written across his sallow face. "Sirana is our lifeblood. Effective immediately, Marina will be taking over my role as CEO. Franko, you will continue to be in charge of packaging and distribution."

Franko stopped twisting his napkin. "*Tata*, I always thought it would be me who would take your place."

"Son, look at your sister. She arrives early to the factory every day, working late alongside the workers. She has learned this business in less than a year, while you've had years to learn it but took no interest. You've done good work with direct distribution, and I know you both will work well together in your respective roles."

"Franko, this was not what I expected," Marina said. "I didn't plan to stay here. But when I'm at Sirana, my life makes sense."

"I won't go against *Tata's* wishes," Franko said.

"Good. I don't want to fight with you. We're on the same side," Marina said.

"But Nikola, all this is meaningless if Horvat sells his shares," Dragica said.

"I have convinced Horvat not to sell his shares until the day before we join the European Union. I hope we will find a Croatian buyer for his shares," Nikola said.

"And if we don't?" Grandma Badurina said.

"I don't know," Nikola sighed. He looked very tired.

"*Tata*, if worse comes to worst, we could take the money Aitor would pay us for your shares, and we could create our own cheese factory," Marina said. "We could begin again."

"Let's hope that doesn't have to happen," Nikola said. "Dragica, love, there will be some difficult times ahead, and Marina and Franko will need your support. Whatever happens, I won't be here to see it. You will all need to make these decisions together."

Dragica nodded absently. Marina didn't know what her mother would do without Nikola to guide her, to provide for her financial well-being. Dragica had always relied on Nikola, leaving the bills and books to his expertise; she had taken care of the domestic realm. Sirana belonged to their family, but in truth, it was Nikola's third child. And now, at least for a time, Marina would shepherd Sirana into the future.

After dinner, Marina collapsed on her bed, sinking into the faded, flowered sheets. She would buy new sheets in Zadar soon, she promised herself. She'd had enough of sleeping on the past.

Marko was still on her list of favorites. She inhaled deeply, touched his name on the screen, and pressed the phone to her ear.

"Hello?" Marko said groggily.

"I'm sorry to call you at work," Marina said, looking at her watch. In haste, she had forgotten to calculate the time difference between Croatia and New York. The wine swirled in her head.

"Is everything okay?" Marko said.

"No," Marina said, her voice trembling. "Are you alone?"

"Yes. What's going on?" Marko said.

Marina felt the comfort of hearing his voice. It was familiar. And yet she didn't know what to say to him. This day had simply been too much for Marina to bear alone.

"*Tata* is dying," Marina said.

There was a beat of silence on the line.

"Nikola is dying?" Marko said, as if he could hardly believe it.

Hearing the words repeated by her estranged husband made the reality seem more urgent. Marina was curled on her bed and began to cry.

"He was diagnosed with late-stage lung cancer," Marina said between sobs.

"Oh God. I'm sorry, Marina," Marko said, with tenderness.

He was thousands of miles away. They were thousands of miles apart, on vastly different islands. But that night, Marina wanted to be held, to have a warm body envelop hers so completely that she disappeared. Even if it were possible, if he could be instantly transported, she didn't know if having Marko beside her would make her feel less alone.

"What went wrong with us?" Marina wondered aloud.

"I don't think this is the time to talk about that," Marko said.

"It's never a good time to talk about anything." She took a deep breath. "You should know, I also found out today I can't have children."

"Come back and get a second opinion," he said.

"What if it's true?"

Marko was silent. "I can't imagine a life without my own children."

"This was not my choice."

"I'm sorry, Marina, but there's a version of life that I had in my head. I can't just erase it."

"You could never accept change. You want all your rows and columns and numbers to add up. This isn't like business, Marko. You can't fix our marriage like a company," Marina snapped.

"You're upset. It's completely understandable, given what you went through today," Marko said in a mollifying voice.

"Don't try to talk me down," Marina said.

"Let's not fight. What can I do, Marina? How can I help? Do you want me to come there?"

"No. *Tata* wants to finish the season, and we have so much to do."

"What do you want?" Marko said.

"I want to stay. I am taking over as CEO of Sirana."

Speaking those words aloud, Marina felt the gulf between them widen.

"My life is here, in New York," Marko said finally.

"Mine isn't. Not anymore."

After she hung up, she curled into a small ball under her faded sheets. She eventually fell asleep and dreamt of jumping out of a plane without a parachute, flailing, falling through the sky above Pag until she desperately reached out for the scythe moon. Her bloody palms stained the silver crescent red, but still she held on, suspended indefinitely, wondering how to land safely home, until day broke and she opened her swollen eyes.

Over the next few weeks, Nikola's health declined precipitously. Radiation treatments, which the doctors hoped would extend Nikola's life past the projected few months, had reduced his immunity, which made him more susceptible to illness. Still, Dragica blamed the *propuh* for Nikola's nasty case of pneumonia, which resulted in complications for his already-compromised lung functions.

The doctors ordered bedrest. Dr. Miletić set up a morphine drip in the spare bedroom to ease Nikola's pain. Marina took over operations at Sirana, sooner than expected. Every day, she felt torn about leaving her father to go to work. She was anxious that he might die before she could say goodbye. But she knew there was nothing she could do to save him. His life's work, though—his company, his Sirana—that was something she could save.

Marina's favorite part of the day was visiting the sheep in the early morning. The flock huddled under a corrugated tin roof for shade, a mass of wooly black-and-white backs. Their bleats made Marina's heart flutter; the lambs, who vied for position and suckled at their mothers' teats, strained to be heard over the flock's chorus, which rose and fell like waves. Standing in the rocky pasture, surrounded by sheep, she faced mighty Velebit; in the clear dawn, surveying perfect layers of stone cut by God—mountains unmoved by any force, not even the *bura*—she felt invincible.

People in Pag Town bowed their heads in sympathy when they saw Marina walk by Tale Bay on route to her midmorning coffee break at the former Café Zec. Everyone was stricken by the news of Nikola's illness. He was a beloved and prominent figure, and the town mourned his departure even before it happened. Tensions with northerners were temporarily set aside, and in solidarity, the island soon entered into an unspoken truce.

Not long after Nikola's diagnosis, the pasteurization machine broke. It was as if Sirana, like her father's body, was finally shutting down. The technician from Zadar came to give a repair estimate, but reported there was nothing he could do. The old Soviet machine had lived its useful life and needed to be replaced.

Over fresh fish and *blitva*, Marina lamented, "*Tata*, it's beyond repair. I don't know what to do." Marina stared into the fish's glassy eye as she removed its delicate bones.

Nikola, who usually had a lion's appetite, picked at the fish's white flesh with a fork. "You've seen the books. We can't afford a new one."

Grandma Badurina took a bite of *blitva*. "Why not do it like we used to?" As she spoke, Marina noticed a piece of green stuck between her teeth.

Nikola stopped picking at his fish. "That's brilliant."

As a child, when Grandma Badurina's mother was still alive, Marina remembered tasting her great-grandmother's homemade cheese, which used the old method of preservation, dusting the exposed surface with ash, creating a black layer of rind. In those days, there was no pasteurization. The sheep's milk was raw, each batch unpredictable, resulting in a rich cheese with complex flavors that exuded an earthiness all its own.

"There are only a few weeks remaining in the season," Grandma Badurina said. "Why not experiment?"

Marina's mind flooded with ideas. They could call it "Grandmother's Cheese," and make each handcrafted wheel smaller, an artisanal cheese, a return to their island's roots.

"Yes, why don't we experiment?" Marina said. "Spain and Portugal sometimes use thistle rennet for sheep's milk cheese, and we could try it, too—and save money, since we wouldn't need to use imported rennet to curdle our milk anymore. Cardoons grow wild all over Pag, and in our groves."

"Where did you hear this crazy idea?" Grandma Badurina said.

"At the World Cheese Awards," Marina said. "I met a Spanish cheesemaker who uses thistle rennet. Maybe he could help us. And I also did some research. Plant-based rennet has been used in cheese production for thousands of years. It's less consistent, but the resulting flavors make thistle cheese more exciting. Plus, it's good marketing."

"What do you know?" Grandma Badurina said. "Those prickly purple flowers that always manage to scratch me on my walks have a purpose."

"Vegetarian rennet? People will laugh," Nikola said.

"Now that the machines are broken we have to try something different," Marina said. "I think there's a market for this."

"People won't buy it," Nikola insisted. "They want what's familiar. Consistency."

"But we're joining the European Union soon, *Tata*. People also want something new. I know I could sell this in America, and they'd love it—the ingredients will be entirely from our island, a small batch using our old cheesemaking methods and an ancient plant-based rennet...." Marina trailed off, glancing at her father. He frowned.

"Give her a chance, Nikola," Grandma Badurina said. "She has a different perspective than us. Maybe she has a point."

Nikola smoothed his mustache. "You really think people will pay so much for a little wheel of homemade cheese?"

"Artisanal cheese," Marina said firmly. "And yes. It will sell."

"Fine, then. If you're sure," he said.

"Will you help me with the old methods, Grandma?" Marina said.

Grandma Badurina chuckled. "My dear, it may have been years since I've kept sheep and made cheese, but even your father will tell you, ours was always the best. Of course, I will help."

The mood in the room lightened as they toasted to their new venture. Grandma Badurina had been industrious her entire life, mostly out of necessity—she had lived through World War II and Yugoslavia's civil war. And Marina saw this was a point of pride for her grandmother, she would almost say it brought her joy, to have given hope to the townspeople in the middle of crisis, to have had her creativity challenged with scarce materials and uncertain outcomes.

Rumors of Nikola's declining health did not take long to reach the north. Some of Sirana's workers had relatives on the other side of the island, or maybe shepherds at a border town spread the rumors at a tavern, loose-lipped and drunk on *rakija*.

Marina returned home from Sirana one blistering afternoon in June to find Josip and Sanja sitting at their table opposite her parents, sipping Turkish coffee from Dragica's fine china cups. Dragica had exchanged Grandma Maržić's crocheted tablecloth for an embroidered white linen tablecloth, which she used for formal occasions. They were having hot coffee despite the day's torrid, salty breath, which bore down upon them, rivulets of sweat trickling down the napes of their necks.

It had been twenty years since Josip and Sanja had sat in the Maržić dining room, during the war, when they were all still friends. Sanja looked stricken. Josip sat bone-straight, his expression solemn and his hands folded in his lap. Marina felt the uncomfortable sensation of interrupting a conversation that was beginning to become grave.

"You're home early," Nikola said, taking a sip of coffee.

As Nikola set the teacup delicately on the saucer, his hand trembled. In the span of a month, her father's physique had drastically changed. His wide girth had visibly shrunk, making his ashen skin appear saggy. Most days, he barely ate, pushing food around on his plate. Like most Croatians, even in summer, they ate steaming soup at least once a day. Besides coffee and cigarettes, soup was sometimes the only food Nikola could stomach. Radiation had ravished his body, and the morphine caused nausea and a loss in appetite. It pained Marina to see her robust father wasting away, the cancer a persistent decay, like a tree trunk rotting from within.

"We finished the last batch sooner than expected. I didn't know you'd have company," Marina said, slipping her bare feet into house slippers.

"They dropped by to say hello on their way to Zadar. Come, join us," Nikola said.

Marina hesitated. "I don't want to intrude."

"Stay," Nikola said, coughing into his handkerchief and pulling out the head chair beside him, as if to welcome the interruption. "We were just talking about the European Union, and the changes we will see in Croatia."

"In less than a month we'll see what happens," Josip said, taking a sip of coffee. The teacup looked like a toy in his giant hand.

"Draga, can you please bring out Sirana's new cheese?" Nikola said.

Dragica nodded absently. Eager for an excuse to leave for a moment, she scurried into the kitchen. She emerged carrying a platter of Grandmother's Cheese, laid out in small triangles arranged like a pinwheel.

Nikola pointed proudly to the cheese. "This is Sirana's latest batch. Come and taste it. I promise, it will bring you back to better times."

Josip dutifully took a slice of the petite wheel of cheese. He passed the platter to Sanja. He bit the entire triangle off the rind and chewed. His laser-blue eyes seemed faraway, reaching into a well of memories. Sanja, too, appeared lost in thought, as if her soul had left the room for a fleeting moment.

"*Bože*," Josip said. "My God."

"Marina made it," Nikola said, nodding in her direction.

Sanja's eyes were misty. "You made this, Marina?"

"Grandma Badurina helped," Marina said. "She showed me the old methods, and we worked together. And of course, my father had a large hand in it."

"Marina is being modest. She doesn't need our help any longer," Nikola said.

"Well, you've created something remarkable," Sanja said. "There's something different about this cheese, I can't put my finger on it."

"Trade secret," Marina said, smiling.

After years of typing vacuous ad copy in New York, leaving the office feeling depleted, Marina felt she had accomplished something tangible, something that mattered. And she did it with her own hands and the gifts of her homeland. She had taken purity from their untamed earth and shaped it into the essence of their island. The thistle rennet had added something unexpected, a pleasant bitterness like the acidity in a crisp white wine, which enhanced the cheese's moreish herbal flavors and floral notes.

"It reminds me of my own grandmother's cheese," Josip said, his eyes still distant.

Marina smiled. "That is what we named it."

Josip's eyes traveled to the wall where a photo of Josip and Nikola used to reside, a space that had been empty for nearly two decades. Marina remembered the photo clearly, the two men at Sirana, their arms around each other; it disappeared after the war, after Josip left the factory to start his own. An unfilled nail hole and the sun-bleached rectangle where the frame used to hang were the only reminders of their fractured friendship.

Nikola followed Josip's gaze and cleared his throat. "Listen, I have some important news to share. First, you should both know, Marina is taking over as CEO of Sirana. Second, I know you've heard I'm very ill, and that's why you're here. But, the fact is, I'm dying."

Sanja sucked in her breath. Dragica dabbed her eyes. Josip stared blankly at the space on the wall. The room became very still. The old fan oscillated above them.

"The rumors are true, then? Lung cancer?" Josip said.

"Unfortunately," Nikola said.

Josip stared into the muddy coffee grounds at the bottom of his cup.

"How long, Nikola?" Josip said finally.

"They said a couple months. That was more than a month ago."

Josip hunched over the table, clasping his hands together. His booming voice became very quiet, as if someone had turned down the volume on a bullhorn. "I didn't want it to be this way between us. I don't want you to die with us being enemies."

"Then why did you do it, Josip?" Nikola said. "All these years I have wondered, how could you do that to me?"

Her father's face crumpled and his eyes moistened. Under his mustache, his lower lip trembled. Nikola deserved an answer. They all did. The question had been waiting for two decades.

Josip ran his fingers through his silver hair and sighed, deep and long. "Nikola, I didn't think we would have this conversation until we were old men. I might have taken it to my grave," Josip said, glancing at Sanja. "When I stole that milk from Sirana after the war, after you and Horvat had privatized Sirana, I was angry. I felt you owed me."

"I owed you?" Nikola said. "I felt you owed me. I shot that Serb who was ready to shoot Luka. I took a bullet in the leg. And I let you have all the glory with Gotovina."

"Let him finish," Dragica said, putting her hand on Nikola's shoulder. "Let's hear what he has to say."

"You're right, Nikola," Josip said. "You were a hero."

Marina wondered if Josip was trying to pacify Nikola, now that he knew her father was dying.

"I didn't try to be a hero. I was trying to save Branko," Nikola said.

"You couldn't have saved him. I saw it with my own eyes. You saved Luka's life, and for that, we are eternally grateful," Josip said.

Marina felt her stomach flutter at the sound of Luka's name. She shifted uncomfortably in her chair. She recalled the scene her father had described, Branko leaping in front of Luka to save his life—a bullet meant for Luka. A bullet that ended Branko's life.

"Branko was a hero, too," Josip said.

"Yes, he was," Nikola said, making the sign of the cross.

"He had his father's courage," Josip said.

"You should be proud," Nikola said.

"No, Nikola. You're not hearing me. He was yours."

"What are you saying?" Nikola said, his forehead creasing.

Sanja pressed her fingers to her lips. Her cheeks were stained with black rivers.

"Branko was your son, Nikola," Josip said.

Marina gasped. Dragica became slack-jawed. Nikola stared at Sanja, who gazed back at him with wide eyes, as if she didn't believe the words had escaped Josip's lips.

Nikola's mustache twitched. With effort, her father raised himself from his chair and started to pace around the room, not bothering to try to hide his limp. His house slippers flapped and dragged like notes in a musical score, one foot sweeping across the floor like a whole note rest, the other interrupting with a half note beat.

"How is this possible?" Nikola said, his voice cracking. He held onto the back of his chair to steady himself.

"I found out I was pregnant when I got back with Josip, and the timing of us getting together was so close to when we broke up, Nikola. It could have been either…." Sanja trailed off.

"Sanja told me after Branko's funeral that he was yours," Josip interrupted. "I married her knowing she was pregnant, but thinking it was mine. I always thought there was something different about that boy. But we tell ourselves stories."

Nikola stopped shuffling. He leaned against the wall where the photo used to hang and wept. Dragica reached for her cup and the contents spilled. She sat perfectly still, watching the coffee stain spread on the white linen tablecloth.

"Sanja, how could you keep this from me?" Nikola said.

Sanja raised her streaked face to the fan and closed her eyes in a silent appeal to God. "When Branko was born, we were given our blood types," Sanja said. "I lost a lot of blood during Branko's birth, and Josip donated his to give me a transfusion. A nurse told me it was impossible Josip was the father. I had married Josip. I knew creating a family with you was impossible, with our families and the way they felt about the division. I had to make a choice, for me and our son."

Marina had had a half-brother. Memories of Branko joining in their adventures at Sirana flooded her head. Branko and Luka and Franko playing soccer together. Branko standing up for Luka when the southern boys teased him about being from a poor fishing village in the north. Branko had always looked so different from Luka; his stocky build was more like Franko's, now that she thought about it. Growing up, she had played games with her half-brother, not knowing they were in any way related. He was dead. She would never know him.

"She didn't tell me until he died that he had your blood," Josip said. "She was tired of carrying such a heavy secret. Do you know what that does to a man, finding out his son is not his son?"

Nikola turned to face Josip. "I don't. But I don't know how you could just walk away from me like that, after all our years of friendship."

"I felt like a fraud. You saved Luka's life, not me. After Branko's funeral, seeing you reminded me too much of him. Even in death, I could see your face in his," Josip said, his eyes wet.

"And so you turned your back on me?" Nikola said.

"I created Janković because I wanted to build a life of our own in the north. I needed to be away from you, Sirana, the south. I needed the same for Sanja and Luka."

"I should have told you. I should have told both of you long ago, and maybe none of this would have happened," Sanja whispered.

"We agreed we wouldn't tell you, but now things have changed," Josip said.

Nikola lowered himself slowly into his chair. "After you left Sirana, I felt you deserted me and I believed you were my enemy. I taught Franko and Marina to distrust northerners, even to despise them, though I'm not sure they listened to me," he said, glancing at Marina. "I should have been better than that. I feel like a fool."

"We've all made mistakes," Josip said, reaching across the table to put his hands over Nikola's. "It's wrong to pass on these old hatreds. It doesn't help anything."

"Does Luka know?" Marina said.

They all turned to her, as if they'd forgotten she was in the room.

"No," Josip said quietly. "I don't want any more bad blood between us."

Marina glanced at her parents. Nikola stared at the Turkish coffee grounds, rotating his cup on the saucer. Dragica hadn't moved her eyes from the stain, which had seeped further into the tablecloth, spreading insidiously.

"Will you tell him now, about Branko?" Marina asked.

"Don't tell him," Nikola said. "Josip is right. We don't need any more bad blood. Our country is joining a new union soon. There is no place for hatred among us."

"And Franko?" Josip said.

"We won't tell him, either. It's better if some things remain unsaid," Dragica said, glancing at Sanja and rising to clear their cups. She removed the tablecloth, which she would later hold over the ribbed metal washboard, rubbing her fingers over the stain with soap until it disappeared.

Marina thought how some stains couldn't be erased, those stains upon history haunting generations, their beliefs about enemies and wrongdoing so deeply entrenched, condemning their children and their children's children to repeat the same mistakes. But they could be different. They could change.

Chapter Eighteen

The cheesemaking season was nearly finished. Marina worked harder, rising earlier than the sun. She felt invisible sweat and tears go into the milk, crystalizing into Sirana's unpasteurized cheese. During those days, everything about her existence felt raw and unpredictable. Each morning, she welcomed the daily hum of activity in the factory, the workers' familiar faces. Anything to distract her from the heavy load she carried in her heart.

When she was alone, the litany played like a song on loop: Her father was dying; her marriage was over; she could not have children; she had a dead half-brother, and she could never mourn him with Franko or Luka. She channeled herself into cheese, and each day, it saved her. Working with her hands was therapeutic, and rubbing each small wheel with oil was like a balm for her soul.

Increasingly, Marina became even more vigilant about the cheese, leaving the production room only for bathroom breaks. She told the cheese all her secrets. She whispered in English, so the workers wouldn't understand, hovering over the vat of curds like a cradle. Sometimes she sang, her soft voice echoing off the tiles. The murmur of machinery had lessened since they'd decided to employ more of the old methods, and the factory assumed a meditative atmosphere. The workers delicately packed the curds and stacked them to drain with care, handling the cheese like a precious object.

The workers gave Marina the same respect as her father, and she had to admit, there was something about having a woman in charge—a Pag woman—that brought a different energy to the factory. They worked hard, with reverence and care. They called her "Gospođa Maržić," despite her telling them the formality was unnecessary, when before they had called her by her first name. Even Igor, who had at first been skeptical of her lack of experience and using thistle rennet, saw she made up for her shortcomings with passion, and he eventually fell in line with the others. But just as Marina felt she was coming into her own, she was losing her guiding force, the man who she had looked up to her entire life. She didn't know what she would do without her father.

She didn't know what she would do without Grandma Badurina, either. At sunrise every day, Grandma Badurina accompanied Marina to Sirana, and she'd also galvanized the other Pag Town grandmothers to help out in the factory, each sharing their own cheesemaking wisdom and lending an extra set of hands. It made Marina proud to see how Sirana continued to bring the town together.

"You're working too hard, dear," Grandma Badurina said, putting a hand on Marina's shoulder.

"I want this one to be perfect," Marina said.

"There's no such thing," Grandma Badurina chuckled, leaning on her cane and adjusting her hairnet.

"I want to make *Tata* proud with our last batch of Grandmother's Cheese."

"You already have. This is the best Pag cheese I've tasted in a long time."

"He's in such bad shape, Grandma. It's so hard to see him like this."

Most days, her father was connected to an IV, which alternately dispensed fluids and morphine. He shuffled from room to room with his IV stand, its metal wheels scraping against the worn wooden floors. Some days, which were becoming increasingly frequent, he rested in the spare bedroom with the shutters closed. In the scorching summer heat, without air-conditioning at her mother's behest, the room felt like a stifling coffin.

"Come, let's take some fresh air. You've barely left this place except to sleep," Grandma Badurina said.

Marina opened the heavy production room door. They squinted into the sunlight. Oppressive heat bore down on them, pressing into their pores.

"I feel like everything is falling apart," Marina said.

"It is a helpless feeling, to see a loved one dying in front of your eyes," Grandma Badurina said. "You were too young to see Grandpa Badurina's slow decline. He got lost, wandered into other people's homes. He started to forget me. Sometimes, he looked at me like I was a stranger, when I'd been his wife for forty years. Eventually, he couldn't recognize your mother. It broke her heart. It broke mine, too."

"With *Tata* it's just happening so quickly," Marina said. "I feel like I should be spending time at home with him. I feel guilty I'm not there. But this is what he wanted, for us to finish the season. I'm trying to carry out his wishes."

"Nikola doesn't want his children to see him this way," Grandma Badurina said. And then she laughed, "It's the first time that he has actually encouraged Franko to go out and play more soccer!" Her face suddenly darkened, and she said, in almost a whisper, "I hope, by the grace of God, he doesn't suffer slowly."

"Let's hope he finds peace," Marina said softly. "I hope to find peace, too. I feel like I'm falling apart."

"Sometimes you need to fall apart to become who you're supposed to be," Grandma Badurina said, embracing her.

Marina squinted up at Sirana's cracked, sun-faded sign. Her family's legacy was contained inside those thick concrete walls. She wanted desperately to protect it, and their cheese family. She felt a kinship with the workers, even with the walls that had sheltered the creation of the cheese that had sustained their family for decades. They had persevered like their ancestors, who had bent over Pag's salt flats for a thousand years, their bare backs blackened by the sun.

"I can't bear to lose *Tata* and our Sirana," Marina said aloud.

"Horvat is keeping his word, isn't he?" Grandma Badurina said.

"We're only a couple weeks away from joining the European Union. After that, Horvat will sell his shares. Probably to the highest bidder."

"Your mother said Nikola was still exploring potential Croatian buyers, who would prefer to be in partnership with you instead of buying your shares outright," Grandma Badurina said.

"Horvat said those offers were too low. He wouldn't budge on the price," Marina said.

"She told me Nikola is speaking with a prospective buyer this afternoon."

"*Tata* didn't mention any prospective buyer coming over today."

It was strange her father didn't mention a buyer stopping by. Nikola was conducting business from home now, and in Croatia, most business was still done face to face. They'd had visits from a cheesemaker from Istria, and one from Slavonia. Neither could afford the price Horvat wanted, which was reasonable by European Union standards but expensive for Croatians.

"Maybe he doesn't want to get your hopes up," Grandma Badurina said.

"I'm not sure I have much hope left," Marina said.

"Keep faith," Grandma Badurina said, grasping Marina firmly by the chin.

Marina was transported to childhood, her grandmother's strong fingers pinched around her jaw. *Chin up,* she'd said, when southern schoolmates excluded her from their games because of Nikola's prominent position, resentful that their fathers worked for him at Sirana. *They're jealous. Just watch. You'll be the one who rises.*

Marina returned home exhausted. She dropped her purse on the bench near the doorway and slid her sticky feet into house slippers. Voices emanated from the spare room, the makeshift office where her father had taken to resting and making phone calls. As she approached the ajar door, she heard an unmistakable voice.

"...pay back over time," Josip said, pausing to glance at Marina, who pushed open the door.

Josip sat on a faded, floral armchair near Nikola's daytime bed. Nikola, dressed in a thin bathrobe, was propped up with pillows against the headrest, curtains drawn. The IV was nearly empty.

"*Tata,* you should be resting," Marina said, rushing to his side. "Where's Mama?"

"She stepped out for some groceries," Nikola said.

"Where is the aide? Your IV is low. It's too hot in here." With nervous fingers, Marina turned up the fan.

"Don't worry, the aide is coming back soon," Nikola said, patting her hand.

Marina still wasn't used to seeing Josip again, especially in their house. Ever since the war ended, he had always been the man who betrayed her father. To come home and suddenly find him sitting by her father's bedside was unsettling.

"What's going on?" Marina said.

"Josip was quite taken with your cheese. We've been talking about Sirana's future," Nikola said.

"Shouldn't I be a part of that conversation?" Marina said, trying to maintain a calm tone. Her temples throbbed.

"I was about to call you. I asked Josip to stop by, because I wanted to speak to him first," Nikola said.

"I heard Sirana is having some financial troubles," Josip said.

"So that's it," Marina said, crossing her arms.

"Give him a chance to speak," Nikola said.

"I was impressed by your cheese," Josip said. "Sanja agreed, we haven't tasted cheese like that on Pag for a long time."

"Thank you. We all worked very hard," Marina said stiffly.

"That cheese needs to be out in the world," Josip said.

"It will. We'll enter it in the World Cheese Awards in November," she said.

November was five months away. She realized, as she said those words, that her father would probably not be alive then.

"I'm sure it will do very well," Josip said.

"Of course, it will do well," Marina said. "Although I'm sure you've also heard the rumors that Sirana might not even be ours anymore."

"Listen. I've never been fond of your father's brother, and what he's doing to your father and to Sirana is low, even for him," Josip said.

"And what about you? About what you have done to my father?" Marina snapped.

"Marina, don't speak that way," Nikola said.

"It's true, I am not without fault here either, and I want to make that right," Josip said. "Horvat put your father, your family, in a difficult position. I'm in a position to help."

Marina's eyes widened. "You want to buy Horvat's shares?"

"I've been blessed with the Janković factory. But it's been a long time since I've worked with my hands. We hired a dairy technologist ten years ago, and I've mainly managed the operations, but these days Luka is doing most of that work. Our families, well, let's say they have a history. I can help Sirana, and I want to do that, if you'll allow me."

Marina turned to her father incredulously. "All of a sudden he wants to help? I can't believe you will accept this."

Nikola took her hand. "Marina, this is ultimately your decision. But please hear the man out."

Josip cleared his throat. "I would buy Horvat's shares at his asking price, and I will relinquish the ability to replace you as CEO. Instead, under the new terms, I would work alongside you as Sirana's dairy technologist."

"You can't be serious," Marina said.

"I would only invest in something that I think has potential, and you have shown me Sirana can be resurrected," Josip said. "Moreover, you've shown you can lead. You had the foresight to seek out the Basque girl's expertise, and you learned from her. When those shit Soviet machines broke, you pivoted and made Grandmother's Cheese, an innovative homage to our roots. You are forward-thinking, Marina. A problem solver. Sirana needs someone like you."

Marina remembered her father always saying that Josip had a propensity for charm, flattering people until they succumbed to his wishes. Still, what Josip was saying was how she wanted to see herself, who she wanted to be. Maybe that was his gift: reflecting a person's potential—how they desired to appear to others. Maybe it was Luka's gift, too.

"What happens if we have different ideas for Sirana's future? Or for the cheese?" Marina said.

"We both want Sirana to succeed," Josip said. "If I would join you in a partnership, I'd have a clearly vested interest. We would work together to continue what you've already started with Grandmother's Cheese. I wouldn't interfere with your vision or management. We can state that clearly in the new terms."

"Tell her about buying back the shares," Nikola said.

"As part of this, you and your family would be able to buy back shares in Sirana over time, as you save money," Josip said.

"Why would you do that?" Marina said.

"You would be buying them back at a higher price, as the value of the shares rise and the company becomes profitable," Josip said.

"So you would profit from Sirana," Marina said. "You would make a lot of money if we succeed."

"I'm a businessman, Marina," Josip said. "Like I told you, I only invest where I see potential. But this is also a way for me to make reparation. I owe a debt to your father."

The aide knocked on the door.

"Come in," Nikola said, coughing.

"Let us discuss this, and we'll let you know," Marina said.

"Take your time," Josip said, rising from the chair. As soon as he'd said the words, Marina could see by his expression that he wanted to take them back. Time was not on their side.

The aide replaced Nikola's IV bag and gave him a dose of morphine. Nikola's face relaxed. To an onlooker who didn't know he was dying from cancer, he might have appeared blissful. After the aide left, Marina sat in the faded, floral armchair, tucking strands of damp hair behind her ears.

"*Tata*, how can you trust that man?" Marina said.

Nikola closed his eyes. "*Mala*, as I said before, this is ultimately your decision. Josip's proposal seems fair, and, like he said, he wants to pay back what he took from us. From Sirana."

"Can you really see us working together?"

Nikola's eyes fluttered open. "Above all else, he respects hard work and craftsmanship. He wouldn't lie about believing in what you've made."

"So he wins. He'll have his successful cheese factory in the north, and also a stake in Sirana."

"If we let foreigners buy Sirana, we will lose what is ours forever. This way, you and Franko can slowly buy it back, bit by bit."

"You think he'll keep his word?" Marina said.

"If he betrays us again, God help him," Nikola said, making the sign of the cross.

"After we buy back Josip's shares in who knows how many years, after we completely control Sirana, we will go back to being competitors," Marina said. "And Josip will have more money than God."

"If Sirana succeeds, everyone will have more than enough money," Nikola said. "Anyway, your Grandmother's Cheese is different than the cheese he is making at his factory."

"And what's to stop him from copying us and doing the same at Janković, once he knows our process?"

"You can specify that in the terms of the contract, and you can always invent something new," Nikola said. "I believe in you, and I am so proud of you. I wish I could be around for more years to see your bright future. I love you, *Mala*."

"I love you too, *Tata*." Marina held back tears.

Nikola yawned and closed his eyes. Morphine coursed through his veins. Marina put her palm under his nostrils and felt a tickle of air. She watched his chest laboriously rise and fall, then rose from the chair, quietly shutting the door behind her.

The screen door banged behind Franko. His T-shirt was stained from sweat.

"Shh, *Tata*'s resting," Marina scolded.

"It's a sauna out there," Franko said, wiping his brow.

"Did you finish the deliveries already?" Marina said.

"Yeah," Franko said. "They were all near Zadar, so I didn't have to go too far."

"Listen, we should talk."

"What about?" he said, opening the refrigerator and popping the cap off a cold beer on the edge of the counter.

"Plans for Sirana," Marina said.

"*Ej*, you're the boss," Franko said, raising his hands in a pose of surrender.

"Franko, I'm serious."

"*Tata* chose you to run Sirana, so why do you need to talk to me?" Franko said, chugging the beer.

"When he leaves us, it will be you and me. I want your input, Franko."

Franko paused, setting the half-empty bottle on the counter. "He always did the best for you. He sent you to America during the war, while I had to stay here and fight. You decide to come back, and he chooses you to take his place."

"You can't blame me for this. You've been here all this time and you haven't even shown an interest in Sirana," Marina said.

"I'm his son," Franko said.

"He chose me. You need to accept that. We're family, and I want you to be involved."

"What is it, then?" Franko took a swig of beer and crossed his arms.

"We spoke to a potential investor today. I know this is going to sound crazy, but it's Josip Janković."

Franko spat the mouthful of beer into the sink. "That's a joke."

"He's willing to buy out Horvat."

"I'd rather see the Basques buy Sirana than have a northerner's claws in our family's business," Franko said darkly.

"Don't be foolish, Franko. Josip wants to make up for the past. He would become Sirana's dairy technologist, at least for a time, but we would have control of the vision and operations. And we could buy back the shares little by little, as we saved money."

"Don't you remember what *Tata* said? Never trust a northerner."

"*Tata* supports this idea. We need to start working with them, Franko. We all live on the same island, and no one else knows or cares about Pag's division. We have to stop our petty fighting and jealousies. The European Union is large, and we will be competing against established cheeses. In order for us to stand out and succeed, we need to be united."

"So, you're saying just forget the past?" Franko said.

"We don't have to forget it. We can embrace it, and move on."

Franko opened the wastebasket and tossed in the bottle. "You're fine working with Luka's father?" he said quietly.

Marina took a deep breath. In the back of her mind she knew, if she lived on Pag and worked at Sirana, she would continue to encounter Luka. They would see each other running errands in Zadar, and at cheese competitions. When she ventured up to the northern olive groves or beaches, Zara and Kata might be there. They would coexist on a skinny strip of land, surrounded by sea, with an imperceptible border marked by stone, a *suhozid* wall that resembled all the others.

"One way or another, we need to learn to work together," she said, placing her hand firmly on her brother's shoulder.

Chapter Nineteen

arina did not buy a new black dress. Her father would not have approved. She decided on a sleeveless A-line with a square neckline and a modest hem that fell just above her knees. She'd bought the dress on sale at a store on Fifth Avenue, justifying the high price tag with its versatility: It could be dressed up or down depending on the occasion. The dress had accompanied her to the office and on dates with Marko, when he used to take her out to restaurants in Manhattan. When she was little and Dragica bought Marina expensive imported dresses for church that she would outgrow in a season, Nikola counted the dresses in wheels of cheese. "That's fifty wheels!" he would say, holding up his hand to emphasize how much cheese he would have to sell to make back the money spent on a dress she would wear once a week, in front of God.

Marina smoothed the fine black fabric. She combed her hair and formed it into a bun. Around her slender neck, she fastened a delicate gold cross, which had belonged to Nikola's mother, her late Grandma Maržić. In the mirror, her grim face staring back at her, she rimmed her eyes with a black pencil and coated her lashes in mascara. She put on lipstick, a shade of light pink appropriate for church.

Nikola died on June 30, the day before Croatia joined the European Union. It was as if he couldn't bear to witness another transition after Croatia had gained its hard-won independence, clinging to their country's past even in death. Like his beloved Yugo, which had eventually stopped running, he never quite recovered from Yugoslavia's demise. In his delirium, he rambled on about Tito's death and the death of Yugoslavia, the breakup of republics that had been forcibly held together by Tito's fist. Marina hadn't realized how much the division of their country had torn him apart. Near the end, Nikola asked for morphine repeatedly, more than the aide could give him. Dragica begged the aide to make an exception, to give the man some peace in his final days, but the woman could not take away his pain. No one could.

Dragica went to wake Nikola that last morning and found him sleeping peacefully in the spare room. She opened the curtains, and when he didn't stir, she'd put her hand gently on top of his and knew then, by the touch of his skin, that he was gone. Marina awoke to her mother's cries; she knew what had happened before she and Franko rushed in the room and knelt by their father's deathbed.

Pag Town had never seen such a crowd. A procession of people spilled out of the Church of St. Mary's Assumption, into the square and narrow cobblestone alleyways that converged into a cross through the heart of the town. From the church façade, the solemn saints, etched in limestone, gazed down on them. When she was little, Marina thought the delicate stone rosette was God's portal through which Mary was swept up to Heaven. Marina hadn't prayed in years, but as she approached the entrance, she said a prayer to Mary, and hoped that the Blessed Virgin had led her father from his earthly life to something divine.

Marina turned her face upward. A flight of swifts darted through the sky: a symbol of hope. She remembered learning in school that swifts spend their entire lives in motion, almost never touching the ground once they learn to fly. Like dark, restless angels, the tiny air pilgrims skim the upper atmosphere, brushing the heavens with their scythe-like wings.

The crowd parted to make way for Marina, Franko, Grandma Badurina, and Dragica. Her mother's eyes were swollen; she had been crying for days. In her trembling fingers, she clutched a rosary. Franko followed his sister under the scorching July sun with heavy steps into the Church of St. Mary's Assumption, passing under the stone portal's lunette. Their dress shoes clicked against the checkered salmon-and-white marble floor. The masses of people were silent. Handheld fans beat the hot air like fluttering wings.

As Marina stepped inside, she dipped her fingers in holy water and made the sign of the cross. The sweet, thick scent of incense filled her nostrils. Out of the corner of her eye, Marina noticed that, despite the overwhelming crowd, Josip, Sanja, Luka, Zara, and Kata had managed to find a pew in the back. Josip bowed his head. Sanja held her hand over the gold cross around her neck. Luka laced his hands together, his eyes trained on the pew in front. Zara held Kata's hand. Kata stared at Marina.

"I know you!" Kata said, piercing the reverent silence. She lunged away from Zara and ran towards Marina.

"Kata!" Zara exclaimed.

"It's alright," Marina said, bending down on her knee to meet the girl's blue eyes, clear as the sea. "I know you, too."

"You look different," Kata said, studying her.

Marina thought back to the person she'd been when she came to Pag the previous summer, not knowing then that she would stay.

"I suppose I am," Marina said. "When I was feeling sad in the olive groves last summer, you made me feel so much better. I'll never forget it." Tears filled her eyes.

"Ivo isn't here, but I can still hear him, all the way from the north," Kata whispered in Marina's ear, cupping her hand on the side of her mouth. "He says you're strong, like him."

Marina smiled. "Only the stubborn and strong survive here. You'll grow up to be a strong girl, too," she said, echoing the words the elders had told her when she was small.

Kata pranced back to her mother, who held her hand firmly. "What did she say to you?" Zara asked, but Kata only smiled.

Marina rejoined her mother, grandmother, and brother. As she passed the overflowing pews, faces blended together: the butcher and the baker's brood, her elementary school teacher, the cashier at Konzum, a barista from the former Café Zec, Dr. Miletić, workers from Sirana, Ivana and her family. People gathered to mourn the life of a man whom many had called the mayor of Pag Town. There were strangers, too, people who had come from the north or the mainland to pay their respects to her father, who had made an impression on them in ways large or small. Through the people who gathered, Marina felt what it meant to be loved. Her father had taken care of people, and they remembered.

Later, Marina would collect their stories: how her father helped an old fisherman repair his boat when the man's gnarled hands had become too arthritic to perform the work himself; how Nikola gave a small loan to a new widow—one of the town's prized lace makers, who relied mostly on summer tourists to buy her expensive handicraft—to carry her through winter; how, one night when the *bura* was strong, he invited a man from the mainland delivering meat to the island during the war to stay overnight in their house until the strong winds passed and it was safe to drive again. Men who had fought with him during the war spoke of his bravery, his leadership on the battlefield, the way he looked after his own and united the island in solidarity. Marina held these stories in the deepest chambers of her heart, where she stored the sound of his laugh—a place it could never be forgotten.

Ascending the red carpeted steps, they approached the altar, which was covered in white roses. Marina fixed her eyes on the statue of the Madonna, cloaked in royal blue robes and seated on a golden throne. Beneath the altar, her father's body rested in a shiny casket. His face appeared waxy, and in the heat, he appeared to be perspiring. They had molded his features into a pose of serenity. But he didn't look like her father—Nikola was nowhere in the slack, absent face. Her *Tata* was gone.

Marina knelt on the hard, marble floor in front of her father's coffin. She touched his hand lightly and recoiled. She prayed his soul was resting. She had never prayed for peace with so much might—peace for her father, her country, her island. And for her own life. She understood now what it meant to forgive: It meant choosing peace. Marina didn't want to fight anymore, not with the northerners, with Marko, with Josip, or with Luka. She didn't want to fight with herself, the raging inner battle that had consumed her since her miscarriage, tearing her apart. They could blame each other for the past, reaching back to the king who divided Pag between two bishops centuries ago; they could blame their neighbors for the war; they could point fingers for centuries to come. And what good would that be, if they could never surrender?

When she turned around to descend from the platform and take a seat with her family in the front pew, she saw Marko's face in the crowd. At first, she thought she was hallucinating in the heat. She became sure of her sight when her mother leaned over and whispered, "Your husband is here."

After their last conversation, when Marina had announced she was staying on Pag to take her father's place at Sirana, Marko wrote to inform her that he would be sending divorce papers, since they'd been legally married in New York City. Only the church ceremony had been on Pag. Marina had married Marko in the Church of St. Mary's Assumption, standing at the very altar where her father's coffin now lay. They had planned to baptize their child in this church, when they thought they would be having a daughter.

Marko had surely heard the news of Nikola's death from his grandparents, who were back for the summer at their house in the north. It was a long way to come for the funeral of an estranged wife's father. Marina was touched by the gesture. She wondered if he had come to try to reconcile, and that possibility sat heavy on her chest.

They rose for the priest, who began his sermon, then sat again at his command. His words echoed off the old stone walls and she felt their vibrations in her body. Marina clutched her handwritten eulogy in her damp palm, nervously tapping her knee. Finding words to express what losing her father meant to her, to their family, to Pag Town, had been excruciating. Each time she completed a draft of what she thought she'd say, she felt like a failure. In the end, she accepted that no words were adequate to convey their loss.

Dragica approached the podium. "Thank you all for coming," she began. "It would mean so much to Nikola to know you were all here. He loved all of you, this town, our island." Dragica paused, her lip quivering. Her eyes rested on the back pew where Sanja and Josip sat. "Nikola taught me that we are connected in ways we don't even realize. He taught me how to love, and I loved him more than anything. He was the bravest man I've ever known. He fought for our country, and for our children. He was the best father. I couldn't imagine a life without him if it were not for our beautiful children. God bless them."

Dragica made the sign of the cross. Tears streamed down her cheeks as she descended the stairs. Marina took her mother's hand, and Franko took the other. Marina had never understood her mother's sacrifices until now. Her mother had known Nikola had loved Sanja, but Dragica loved him more.

"Marina, it's your time." Dragica squeezed her hand.

Marina ascended the stairs to the podium and adjusted the microphone. "I was fortunate to have Nikola as my father. As many of you have told me, he was like a father to so many on Pag. Like my mother said, he loved all of you, and he always wanted the best for everyone. He was a generous man, and did whatever he could to help others."

Marina glanced up from her paper. Fans fluttered like a flight of a thousand swifts.

"We have immense pride in our island, our people, our salt, and our cheese. Over centuries, we have constructed barriers to divide ourselves, walls that rely on tradition over reason. In one of my favorite poems, a neighbor keeps pointlessly rebuilding a stone wall as a ritual every spring, even though it's unnecessary, because his father taught him that good fences make good neighbors. For him, following tradition is more important than practicality or innovation. My father believed in tradition, but he also believed we need to reinvent ourselves. He believed the next generation needs to usher in a new age on Pag. As most of you know, I am taking his place at Sirana, and I can't imagine how I will step into his large shoes. Some of you might not know that Josip Janković has helped us save our beloved Sirana."

Murmurs rippled throughout the congregation.

"It was my father's dying wish that we find a way to heal our divisions. We inherit many good things from our fathers, but we must question ritual for the sake of ritual. Old walls serve to keep us apart; when they crumble, as they do over time, we don't need to rebuild them. My father believed we are stronger without our walls."

Marina took a deep breath. "I hope you will all honor my father's memory by embracing your neighbors in a new way, whether you are from the north or south. In the future, let's build *suhozidi* to corral our sheep, not to divide ourselves."

The sound of fluttering fans died down. And then, Josip made his way towards the front of the church. He adjusted the microphone and surveyed the pews. He bent his head and cleared his throat.

"I wasn't going to say anything, but now I feel I must," Josip began, grasping the edges of the podium. His voice had grown softer. "As Marina said, we must honor Nikola's wishes and find a way to heal our divisions. Nikola was my best friend for many years, before our falling out. He was like a brother to me. I valued his friendship, and I valued who he was as a person: his honesty, his selflessness. We fought side by side in the war. He was braver than me, and a better man."

Josip paused, wiping perspiration from his forehead with the back of his giant hand. "Nikola was a hero. He saved Luka's life."

Hushed whispers filled the pews. Marina glanced at her mother, whose eyes were wide. Marina craned her neck to glance at the back pew. Luka's face was ashen.

"He watched out for everyone," Josip continued. "I remember how he always took care of people, even singing to the men when we were heading off to Operation Storm, and they would start singing with him. He had a way of making everyone feel better and he always kept up our spirits. He was a true leader, like his daughter. I missed his companionship over the years, and I regret spending so many years apart now that he is gone. I regret many things. I wish I'd come to explain myself to him sooner. Maybe we could have understood each other and reconciled, if I had just been honest about the past." He looked up at the domed ceiling. "Nikola, my friend, may you rest in peace."

In the square after the funeral, people came to give Marina's family their condolences and express how touched they were by the service. Marina knew old wounds took time to heal, especially on Pag, but at least this was progress. She hoped her father, looking down on them, would approve. She had done her best to honor his memory. As he'd always told her growing up, "Do your best, Marina. That's all you can do."

Uncle Horvat, who had been lurking in the back in a black suit and dark sunglasses completely inappropriate for church, approached to give his condolences. He was barrel-chested like Nikola, with the same thick fingers. She couldn't see his eyes behind his dark sunglasses. A wide-brimmed black hat shaded his face.

"My best to you and your family during these very sad times," Horvat said, reaching out in an awkward embrace.

People milled around the square, watching Marina's reaction out of the corners of their eyes. Crooked as he was, Marina knew she had to forgive him, at least in appearance. If her father could forgive Josip, she could forgive her uncle. For now, she had to set an example. Marina took a deep breath.

"Thank you, Uncle," Marina said, leaning into his arms.

"I'm glad it all worked out," Horvat said, patting her back.

"We are, too," Marina said, forcing a smile.

"My brother was a good man," he said. "And you are your father's daughter."

"I'm blessed he was my father."

She knew Nikola would have praised her diplomacy.

After giving his condolences to Dragica, Franko, and Grandma Badurina, Uncle Horvat tipped his hat and disappeared down a side lane. At least he had made an appearance out of respect. Nikola had told her about feuds in their family where siblings didn't even bother to turn up at funerals, perpetuating grudges with their children and their children's children, generations of spite. Marina hoped that if anything could come of her father's death, it would be small gestures of forgiveness, the ability to repair.

Marko lingered at the edge of the square, waiting until the last of the congregants had paid their respects. Marina had been watching him, nervously glancing in his direction on occasion. At last, he approached.

"Marko," Dragica said, taking his hand. "Thank you for coming."

"Of course," Marko said. "Deepest condolences for your loss."

"Thank you for coming," Marina echoed, in a tone she knew sounded unnecessarily formal. After a year of not seeing him, her husband appeared like an apparition from a long-ago past, a surreal reemergence through her opaque grief. He looked weary.

Marko cleared his throat. "Marina, could we take a walk by Tale?"

"We have to get home and lay out all the food," Dragica said, tugging at Franko's sleeve in the direction of home. "Marina, you go."

"Are you sure, Mama? So many people will be stopping by. You'll need help."

Dragica pulled Marina into a tight embrace. "You've done so much already," she whispered. "Your father would have been proud. I'm proud, too."

In those simple words, Marina understood that her mother finally saw her. She saw the woman she had become. "Mama," Marina said, wiping her eyes. "You've done so much for us. You've given us everything."

Marina and Marko walked in silence towards Tale Bay, down the lane of white cobblestones leading to the sea. In the sunlight, the water glittered like millions of glass shards. Marina recalled the beer bottle she had knocked to the floor the summer before when Marko had told her about his affair, how it caught the light like dangerous gems, reflecting her rage. She realized how lonely she'd been, standing in front of him.

"What you said in there was beautiful," Marko said, taking off his shoes.

"Thank you," Marina said, taking off her heels and letting her bare feet press on the stones.

"It made me think about us," Marko said.

"In what way?" Marina asked.

"Everything you said about healing our divisions. I thought about our marriage."

Marina gazed at the bald hills on either side of Tale Bay that plummeted into the sea, forming a gaping mouth that led into open waters. She wondered how much of their island wasn't visible, how much of the foundation lay beneath the clear, deep saltwater.

"I've done a lot of thinking about our marriage, too," she said.

"I know I've been distant, and you always say I'm unavailable. I couldn't understand how to move past losing our daughter. But hearing you speak—I thought it might be possible for us to repair, too."

Marina breathed in the salty air. "Our unhappiness began long before we lost our daughter. We never quite saw each other, I think.

And if I've learned anything in this past year on Pag, it's that you can't live in what used to be."

"I just thought," he began. "I thought we could try again, here. I could move to Pag, and we could see. I could help you with Sirana. For God's sakes, it's what I do for a living."

Marina thought of Marko's rows and columns, the spreadsheets he used to organize and make sense out of messy life. He distilled people's problems into figures, but numbers couldn't fix them.

She stopped and reached for Marko's hand. "I can't go back to how things were, Marko," she said. "Things are different now."

"I can see that," Marko said, his eyes filling with tears. "I can change, too."

She led him to a nearby bench—the same bench, she realized, where she had spoken with him last summer, when she'd thrown her phone and cracked its screen. Marko's eyes were fixed on two young children tossing rocks, tiny explosions disturbing the sea's calm surface. Their shrieks pierced the air.

"You want children," Marina said.

"I don't have to have them," Marko said.

"No," Marina said, shaking her head.

"I want you," Marko said.

How badly she wanted to be wanted; how badly she wanted to believe him. She knew how easy it would be to fall into their old, familiar patterns, the ease of sliding out of the driver's seat into a cozy, supporting role. He would always want her to be someone else. He would always want children of his own.

"No," Marina repeated, tears filling her eyes. "Our time has passed, Marko."

Marko put his arms around her. She felt numb; he could no longer touch her in a way that cut beneath the skin.

"We need to let each other go," Marina said.

"God, Marina. I don't know how to do this."

"I don't either," Marina said. "But we have to learn."

The children shrieked. Marina stared at the Adriatic, its alluring, aching blue. She wanted to plow into the depths beyond Tale Bay, into the gaping mouth, broaching the wide, open sea.

Chapter Twenty

Marina and Franko exited the Tube stop in the dreary Docklands. It was Franko's first time to London, and Marina noticed her brother's wide eyes. "Look at the crowd," he said. The sea of black suits emptied from the train. Franko had visited her once in New York, fascinated with the subways and crowds of people that seemed to flow through the procession of stops in uninterrupted streams that collided and dispersed. Everyone on their way somewhere, and always in a hurry. The November weather was brisk, heavy with impending rain. This time, Marina came prepared with umbrellas.

They entered the enormous hall under a banner with an image of a globe and a gavel that read: World Cheese Awards, London, 2013. Josip had offered to arrange for a cab to transport Sirana's and Janković's materials. Marina told him they should split the fare in half, reflecting their divided shares in Sirana, but he had insisted on paying. "Let me at least do this," he'd said. Since her father's death, Josip had reached out regularly, asking if their family needed any help. Dragica politely refused any financial help, indicating that what he had done for Sirana was enough.

This year, since Croatia had joined the European Union, they were not grouped with their Serbian and Bosnian neighbors. Croatia's Slovenian neighbors to the north, also EU members, shared half of the table, while the other half was divided between Janković and Sirana. As Marina and Franko approached, Josip stepped in front of the table to greet them.

"I took the liberty of setting up," Josip said. "I hope you don't mind."

Sirana's pamphlets were neatly arranged at the end of the table, along with a wheel of Grandmother's Cheese from Marina's final batch made in late June, as the season was ending. Just before her father passed away. It bore a new label, an old *nana* dressed in black, surrounded by sheep on a rugged limestone pasture overlooking the azure sea. The grandmother hunched over a barrel, stirring milk with a paddle, patiently waiting for it to curdle. Marina had designed the label as an homage to the women cheesemakers of Pag's past. Women had milked the sheep; they had stirred countless batches of milk with their strong arms; they formed curds into wheels with able hands; they coated them with salt and submerged them in brine; they turned the wheels as they aged, tenderly rubbing them with rich oil from the fruits of the island's ancient olive trees.

A piece of Pag lace, framed with olive wood, was displayed on an easel. In school, Marina was taught that the olive branch, a symbol of peace for the ancient Greeks, was also used by the ancient Romans, who had inhabited Pag; during war, they would hold an olive branch to indicate they were pleading for peace. Marina had often wondered whether that was the reason the Venetians had left the olive trees to thrive on Pag, cutting down all the others for wood to build their ships and city, shaving the

THE CHEESEMAKER'S DAUGHTER

island bald. Over centuries, the olive trees remained, timeless columns—*stupovi*, as locals called them—bracing against the *bura* and marked by families who claimed them.

"It's a nice touch," Marina said, gesturing to the intricate web of lace.

"Luka's idea," Josip said, nodding to his son, who was busy arranging boxes of cheese beneath the table. "It was also his idea to display our cheese on olive wood from our northern groves."

"I brought one for Sirana, too," Luka said, rummaging in a box and handing the olive wood cutting board to her.

"That was very thoughtful," Marina said.

The patterns of the grain told the story of the tree's life. Like all the others, it had endured favorable and less favorable conditions, drought and cold, years of *bura*, which had bent its limbs and forced its trunk to bow. It was dead, this piece of wood cut from a cross section of its body.

As Marina accepted the cutting board from Luka's hands, their eyes met. She hadn't seen him since the funeral. She could hardly believe that just a year before, they had been together in this city. They had sat in a dark pub talking about Branko, the half-brother she never knew she had. Luka knew her in a way no one else did. He held parts of her no one else could understand. Now, she held his parents' secret.

It was a burden, keeping Branko's paternity from Luka; in another way, it bonded them. Marina didn't want to risk rekindling the feud between their families. So much would remain unsaid. They would have to live that way. As much as she yearned to return, they could never go back to that place. She could never be as she had been.

"How have you been?" Luka said, trying for a casual tone.

"Busy. Catching up with the business, and *Tata's* affairs," Marina said.

For the remainder of the summer and well into fall, Marina had sequestered herself in her father's office, poring over paperwork and trying to learn parts of the business her father hadn't had time to teach her. She'd sat at her father's desk for hours, deciphering his shorthand, calling up distributors and sending Franko to collect money that was owed to Sirana. There was nothing more she could do to prepare for the World Cheese Awards. The cheese had been made back in June and had gestated in the aging room, rotated and caressed by careful hands. Her father had tasted early batches of Grandmother's Cheese, but had died before the last one was ready.

"And you, Franko?" Luka said. "How is it out on the field these days?"

Franko, who had been silently taking in the buzz of the hall and the staggering rows of tables overflowing with cheese, turned his attention to Luka.

"I haven't been playing much," Franko said flatly.

"That's not like you," Luka said.

"There are more important things than soccer," Franko said.

Marina raised her eyebrows in mock surprise. Her brother was serious.

"Hello, John," Josip said in accented English, reaching out to shake their distributor's hand.

"Good day," John said. "I see you're all set here."

"Yes," Josip said. "You remember Marina, from Sirana? You met her here last year, and at SIAL."

"Of course. You were really on to something there, with that cheese," John said, referring to Céline's batch.

"Marina, you remember John, our London distributor from Dissa?" Josip said.

"Nice to see you again," Marina said.

"What's this?" John said, pointing to the wheel of Grandmother's Cheese.

"This is something special," Josip said, before Marina could reply.

"It's called Grandmother's Cheese," Marina said. "We went back to our old island methods, coating the cheese with ash, and also made some new, modern improvements."

"Interesting," John said. "I've been to Pag and tasted homemade cheese from makers selling along the roadside. Is it like that?"

"Why don't you try it," Marina said, slicing open the wrapping with a knife.

Marina cut the cheese on the olive board and offered it to John. He examined the slice, taking in its pale golden color, the ash rind like a slash of seaweed on their shore's cheek. John bit into the cheese and chewed. They all watched his ruddy face transform as his blissful expression turned contemplative.

"This is something extraordinary," John said finally. "It's familiar, ancient in a way, but it's also something completely new and unique."

"Thank you. We did our best," Marina said.

John would never know all that went into that final batch. It possessed the flavors of their island, but also something intangible that unlocked memory for those who tasted it. Grandma Badurina had explained the unpredictable alchemy of the old cheesemaking methods. "You think you can control the process, that it will turn out one way, but the cheese has a mind of its own."

So John would never know that what he tasted was Marina's tears, her deep longing for home, for family, for belonging; the pride of Sirana's workers, who cared for the cheese like children; their fight for survival. It held all her secrets, but it held the truth as well. It was a noble cheese. She had made it for her father.

The Best Central and Eastern European Sheep's Milk Cheese awards were held in the same South Gallery Meeting Room. A panel of five judges sat on the stage behind a long table. Marina and Josip were sandwiched between Luka and Franko on stiff auditorium seats. Marina could hardly believe that only a year before, she had sat next to Luka on these same seats as the judges decided their fates. This year, she was not nervous. She heard her father's voice: "Do your best. That's all you can do."

"Welcome," the announcer said. "We're pleased to announce the winners of the 2013 World Cheese Awards in the Best Central and Eastern European Sheep's Milk Cheese category."

Marina glanced at Franko. His expression was solemn. She took her brother's hand.

"This year had strong contenders, and our judges made some difficult decisions. The depth and variety of flavors were truly astounding."

Marina looked to her left, at Josip. His eyes were fixed on the judges. For both of them, it was not just a matter of bringing home an award for the sake of glory. Awards affected distribution and future financing. A win for either of them would be good for Pag and their island's cheese, Marina reminded herself, increasing their visibility in the European Union marketplace.

"For bronze, in third place, Kovač Bovec cheese from Bovec, Slovenia. Congratulations on a total score of forty," the announcer said.

A voluptuous woman with rosy cheeks took her place on the stage. Marina remembered her from the previous year, when her cheese placed second. The audience clapped as she shook the judges' hands and accepted her award with a broad smile.

"For silver, in second place, Janković, Pag cheese from Pag Island, Croatia. Congratulations on a nearly perfect score of forty-nine."

"Congratulations," Marina said, shaking Josip's hand as he rose from the chair.

"*Hvala*," Josip said.

Luka and Josip ascended the stage and shook the judges' hands.

"And the gold winner of the 2013 World Cheese Awards in the Best Central and Eastern European Sheep's Milk Cheese category is…"

Marina sucked in her breath and squeezed Franko's hand.

"Sirana, Grandmother's Cheese, also from Pag Island, Croatia. It's our first time awarding two cheeses from the same island, with such close scores. Congratulations on your gold award, with a perfect score of fifty," the announcer said.

Franko pounded the arms of the auditorium chair with an enthusiasm usually reserved for when his beloved Hajduk Split soccer team scored a goal. He kissed Marina on the cheeks. "*Bravo, sestro*," he shouted. Bewildered, Marina ascended the steps to the stage with Franko. The announcer handed her the microphone.

"Thank you," Marina said, squinting into the bright lights. "Sirana's cheese this year was a labor of love. We did something different, and we are so proud of our Grandmother's Cheese, a homage to Pag Island's cheesemaking roots, to our tradition, and also our ability to transform in new ways. As my own grandmother told me, 'Great cheese always requires a little magic.' I'd like to dedicate this award to our father, Nikola, who was the soul of Sirana. And to the entire Janković family; without their support, we would not be standing here today. This gold belongs to Pag—to our entire island."

Josip and Luka were the first to clap. The auditorium slowly erupted in applause. It was unlikely anyone in the audience knew what Marina meant about the gold belonging to Pag, but Josip and Luka understood. Centuries ago, their island's gold had been salt. Now, Pag's gold was cheese. And their entire island would share the wealth.

As they exited through the sea of people, Marina cradling the golden plaque in her arms, a familiar face emerged.

"Congratulations," Céline said. "I see you learned to listen to the cheese."

"I talked to it, too," Marina said.

"Our condolences. We heard about your father," she said, fingering her pearl necklace. Céline liked to fidget, never staying still for long.

"From Horvat?" Marina said, narrowing her eyes.

"Horvat called us after the funeral. He's helping us broker another deal with a cheese factory in Slavonia. It's in distress. Some unpaid debts."

"For months, I've been wondering, how can you do this to people?" Marina said.

"It's business, Marina," Céline said.

"This was personal. You know it was."

Marina wanted to say she thought they had been friends. She hadn't realized how dangerous Céline was, the strength of her seduction. Marina studied her bright eyes; she was a mesmerizing viper.

"I'm sorry, but for me it was truly just business," Céline said.

"Was it?" Franko said.

Marina felt her brother's presence looming behind her. Céline's mouth twitched. Her face dropped for a second to reveal a glimpse of tenderness; had Marina blinked, she would have missed it.

"I'll let you two talk," Marina said.

She did not want to carry hatred, but it would take longer to forgive Céline than Horvat. After all, Horvat was family.

Marina turned around and bumped into a very attractive man with tanned olive skin and warm green eyes. "Excuse me," she said.

"No excuses needed," he said, smiling. "I was looking for you, but you disappeared."

"Oh, really?" she said.

"Marina, right? I'm Andy," he said, extending his hand. "I was sitting with my boss in the audience. Congratulations on your gold, really well-deserved."

"Thanks," she said, shaking his hand. Her stomach fluttered.

"He's a Croatian winemaker out of Napa. My boss, I mean." He shifted his weight from one foot to the other.

"Oh, okay. I thought you were a cheesemaker."

"Nope, just wine. Well, actually, we have a new collaboration with a northern California cheesemaker. We're producing a Merlot goat's milk cheese together. We're calling it, 'Goats Love Vines.'"

"That sounds delicious," Marina said. She couldn't look away from him.

"It's incredible. You should try it, I'll send you some. But I wanted to talk to you about something else. I'm sure you know zinfandel is originally from Croatia."

"Most people don't know that," Marina said, smiling.

"Right? When my boss told me, I couldn't believe it. He brought some old vine zinfandel cuttings over from Croatia when he came to America. Anyway, we thought it would be interesting to do a collaboration. Your cheese, infused with our wine."

"Grandmother's Cheese, with zinfandel?"

"It could be a love story. A Croatian cheese made with old methods, with wine from ancient Croatian vines, grown on American soil."

"I love it," Marina blurted. Her mind was already working.

"Oh, good," he said, blushing. "I'm relieved. I was really hoping to get the opportunity to work with you. I love what you've done with Grandmother's Cheese. People have been talking about it here, even before it won."

"Really?"

"Yeah. It's impressive how you went back to your roots. You managed to do something different, but still honor tradition."

"That's nice of you to say," Marina said, blushing. "Living half my life in America gave me perspective. I don't think I could have made this cheese if I'd lived my entire life on Pag."

"I know what you mean," he said. "My ancestry is from Sicily, and my family used to be winemakers there. When they came to America, a lot of that connection to the land was lost. I think that's one of the reasons why I got into wine. That, and the fact that I can't sit in an office all day."

Marina laughed. "Actually, that's mostly what I do."

"Have you ever been to Napa?"

"No," she said.

"We'll have to get you out West," he said, winking. "Let's keep in touch. I think this could be really exciting."

"Me too."

"See you in California," he said, waving and disappearing into the crowd.

"Careful!" Marina shouted above the hum of machinery.

The *bura* was strong that cold December day, and Sirana's cracked, sun-faded sign wavered on a crane above them. Marina had instructed the installers not to damage the old sign. She planned to display it inside the factory, in the production room, as reminder of Sirana's past. A memory of her father.

Sirana's new sign had bold lettering on a background of delicate Pag lace. Marina used a portion of the money collected from vendors to pay for the sign; Franko had finally convinced them to make good on their back payments. She didn't ask how Franko went about obtaining the money, but she wondered if he channeled his old rage from the soccer field into his new job. He seemed to throw himself into the work with a passion, the collections and distribution, too. And he had plans to introduce tours of Sirana's factory for the summer crowds next year. She wondered if Franko, like her, had been struggling to find his place. It seemed, at least for the moment, he'd found it.

Sirana's old sign lowered gently to the ground, and the installers released the heavy hooks and chains. Marina touched the sign's rough surface, blistered from the sun and marred by sea salt carried by the *bura*. She remembered when her father had the sign installed, one summer when she'd returned home after the war. He was proud to erect proper signage; previously, the factory's name had been painted on the side of its chipped concrete wall. Sirana had not been able to afford a proper sign during the Yugoslavia era, and after Croatia gained independence, the sign became a beacon of change for Pag Town.

She stepped into the hallway, blowing on her hands to warm them, then ascended the stairs to her father's office, pausing at the window that overlooked the production room. Igor was cleaning the *salamura* tank, which was drained of its saltwater. The workers had removed the old Soviet machinery that was no longer in use, and those pieces that were broken beyond repair. Sirana's production process had changed; most everything now was done by hand, following the essence of the old island cheesemaking methods. The townspeople applauded her, since this labor-intensive method also meant hiring more workers at Sirana. With money flooding in for Grandmother's Cheese from across Europe, Marina had funds to hire new employees.

In less than a month it would be January, and a new season would begin. There would be young lambs sucking at their mothers' teats and fresh milk for making cheese. Sirana would continue to produce Grandmother's Cheese, which had become popular overnight in European gourmet circles, and also introduce a new cheese, made with cow's milk from the mainland. After the World Cheese Awards, demand for Sirana's cheese had exploded. Due to the limited supply of sheep's milk on the island, Marina decided to expand Sirana's offerings. Some people on Pag felt she was straying too far from their traditions by incorporating milk from the mainland, but Marina felt that new cheeses made with other Croatian milks would strengthen Sirana's profits, since they could produce cow's milk cheese in the off-season. Next, she would attempt goat's milk cheese. And once the season was well underway, she couldn't wait to visit Andy in California and discuss the possibility of a cheese made with zinfandel.

Marina relished the silence at this time of year. The holidays were quickly approaching, and most of the workers were already on break, save the core crew that periodically vacuum-packed cheese for distribution and attended to wheels in the aging room. A creased copy of *Free Dalmatia* lay on her father's desk, touting Sirana's success. The Dalmatian papers had been kind to Sirana, celebrating their World Cheese Awards win for weeks.

She settled into her chair and started on a pile of paperwork. Her pen paused; she gazed at the World Cheese Awards plaque, and a photo of Nikola in front of Sirana. Months after her father's death, it was still strange to sit at his desk. The smell of smoke had long since faded, but she could picture him reclining in his chair, the unoiled wheels squeaking, holding a cigarette.

Josip's sharp knock startled her.

"Come in," she said, gesturing to the seat across from her.

"I was just heading to Zadar, thought I'd stop by," Josip said. "I figured you'd be here."

"The paperwork never ends," Marina sighed, setting down her pen.

"Anything you need help with?" Josip asked.

"Thanks, but no. I just need to get through it before we start production."

"The good news is, with the EU funds, Sirana can finally afford new machinery."

"I wanted to talk to you about that," Marina said. "I feel like the small batch production is really working for us. I don't want to invest in new machines, at least not now."

"What about the cow's milk cheese you're planning to produce? Your margins will be slimmer if you produce it almost entirely by hand. People won't pay a premium for cow's milk cheese like they do for Pag cheese."

"I believe the handcrafting method is in demand. It's more expensive, but I think it will pay off."

Josip chuckled. "We move forward, only to move backward."

"It's a different kind of progress," Marina said.

"If you had told my grandmother that we'd be using the old methods when we have machines that can do these things now, she would laugh," Josip said.

"Machines aren't people," Marina said. "You'll never get the same results. Plus, like my grandmother says…"

"I know," Josip said. "Cheesemaking always takes a bit of magic. You are a wise woman, just like your grandmother." He looked at his watch. "I should be on my way. Sanja needs Maraschino for Christmas, and Konzum is sold out already, would you believe."

"I should get some for my mother, too," Marina said.

"I'll pick you up a bottle," Josip said, rising from the chair. He paused. "I always drank cherry liqueur with your father."

"It was his favorite," Marina said, her eyes moist.

"We'll toast to him, when we start the new season," Josip said, closing the door softly behind him.

Sirana had survived. Marina thought about everything that had been stripped away. She was free to cast her sails in any direction, but for now, she chose to remain here. This year she would continue to live with her mother and brother, but she imagined a place of her own, an apartment or a house with a sunny window that overlooked the sea, a place to enjoy her morning coffee before heading to the factory. A place to watch the island continue on. She would watch over the shepherds and the sheep's milk; she would watch over the workers who molded the curds into wheels; she would watch over the women who rubbed the wheels with oil as they aged, turning them as they matured.

Marina opened the heavy production room door, bracing herself against a strong *bura* gust. The installers gripped and steadied the new sign, which swayed dangerously on heavy chains, as if the *bura* wished to claim it. Marina watched as it filled the space where Sirana's broken sign once lived.

Acknowledgments

This novel is my love letter to the island of Pag and its people—this book would not exist without the hospitality and generosity of the people of Pag. I am especially grateful to Martina Pernar Škunca, who was not only my guide and occasional translator, but my friend. I'm thankful for an early reporting assignment for the now-defunct *Croatian Chronicle*, where I covered a cheese festival on the island and became smitten with Pag and Pag cheese. The seed of an idea was planted back in 2011, and many years later, a story finally bloomed. Thanks to my husband, Jaidev Shergill, who encouraged me to keep going when I felt like giving up, and to my daughter, Uma, who reminds me that we are always learning and growing. Thanks to my parents, Phil and Kathy, who supported my education and writing journey from the beginning, and to my father, who fueled my obsession with Croatia as he researched deep into our family history.

This story was inspired by Croatia and written in America. I am indebted to Lynn Steger Strong and her epic 2020 Catapult Novel Generator workshop, which kept me sane and focused on writing this story during the pandemic, and resulted in the first real draft of this book (shout-outs to all the amazing authors in that workshop, especially Claudia Cravens and Cherry Lou Sy, whose novels also found homes). Thanks also to Taylor Larsen and her Catapult Novel Generator for early feedback and inspiration. Gratitude to Jean Kwok, who I met at the unicorn Catapult/ WME Writer's Winter Break Conference in Florida in January 2020—under her expert guidance, this story became Marina's story, and found its structure and narrative engine.

Thank you to the early believers, first and foremost Caroline Leavitt, whose faith in this novel propelled me to persist—thank you, Caroline, for being the best guardian angel I could have hoped for and one of the most generous human beings and literary citizens around. Thank you also to Brenda Copeland and Andra Miller, whose sharp eyes and expertise helped shape this novel into its final form, and to Julia Phillips, whose keen insights and advice pushed this manuscript across the finish line. Thanks to JVNLA and my agent, Alicia Brooks, who kept the faith through revisions and encouraged me to make this story more hopeful—and for finding my dream editor, Adriana Senior, who was meant to edit this book. Thanks to Aleigha Koss for helping this manuscript become a novel. Thanks to Regalo Press and Gretchen Young for taking a chance on a new novelist, and for believing this story deserves a place in the literary landscape.

I am indebted to friends who provided inspirational background information and cultural context for this novel, including Ivana Klanac-Stern and Vesna Jakšić Lowe. Thanks to the National Federation of Croatian Americans Cultural Foundation and Steve Rukavina for their early support—and to Sara Nović for the "40 Under 40" nomination (it did come in useful, Sara!) Thanks to Sirenland—and Dani Shapiro, Michael Maren, and Hannah Tinti—for the space to workshop and create, and to Jess

Walter for his feedback on what became my first chapter. Thanks to Milda De Voe and the Tuesday morning Pen Parentis group for their support and encouragement while I revised the beginning of this novel for what felt like the thousandth time, and for all the shared goal setting that pushed me through many weeks of reworking. Thank you to Paragraph, the treasured space away from home where I was able to write and revise in peace, and to the entire community of Paragraph writers, whose clicking on their keyboards fueled my own strokes.

Special thanks to all the editors over the years who have let me indulge in my obsession with Croatia, in particular Anne Banas from *BBC Travel* and Ellen Carpenter from *Hemispheres*, who commissioned very personal features about Croatia, and Dan Saltzstein, who gave me my first big break in the *New York Times*. Thanks to Ivan Miletić, who helped with our family history research and background information about the history of Croatia. Special thanks to the Croatian National Tourist Board for their support, and for the Zlatna Penkala (Golden Pen) award for my writing about Croatia. And *hvala* to Ina Rodin for her help connecting me to people in Croatia.

I am grateful to Katie Freeman, and also the AME team, for their help ushering this book into the world. Thanks to Ariana Phillips at JVNLA for helping this book get heard. And thanks to all the people who have believed in my writing along the way and helped me on my journey—including Leslie Sharpe and Phillip Lopate. And Lita, I hope you're looking down and smiling.

About the Author

Author Photo by Sylvie Rosokoff

Kristin Vuković has written for the *New York Times, BBC Travel, Travel + Leisure, Coastal Living, Virtuoso, The Magazine, Hemispheres,* the *Daily Beast, AFAR, Connecticut Review,* and *Public Books,* among others. An early excerpt of her novel was longlisted for the Cosmonauts Avenue Inaugural Fiction Prize. She was named a "40 Under 40" honoree by the National Federation of Croatian Americans Cultural Foundation, and received a Zlatna Penkala (Golden Pen) award for her writing about Croatia. Kristin holds a BA in literature and writing and an MFA in nonfiction writing from Columbia University, and was editor-in-chief of *Columbia: A Journal of Literature and Art.* She grew up in St. Paul, Minnesota, and currently resides in New York City with her husband and daughter. For more information, please visit *kristinvukovic.com.*